SLIPPED

Chantelle,
Lunar Blessings,
Jules
x

SLIPPED

JULIE WALKER

Matador
Unit E2 Airfield Business Park,
Harrison Road, Market Harborough,
Leicestershire. LE16 7UL
Tel: 0116 279 2299
Email: books@troubador.co.uk
Web: www.troubador.co.uk/matador
Twitter: @matadorbooks

ISBN 978 1803136 752

British Library Cataloguing in Publication Data.
A catalogue record for this book is available from the British Library.

Printed and bound in Great Britain by 4edge Limited
Typeset in 11pt Adobe Garamond Pro by Troubador Publishing Ltd, Leicester, UK

Matador is an imprint of Troubador Publishing Ltd

For my special 1987's:
Antonia, Alexandra and Katie

ONE

WOLF MOON

They say that if you consistently wake between the hour of 3.30am to 3.40am that a ghost is watching over you. If only that was true for Jessica, but that's when she *slips.*

Her father died the night she was born.

In the early hours of the Great Storm of 1987, he was racing to the hospital when a telegraph pole fell and struck his car, killing him instantly. At that same moment the electricity failed in the hospital and her mother, Isobel, felt her pregnant belly disappear and then reappear ten minutes later. The hospital staff hadn't noticed, and she was born as the power was restored at 3.40am on the 16th of October.

Three weeks later Isobel was feeding baby Jess, sitting with her grief in the nursery, when she disappeared again.

Dumbstruck, she had just sat there. Her world had already been turned upside down and she had considered ending both their lives, but she couldn't move. She felt that she was being punished for having those thoughts and now Jess had vanished.

At exactly 3.40am Jessica reappeared. As she enveloped her baby, Isobel's face softened, the drum beat of her heart slowed and she vowed to protect her. She was determined but waking each morning her mouth was dry, her stomach knotted and the loud drumming of her heart was now accompanied by a percussion in her head.

It never went away.

The scales were always tipping from love to disdain towards Jess when she found out where she was going. Prior to that she had no idea how or where she'd been and where she continued to go at every full moon from then on.

Jess had no memories of those early times except for a feeling of contentment. As she grew, she began to recognise his face, the same one that sat in a photo frame on the coffee table.

When finally, she could speak, she could answer the same question that her mother had asked her every single time.

'Where have you been, Jess?'

Her first words were, 'Papa-ji.'

*

Jessica's aunt, Viv, had invited her to stay at the hotel she ran, safe in the knowledge that her sister, Jess's mother, was safely locked up in psychiatric care. The hotel was normally a wedding venue, but today it was a wake that was being held and Jess had volunteered to work as one of the regular girls hadn't turned up.

In the main bar stood an easel with a photograph of a woman, approximately in her late forties, whose life was being celebrated. It was a small gathering, and everyone seemed to be in couples except for a young man who Jess thought was a similar age to herself. She had noticed him immediately, describing him to Viv as tall, dark and handsome. That wasn't strictly true as she noticed his unusual piercing feline green eyes straightaway. Jess thought there was a sadness about them before chastising herself and remembering that this wasn't a wedding breakfast.

He'd been up to the bar so many times, a pint and a double whiskey chaser on each occasion. Nothing for anyone else. Each time he lingered a little longer, looking to engage Jess in conversation. It was the usual banter, initially, and then she discovered that he had buried his sister and was angry that his only other sibling wasn't there.

He extended his hand. 'Josh, and you are?'

'Jessica. I'm sorry for your loss.'

'What does that even mean? How can you be sorry? You didn't even know her!'

'It's what people say, isn't it? What would you rather me say?'

'I don't know, I didn't think it would be this difficult…'

His voice trailed off and he wandered back to his seat in the corner, alone, surveying his surroundings. His cousins were openly weeping and consoling each other. One by one the guests began to leave. All of them came up to Josh to say goodbye with some heartfelt words about how Gail had been so proud of her little brother. He nodded politely but inside he was incensed. Anna should've been here too to support him.

No amount of begging, pleading or cajoling would change her mind. He wouldn't forget this.

Josh was glad when the last people left, and he sauntered back up to the bar. Jess was busy tidying up, hoping he would leave soon so she could get to bed.

'Will you join me now that you've finished working?'

'I don't finish until you leave, but I could do with a drink, I guess that would be OK.'

Jess never normally drank alcohol on the full moon; she liked to have total clarity. She felt sorry for this guy, though; his grief was hanging heavily on his shoulders for all to see and so thought she'd make an exception.

Josh went on to tell her that fate had intervened when his girlfriend had thrown him out after hooking up with another guy and how he'd gone to Gail's for a couple months to get his head straight. Then the cancer came for her, and he'd nursed her to the end. He told Jess about Anna, his other sister, who claimed she was a "free spirit", which Josh said was just a euphemism for doing exactly what she wanted with no consideration for anyone else.

'My mum deserted us when I was a baby. Anna never cared but Gail was like a mum to me. My dad has dementia and is in a care home. Life is shit.'

'My papa died the night I was born, so I never knew him, and I seem to spend my life saving my suicidal mum.'

'Are we playing Top Trumps?' Josh laughed.

Jess's face flushed as her body temperature rose. It wasn't her intention, and she wasn't normally so forthcoming about her mum's mental health. She thought she just wanted him to feel better, before reminding herself that she of all people should know that was an impossible task. Grief was the strangest emotion and she had never been able to successfully navigate it. She had her back to him now as she wiped down the preparation area. On the one hand she was tired and just wanted her bed, but on the other she was intrigued by this man.

'My sister, the other one, she's living in India, on some "journey", apparently. It's just an excuse, it always is with her, she's so cold,' Josh slurred.

Jess turned back to face him. 'My grandparents live in India; I've never been, though.'

'Trumping me again?' He laughed. 'How long have they lived there?'

Jess was now laughing. 'They were born there! Did you think I just had a tan?'

'No offence, but everyone is a melting pot, there's some Jamaican in me somewhere along the line. These days everyone wants to claim their 6%.'

'Yes, but that's normally white people! My papa was Asian, my mum is white. I'd say that was more than 6%!'

Fortunately, Jess was laughing. Josh was glad, as he hadn't intended to upset her. He liked her and certainly didn't want to alienate her. In his drunken state he couldn't tell if she was flirting or not.

'Jess, can I call you Jess?'

As she nodded to him, he then continued, 'Jess, Jess.'

'I think you may have had too much to drink, best call it a night, eh? Shall I call you a cab?'

'No, Jess, I want to tell you something. It's really bugging me, and when I asked Anna, she told me I was being stupid and there were no dark secrets. But, Gail, as she was dying actually said to me, "Now you'll find out the secret." What do you think she meant?'

Jess was shaking her head as she towel-dried some glasses, 'How the hell should I know? What I will say is that *every* family has secrets, it's not unusual. Now, let me call that cab for you.'

'No, no, Jessie, listen, I know Gail, she meant it and it'll be something big! What do you think?'

'I didn't say you could call me Jessie…' That nickname was reserved only for her father.

'Sorry, sorry, I'm tired. I've not been sleeping trying to figure it out.'

'And that's exactly why you need to go home. For all you know, maybe Gail was really your mum?'

'It's 2017, no-one does that anymore! What kind of Victorian life are you living in? My mum left us when I was young, she didn't care – how does someone leave three children? I can't go home; no-one is there and everywhere I turn it just reminds me of Gail.'

Josh sat silently sobbing; he tried to stop it, but it just made the tears flow more.

'I'm sorry, it just seems as if my bladder is too close to my eyes.'

Jess laughed as she wiped her hands with the tea towel and lifted the bar flap to walk around to his side. She put her arms around him, instinctively consoling him. No-one deserved to feel that way, but she knew that life wasn't fair; the good people died as easily as the bad, and who was she to be judge and jury?

'I'm sorry, Josh, you *asked* me, and it was the first thought that came into my head. You said she was like a mother to you and she's obviously old enough, I'm sorry. Let me make us both a coffee.'

Jess went to get him a tissue from her bag before firing up the coffee machine. She'd already cleaned it and knew what a stickler Viv was about hygiene so that was something else she'd have to factor time in for. Viv, unlike her sister Isobel, prided herself on her cleanliness and proudly displayed her award for winning the TV programme *Four in a Bed*. They'd not found an iota of dust or even a stray pubic hair when they filmed the show. Isobel could barely wash and dress herself. Jess wondered about the differences between her aunt and her mum, pondering about how different their lives would've been if her papa was still alive.

Bringing herself out of her daydream she glanced at the clock and could see that it was nearly 2am. She was sure she'd be able to get rid of him within the hour, but truth be told she didn't want to.

She had to, though.

Looking out of the window Jess could see that it had started snowing, not unusual for a January night but that might make him more reluctant to leave. The moon was visible despite the weather; she knew this one was called the "wolf moon" and it was the worst of all of them for her mum. She knew that the word "lunatic" originated from the Latin word for moon because it was observed that some fragile people were filled with psychosis at this time, as was the case for her mum. The fact that neither of them dared tell anyone the truth added to the difficulty of managing her mother's mental state and Jess had never broken the promise they'd made to each other. In her mum's more lucid times she had expressed that Jess would no longer see her father if it became known and it might change the "space-time continuum". She'd been a small child at the time of their pledge and whilst she didn't know what that meant she never saw a reason to doubt her. Jess knew that her mum wanted what she had and that had led to a fractious relationship when she became a teenager. The usual angst was there, but it was Jess who had to be the adult. Sometimes she almost wished her mum would succeed in her efforts to end her life; it would be some form of release. Jess's father thought the opposite. So, the secret was kept, and Jess kept rescuing her mum.

'Would you like me to book you into a room? I'm sure there are some free.'

'Jessie, err, Jess, Jessica, I don't want to be alone, I really, really don't want to be on my own. Can I stay with you? Where do you live?'

'I'm staying here tonight – there is a sofa in my room if you want.'

Jess was surprised by her own reaction but figured that he'd had a long, traumatic day and had definitely had way too much to drink. With any luck he'd pass out as soon as he laid down.

'Thank you, thank you, I promise I won't be any trouble.'

As they finished their coffees, Josh was still going on about the secret, Anna, Gail and his family. He said he felt like an orphan as his dad barely knew who he was. He didn't visit much anymore, but every time he went his dad was worse than the previous time. Josh reserved all his vitriol for Anna, saying that she had abandoned the family and how it was all left on Gail's shoulders and that's what had made her ill. Jess doubted that but didn't correct him; he'd been through enough today. She didn't realise she'd been intently looking into his eyes.

'Are you eye-fucking me?'

Jess laughed; she'd never heard that expression before. It was definitely more direct than accusing someone of having "come-to-bed eyes". The surprise was evident in her face.

'I'm only joking, but you, you have the most amazing black eyes.'

'That doesn't sound right either!'

'No, I mean, you have black saucers for eyes – I can't see where the pupil ends and the colour begins. I have never seen anything like it, are you wearing contacts? Actually, it's me that is eye-fucking you!'

They both laughed now.

'No, I don't, everyone thinks that. Come on, let's get you to bed, in the literal sense, that's all.'

Josh followed her like a baby giraffe, stumbling as he tried to put one foot in front of the other. Fortunately, Jess's room was on the ground floor; she doubted if he would make any stairs in his inebriated and grief-stricken state.

'So, here's the sofa, slip your shoes off, I'll get you a pillow and some blankets. I hope you don't snore!'

Josh nodded and attempted to untie his laces unsuccessfully, so Jess found herself on her knees treating him like a small child. She felt like she was yet again mothering someone who wasn't her child. There's probably a word or syndrome for someone like that, she thought, but it was just second nature to her, having looked after her own mum for as long as she could remember.

'Gail taught me how to tie shoelaces. Gail taught me everything.'

How Jess wanted to take away his pain, but she felt she'd failed to do that for her mum, so what chance would she have with this beguiling stranger? She didn't want to have to care for him as she did for her own mum, especially not tonight. It appeared as if she'd swapped one nightmare for another, but it was just not in her nature to abandon anyone.

As she picked up both of his legs to swing them onto the sofa, he lurched forward to kiss her.

She didn't pull away.

Jess also realised that he wasn't as intoxicated as she'd first thought; he was just utterly and hopelessly "grief drunk".

'I'm sorry, I promised I'd behave, and I didn't even last five minutes. Will you sit with me until I fall asleep?'

Jess nodded and replied that she didn't exactly push him away, but it was probably better for him to sleep. She glanced at the clock for what seemed the umpteenth time; each minute brought the full moon closer, and Josh didn't show any sign of falling asleep. She had less than an hour. If he didn't fall asleep soon, she'd have to excuse herself and go to the bathroom, but she was frightened. For as long as she could remember she'd followed the same ritual every month and if she veered from that it may not work. She always showered, put on her papa's old T-shirt, lit a candle, said a quiet prayer and then lay flat on a bed, wherever she was.

'You seem distracted, Jess. Listen, if you're not comfortable with me being in your room, I'll go and—'

'No, it's OK, please just go to sleep. I'm going to have a quick shower.'

The thoughts seemed to be running through her head as fast as the water through the shower head. Mostly she was hoping that by leaving him alone with no distractions he would be sleeping by the time she came out. Taking a cleansing wipe out of her wash bag, she began to liberally rub what was left of her make-up from her face. Staring at her reflection, she started to look deeper into her own eyes; an ex-boyfriend had once described them as "obsidian eyes". It was always the feature that people noticed the most; she just thought they were good at misdirecting people. So focused on the unusual that they didn't see the pain or fear of one day losing the special time she had with her father. It was only ten linear minutes a month, but for them it could seem like all day; time didn't exist where they were, wherever that was. Jess was always fearful of asking questions in case she changed the dynamic of the situation. Over the years she'd adjusted her thought process so that she considered it to be like having a divorced dad who only had visitation rights once a month; it helped her. The trouble was that there wasn't any physical touch – no kiss on the cheek or a well-done hug. They mostly played chess on the beach while they talked, but neither moved the pieces, just thinking it made it so. Jess was always the first to say, 'Checkmate.' When she was little she thought her papa let her win but became quite the expert over the years.

After she finished drying herself off, she glanced at her smartwatch. It wasn't the 17,000 steps she was looking at, though she smiled at the unsurprising number considering she'd been on her feet all day. 3.12, hopefully Josh was asleep by now. She slipped on the T-shirt, put on some fresh knickers then quietly tip-toed out, gently closing the bathroom door behind her.

'You look gorgeous, even in that bedraggled Rolling Stones T-shirt!'

'Josh! I'd thought you'd be asleep by now, the state you were in!'

She felt vulnerable; it was her dad's T-shirt that she wore as nightwear every month. She recalled how it had hit her ankles when she was little and now it barely covered her bottom, and she tugged at the fabric, trying to pull it down. Josh now looked stone-cold sober. She felt herself becoming anxious and tried to equalise her breath as Viv had taught her, breathing in for a count of four and blowing out for a four count. It wasn't working. At least he was still on the sofa. Jess climbed into bed and lay a couple of the pillows lengthwise beside her, looking to tuck down behind them in the hope that if she *slipped* that he wouldn't see.

'Goodnight, Josh.'

Tonight was not going as she had hoped at all – well, sort of. She was glad she'd met Josh; she just wished it had been on a different day.

'Why are you hiding from me? I can't see you, but I know you're there. Jess, don't go to sleep yet, please, I feel wide awake. The coffee's kicked in and I can't stop thinking about Gail and her secret. I feel so angry, and I don't know why.'

'Grief, Josh. The anger is just grief. You know how you felt about your sister and I'm sure she felt the same. Cherish that, think about some nice memory of her, that's what I do with my papa, and please try to sleep.'

3.26am. Jess took a deep breath; she considered going into the bathroom as it didn't seem like he would shut up, and then she would just hope for the best. She should've insisted on calling him a cab and then none of this would be happening. More deep breathing – one, two, three, four, one, two, three, four.

'You never knew your dad; how can you have nice memories?'

Whoops, she wasn't thinking there, but she had to act now, and fast.

'Have you never heard of using your imagination? My mum told me stories about him, and I just insert myself in those stories,' she lied.

'Uh-huh, OK, I'll let you sleep then, but can I have a kiss goodnight?'

Without waiting for a response, he walked over to the bed and noticed she was lying flat on her back, one hand on her heart, the other resting on her tummy. He thought she was stunning, even more so in the tatty T-shirt and bereft of make-up. He knelt one knee on the pillow fort and swung his other over her, straddling her. Very gently he rested on his hands either side of her on the bed and leant in for a kiss. Just as his lips brushed hers, he face-planted into the space that a second ago Jess had been occupying…

'What the f…! Where is Papa? Why are you here? Oh my God, you've ruined everything, Gail, how did you do that? Why did you do that?'

'At least you know who I am! Glad I didn't have to watch you making love to my little brother!'

'I wasn't going to, I don't need your approval anyway, but what have you done to my papa?'

Jess's breath was running too fast; she could just about hear her father in the distance, calling her.

'Papa-ji, I can hear you, where are you?'

'Look, I don't know how I did that and I'm sorry I wasn't who you were expecting, but I just saw you together and as the entryway opened, I sort of accidently fell in front of the guy who was waiting.'

'No, no, Gail, you can't do that! But you have and now I may have to spend all of my life with you instead of him.'

Jess began to sob; she wasn't even thirty yet. Her mind became like a jigsaw puzzle with one piece missing. In her head she could see images of her mum and for the first time in her life she kind of understood why she was desperate to meet him and how it had actually driven her insane.

'Look at him, he thinks he's dreaming!'

At this moment Jess couldn't care less about Josh, though she knew she would have to come up with some plausible excuse. If only she could arrive back in the bathroom, but she'd only ever arrived from where she'd left. For roughly 351 full moons she hadn't dared changed her routine. She always believed that any deviance from her first cognitive memory would destroy the connection. And now? Who knew?

Josh had his head in his hands and was repeatedly swearing. Every couple of breaths he looked around in case he was mistaken, but no, she definitely wasn't there. He wondered if this was some spooky hotel, like in a horror movie, and maybe Jess had been just an apparition, a figment of his grief-stricken state of mind. If he was previously still feeling a little intoxicated, he had immediately fully sobered up and was now pacing the room, constantly repeating, 'I'm not imagining this.'

'Let me tell you about Josh, when he gets the bit between his teeth he doesn't let up. He's so stubborn and so loyal but totally lovable. That's why I'm here. I wish I hadn't mentioned the secret—'

'What, that you're really Josh's mum?'

'Don't be silly, I'm not his mum! But you must convince him to stop looking – it'll serve no purpose but heartache. He won't give up, no more than he will finding out the truth about you.'

'Don't you think you should've thought of that at the time?'

Gail went on to explain that in her morphine haze she'd thought it was the right thing to do but instantly regretted it, and before she had the chance to rectify it, she died. She'd been on the other side for just over four weeks now and after a few days she'd seen them all gather on the beach. She also said that Jess was unaware that she and Josh were in the same nightclub; he'd held the door open for her as they both left, but instead of following Josh, for some reason, she chose to follow Jess. It was then that she began to see all the "16/87s", as they called them, and no-one ever bothered them; it was some unwritten rule.

'Did you think you and your father were the only ones? You can only see one person, as the others can too, but all of them are on the beach right now. You're all celebrities over here.'

'You're lying, how do I even know I'll see him again? And what the hell am I going to say to Josh?'

'I don't think I *can* lie now, and I'm sorry I interrupted by my presence. I'll probably be in trouble. Josh will understand – you'll love him when you get to know him. I'm sure that there is some reason all this is happening right now after all these years.'

The enormity of what Jessica was hearing suddenly hit her like a ton of bricks. 'Whoa! Back up, back up. Others? "16/87s"? Celebrities? What the hell do you mean? Others?'

Gail took a deep breath; she hadn't meant to upset the gorgeous woman with the white streak in her jet-black hair and the most unusual eyes she'd ever seen.

'As I understand it, there must've been some seismic shift on the night of the storm, I guess. No-one knows. Everyone here watches their loved ones – sometimes we're seen, most times not. But those born on 16th October 1987, or the "16/87s", as they call you... no-one really knows.'

Jess closed her eyes tight and put her hands over her ears, whispering to herself, 'This is not happening, this can't be real.'

As she reopened her eyes, she was back in the hotel room and Josh was sitting there wide-eyed. Where did she begin? How could she explain something she didn't understand? Before she had a chance to even come up with a believable excuse, Josh spoke. 'What the fuck happened? I knew I wasn't dreaming, are you real? Are you dead? What century are you from? Are you a time traveller? Can I come?'

Jessica laughed at the last of his quick-fire questions. He definitely didn't seem to be afraid, nor disbelieving of the situation. All her life she'd wondered what would happen in an event like this, but her fear had made her sure never to put herself at risk of losing the one thing she held dear. The way she saw it, she could either make up a convincing excuse, though what that would look like she had no idea, or tell him the truth. Her mum had drummed it into her so many times that if she ever did tell anyone it would disrupt the "space-time continuum", whatever that meant. Jess now felt she had nothing to lose, in this moment doubting that she'd ever see her father again. Maybe the pressure would be taken from her; maybe her mum would get better if they were both in the same "forever-grief" circumstances. So many questions that she didn't have the answers for.

'I'm waiting, Jess. This isn't going to go away, so you may as well spill the beans. I'm not leaving until you do.'

Gail was right, she thought. Stubborn and relentless, she could just tell by the tone of his voice. One, two, three, four, one, two, three, four, breathe…

'I can hear you counting, what's that going to do? Are you going to disappear again? Can you do this at will? Can I come with you?'

She hadn't realised she was counting out loud; what she had recognised, though, was that he'd asked a couple times if he could come with her. What was he running away from? Jess took another deep breath. Grief, she decided, that was what he wanted to escape from. She knew that feeling, except for her it wasn't the grief of her father; it was the living grief of her mother.

'OK,' she began, thinking in her head that she needed to tell the truth.

Josh laughed. 'You still think you're talking in your head, don't you? Or am I now hearing you telepathically? Have I got some gift now? Can I come with you?'

There it was again, his fearless desire to come with her.

'You aren't telepathic. I realised I said it out loud when I didn't mean to. You're confusing me and Gail has confused me even more!'

'What's Gail got to do with this? Have you seen her?'

Jess couldn't believe that would be one of his thought processes. She'd run scenarios like this through her head ever since she was old enough to, which was why she always made sure she was alone, but not this time. She began shaking her head.

'So, you didn't see Gail, OK, that was a bit far-fetched, but then every possible thought I'm having right now is—'

Jess interrupted him and began to explain, right from the beginning. Half an hour later she realised he was holding her hand and looking into her eyes. There was no disbelief on his part; that was what surprised her the most. It felt good to finally shed the façade she'd presented all of her life. She had no idea where to go from here. She explained to Josh that her biggest fear was never being able to see her father again.

'But don't you see that maybe it is time, time for you to get on with your own life? Anyway, you don't know for sure, do you?'

Jess was quietly sobbing now. As if all that pent-up secrecy over nearly thirty years had to be cried out.

He lifted her chin. 'One more question: ten minutes ago your hair, well, it didn't have that big streak of white through it!'

Jess smiled weakly. 'Side effect. It goes away, well, I think it does. I dye it in the morning, always carry one, and it doesn't grow through, but every month I'm back to square one. I actually thought Caitlin Moran was like me because of her hair, but then I figured I was the only one. Well, I always thought that till now. I couldn't see them, but Gail could.'

'Maybe she was lying.'

Jess stood up. 'That's the point, Josh, *they* can't, it's impossible!'

'You said that it should've been impossible for Gail to do what she did, but unless *you* were imagining it—'

'*No*, definitely not. Anyway, she says to forget about the so-called secret.'

'I can't, I won't, I need to find out.'

Jess remembered that Gail had said how obstinate he was

and doubted he would let it go. She'd have to somehow solve his problem but had no idea where to begin. Sensing that Jess was considering her next move, Josh decided to step in.

'OK. Today, I've buried my sister with her secret, I've fallen for a girl who disappears and sees the dead and comes back with a white streak in her hair and expects me to just get on with the rest of my life—'

'Hang on a minute! I never said *you* had to do anything. No, you can't just pretend nothing has happened, but we haven't even discussed what to do next.'

Josh took her hands and sat her back down beside him on the bed. He gently kissed her before saying, 'Did you hear me say I'm falling for you?'

'I ignored that. Grief, it's just your grief speaking. If my secret gets out it could ruin my life, Josh. This could tip my mum over the edge. I need you to understand the gravitas of this.'

Josh hugged her tightly, promising not to reveal it to anyone. He didn't think anyone would believe him anyway. What worried him was that she'd been burdened by this for her whole life, having no-one else to share it with, apart from her mum, who Josh realised was just as much of a responsibility. Questioning her about how she'd avoided previous boyfriends finding out seemed a silly thing to ask; his ex-girlfriend had managed to hide an awful lot and he'd been none the wiser.

Then he had an idea.

'Let's find them!' he announced.

'Find who?'

'The others, the "16/87s", as you called them. They could help you understand and vice versa.'

'I wouldn't know where to begin, and God knows how many of them there are, Gail didn't say.'

'You don't even know what I do for a living. It's my speciality, finding out about people. If you help me find out Gail's secret, I'll help you locate all of them, however many there are.'

'Blackmail? I may never see Gail again, so how can I help?'

'Firstly, not blackmail, definitely not. It's just that in my experience you have to take a step back to see things clearly and I'm too close to the situation – same for you with your dad and his cohorts.'

'I don't think my papa knows – he would've told me. Maybe he can't see them either.'

'Listen, they're all probably scared, just like you. That maybe any change to what they've been doing all these years might alter the trajectory forever. I don't mean it like this, but we don't need them. We can figure this out ourselves.'

'OK, Sherlock, so you want me to be your Watson?'

Josh laughed. 'My surname is Holmes, but no relation to the character!'

'We're really going to do this?'

Josh nodded. The sun was just beginning to rise. He glanced at his watch; it was just after eight. They had been talking for over four hours. She was no longer fearful; taking this adventure with a stranger seemed almost the most natural thing in the world. Jess thought she needed to see her mum, but she wasn't ready to take Josh with her to the hospital.

'So, what are you proposing? You can't exactly put an advert in the newspaper or invite everyone who shares my birthdate to a party on the next full moon now, can you?'

'True, but we'll figure it out.'

'I have to go; I don't even have your phone number.'

'That's an easy one to solve – I doubt everything else will be.'

TWO

SNOW MOON

'Ow, ow! Rach, call my mum!'

'I have, babe, she can't get here, the snow is too bad for her little car. I'm going to have to call an ambulance.'

'*No! My mum is my midwife, and look at the time, we can't chance it!*'

'Please don't shout, Lexi, it's not my fault our baby is coming early.'

Rachel sighed; this was no-one's fault, and she'd never sat with a woman in labour before. The antenatal lessons covered the emotions of a woman giving birth but not one in their circumstances. Having a baby on the full moon was something they'd deliberately tried to work round, but babies have their own agenda and come when they're ready.

'Sorry, ouch, sorry, ouch, I know I'm being cranky, but I have no idea how to navigate this. Can you check me again, please?'

Lexi's mum had explained to Rachel how to check her dilation on the last phone call. She was only 4cm on the first check and thought they still had plenty of time. Rachel carefully examined her partner before saying that she'd already moved to 8cm, and they'd better call an ambulance. Finally, with her eyes not daring to blink and her heart in her mouth, she allowed Rachel to call. The emergency services were backed up due to the bad weather and a couple of serious car accidents. There was nothing for it but to drive Lexi herself.

Rachel picked up Lexi's hospital bag and took it to the car. It started on the second turn of the ignition, then she put the heaters on and sprayed the window with de-icer before returning indoors to help Lexi to the car. She managed to make Lexi laugh despite the pain she was experiencing as they made their way to the hospital. Rachel glanced at her watch – 3.05am, there wasn't much time. They'd only driven two and a half of the six-mile drive before the car stopped and the lights turned off. Quickly Rachel grabbed her mobile phone and turned on the torch, shining it in Lexi's face, putting on an accent to announce she was being interrogated, in the hope that she would laugh. Rachel had always been a bit of a comedian, usually managing to find a funny line in any awkward situation.

'Call my mum, she'll guide you through the delivery, we can't do it on our own.'

But there was no answer from Lexi's mum. Rachel suggested that, knowing her, she probably would have attempted to drive to their house and left her phone at home.

'Ow! *Ow!* Now what are we going to do? Oh, Rach, this isn't what I imagined. I wanted the water birth in that warm room with that lovely music we picked, not stuck here in the middle of winter, ow, ouuuuch! They're worse now, babe. I think he's coming!'

Rachel took matters into her own hands and called 999. They told her they would divert the original ambulance and that they would put through someone to guide her if they didn't make it in time. She could feel the goosebumps on her arms; her mouth was so dry she could barely put two words together. Rachel didn't want to be responsible for bringing their baby into the world. It had been an arduous three years for Lexi to carry a viable baby. All the disappointment and sadness would be for nothing if she messed this up. She put her phone on speaker.

'Rachel, Rachel, can you hear me OK? My name is Maria and I'm the midwife on call.'

'Yes, yes.'

'I'm going to guide you through this, step by step, just listen carefully.'

Rachel nodded before Lexi called out their agreement. She thought that Rachel looked like a rabbit in the headlights, dumbfounded. Maria asked her to put her timer on the phone and count the time between the contractions. Then Rachel went into the boot of the car to collect a blanket. The heaters had stopped working when the car had and the windows inside were steamed up until the bitterly cold air swept in as she opened the car door. Lexi was shivering by the time Rachel returned with the blanket. Looking at the time, she could see it was already 3.28am now.

'You're both doing great. Deep breaths, Lexi, in through the nose and then blow the air out through your mouth as if you were blowing a feather slowly away from your hand. You too, Rachel, do it together. We're almost ready to push, but not yet, Lexi – is the urge strong? We think you're 9cm now, if you feel like pushing, hold on and blow your breath out as if you had a birthday cake and were blowing the candles out individually. Can you hear me, ladies? Rachel, are you there?'

Rachel was, but where Lexi had lain on the backseat was now empty. She blew her breath out, but not like Maria had suggested. The midwife was still calling out to them to no avail. Rachel was mute and had no idea what to say or do. Quick thinking was needed; she wondered what would happen if Lexi gave birth over there, wherever *there* was, but that wouldn't pacify Maria.

Holding the phone away from her ear, she disconnected the speaker and started talking. 'Can't hear you, battery is dying, will try to find a char…'

With only half of the last word said she ended the call. These ten minutes were going to be the longest ever. So many questions were running through her brain. At least the blanket didn't go with Lexi as she was freezing cold now. What would she do if the ambulance arrived? What if the baby died *over there*? Before she could answer her own questions, Lexi's phone began to ring.

'Crap, now what?' Rachel rummaged in Lexi's bag, praying that it was her mother-in-law, but the number was unknown. Yes, it could've been a spam call, but surely not at this time – more likely the hospital had found Lexi's phone number. Rachel didn't want to press "end call" so she just let it ring until it didn't. Hopefully they'd think she'd left it at home.

Rachel began to pray; she didn't think she believed in God, especially any god who thought homosexuality was a sin. Her strict Roman Catholic parents had disowned her when she came out as a young teenager. Lexi's mum had taken her in, proclaiming she only went to church to get Lexi a place at the school in the first place and that "love was love was love", and who was anyone to tell another who to be with?

In the distance Rachel could see and hear the sirens heading her way, glancing at her watch for the umpteenth time – sixty seconds left, hopefully it would be before the ambulance arrived. She could also see a car overtaking the emergency vehicle at high speed. Idiot, thought Rachel as she looked at her phone for the time, as if that would be different to her watch. In her head she began counting twelve, eleven, ten, nine, eight, seven, six, five, four, three, two…

'*Lexi!*'

Laying exactly where she was before was a resplendent Lexi; only she wasn't alone: the baby was laying on her chest and she had the most serene smile that Rachel had ever seen. It was also the first time ever that Lexi had seen Rachel cry. Tears of joy, tears of pride, they kept falling.

'Dad delivered him, oh, Rach, it was amazing, I felt no pain over there. Shall we call him Chris after him?'

'I thought that was a given, though it's more poignant now. Christopher, the patron saint of travelling, well, no-one said time travel didn't count!'

Rachel leant over to her wife, first kissing her then their new-born, but was rudely disturbed by a man banging on the window.

'Hi, Avery Shepherd, from *The Herald*. So, you delivered the baby yourself?'

Rachel was blinded by the flashing camera of another guy beside this Avery person.

'Act normal, Rach. Say yes.'

Just as she opened the door a paramedic arrived to take care of Lexi, leaving Rachel to deal with the reporters.

'Yes, I delivered our baby.'

'And you are?' said Avery as he thrust his phone towards her face.

'I'm Rachel Holby and she is my wife, Lexi – our car broke down and the ambulances were busy.'

She felt like her heart was beating outside of her body but hoped she sounded convincing.

'So, Rachel, what are you going to call the baby?'

'C-Christopher, after Lexi's dad.'

Rachel went on to tell him that Chris had died in the Great Storm of 1987, which coincidently was when Lexi was born. She felt she'd said enough to appease the reporter. He got his story, but she was grateful when Lexi's mum arrived.

'I've been driving at a snail's pace – by the time I got to your house you'd left, and I couldn't answer when you rang because I was concentrating on my driving.'

'It's OK, Lexi is fine, and we were *alone.*' Rachel winked slightly at Lexi's mum, and she fully understood.

'Great, good, yes, yes. Let's get her to the hospital and you can come in my car with me.'

She hugged her daughter-in-law before checking that Lexi was OK.

All was right with the world.

*

Rachel looked down at her little baby boy; she couldn't believe she could love someone so instantly. Lexi wasn't pleased with Rachel's choice of middle name for him, but at least they'd decided against calling him "Harrison", which was one of Lexi's own choices. Rachel knew people would shorten that to Harry and he was still her nemesis even though they hadn't seen him since they left school. Rachel had gone to register his birth and came back, proudly waving the certificate stating "Christopher Snow-Moon Holby". She'd said that having blurted that out to the reporter she felt she had no choice but to go through with it. That was the thing with Rachel, thought Lexi, she always carried out whatever came out of her mouth. Her thought processes often astounded Lexi, but she was definitely an honourable woman.

Rachel knew from a young age that she wasn't interested in boys; Lexi didn't know either way. They'd been best friends since primary school, having always told each other that they loved one another, but it wasn't until they were fifteen that feelings had changed on Lexi's part. Unbeknown to her, Rachel had been in love with her since they met in the playground. Lexi always said that she admired the confidence that Rachel had which seemed to be lacking on her part, for a very good reason. Keeping her cards close to her chest was Lexi's preferred way of living, always fearful that her secret would be found out. It was easy when they were small children, her mum would make excuses if a sleepover coincided with a full moon, but when they were teenagers, it occasionally caused arguments.

Rachel remembered the first one they ever had. Girls Aloud were having their first concert and she'd bought them tickets, declaring that Lexi should stay overnight as she was home alone that weekend. She didn't know it but that was when Rachel had decided she would declare her undying love to her friend, so with this added significance heightened, it caused such a rift between them when Lexi said she couldn't go. Rachel had flown into a rage, completely losing all sense of reality, throwing things around and screaming at the top of her voice. Rachel thought she had irrevocably broken their friendship and Lexi would not speak to her, so she was acting the same.

Lexi had been dating Harry even though Rachel seemed to have a problem with him, for good reason. Their group of six friends were out in the park, having climbed over the railings after dark. Rachel normally enjoyed it when they all hung out drinking Smirnoff Ices or Blue WKDs; Harry's older brother used to buy the alcohol for them. Lexi had expressed on more than one occasion that she had to be home by midnight, but none of them were taking any notice. Harry had joked that she was Cinderella and that Rachel was both of the Ugly Sisters. Rachel never showed she was upset by the name-calling; she was used to it and usually got in first before they did, being disparaging about the size of her own body. It was a deflection tactic. It really cut deep, but there was no way she would let them know; she acted like one of the boys and despite yet again enduring the name-calling about her sexuality and her body shape, there was no way she would leave Lexi on her own with Harry. He often bemoaned the fact that they were never alone, but tonight was different. He knew that they'd had a falling-out and weren't speaking to each other. Harry didn't understand why Rachel had even bothered turning up this evening. Rachel wanted to be there; she'd felt so bereft since their argument, but at least she could see Lexi. Harry had a bottle of vodka in his pocket, and whenever Lexi wasn't looking, he was pouring some into her alcopop. Rachel saw him do it several times and wanted to say something, but every time she went to speak to Lexi, the girl turned her head away.

Harry convinced Lexi to go for a walk on their own; by this time she was absolutely intoxicated and had no idea of the time. He was limping from a football tackle the day before, which was just as well seeing as he was trying to push her further than the usual kisses. Rachel could hear Lexi saying, '*No*,' repeatedly, but he wasn't taking any notice. She saw in the darkness the glow on Lexi's watch as she looked at the time and then she suddenly tried to get out of Harry's grasp. He tried to chase her but fortunately because of his injury he couldn't keep up, but Rachel could, and she ran as fast as her body would allow, kicking Harry down as she passed him. She saw Lexi go behind the big oak tree on the far side of the tennis court, but when Rachel rounded the corner, Lexi wasn't there. She'd sat on the floor, stunned, trying to figure out which way Lexi must've gone, befuddled as to why she didn't see the direction; there was no shelter anywhere. Rachel didn't want to go back to the impromptu party; it was only Lexi's presence that made her come in the first place.

She looked at her own watch; it was the same make as Lexi's. They'd bought them together; made by Timex they had a button on the side which lit the watch face up in neon green. 3.38am, time she headed home, but she so wanted to make sure Lexi was OK. She considered telephoning Belinda, Lexi's mum, to see if she'd gone home. They weren't far and she could've easily made it by now. Rachel loved Belinda; she was such a "cool mum" and Rachel could speak to her in a way that she couldn't with her own straitlaced mother. Even so, she didn't want to worry her; she decided to wait a few more minutes and had laid down on the damp grass to consider her next actions. She saw Lexi's phone. She'd obviously dropped it, and it was switched off. As she turned it back on it began to ring. It was Belinda; gingerly Rachel answered it at the exact same moment as Lexi appeared beside her.

Lexi took the phone from Rachel's shaking hands and said to her mum, 'I'm OK, I'm back, Rachel's with me, I'm *so* sorry, but she really did save me from Harry.'

Their first argument ended there, and a shared secret bonded them forever. Rachel often thought back to that night, and looking down at their baby now she began to wonder if he too would be a "disappearer". It was an affectionate word that Rachel had made up when they were fifteen and it had stuck. She'd always been interested in UFOs and aliens, and after Lexi had spoken to her mum that night in the park it was the first thing she'd asked her. She laughed now at the recollection of her saying, 'What was the spaceship like? What did the aliens look like?', so convinced that Lexi had been abducted she couldn't comprehend any other possibility. The reality seemed more improbable to Rachel, but she could always tell if Lexi was being untruthful – she definitely wasn't – and the two girls had hugged each other for the longest time. Rachel also wanted to know why Lexi's hair now had a white streak in it. The words of love would come later. Rachel had just been grateful that she had her friend back in her life. It was a couple more years before they became intimate and Rachel mused that it definitely was the best night of her life, until now. She vowed then to protect baby Christopher as she did his mum. If he was a "disappearer" she would make sure no-one found out.

Rachel was disturbed from her daydream by Lexi coming into the room, rubbing her wet hair with a towel.

'That feels so much better! How's our little snow boy?'

'I promise you, Lex, if he is like you, I will go to the ends of the Earth to make sure it never becomes public knowledge. If he is like you, I promise to keep you both safe.'

Lexi was shaking her head. 'Dad has met him in the most marvellous, wonderous way, which was amazing, but I don't think he'll be coming on any more of my travels.'

'We can't know for sure, but we've only got three weeks and then we'll really know. Would you like a cuppa? My arm has gone dead, I never knew babies would feel heavy like this!'

*

Rachel regretted that she and Lexi had disagreed with each other on that first full moon night. Lexi was being stubborn about having baby Christopher laying on top of her so that if he came too, she would be holding him. Rachel felt that she didn't want their baby to faceplant on the bed if he didn't go with her. She gave in in the end as the fall would be soft, and she was too tired to argue. She never normally sat up with Lexi on those nights, but this was the first one with Christopher. He did indeed faceplant on the bed, and Rachel swiftly picked him up, holding him to her chest, grateful that he wasn't going to be a "disappearer".

Rachel and Christopher were sound asleep when Lexi returned; she lovingly gazed at them, deciding to make breakfast as a treat to make up for her obstinance. Her dad was so chuffed that they'd named the baby after him. He casually told Lexi that he'd already seen him before he was born, in the so-called "waiting room". When pushed to explain at Lexi's request he tried to make sense of it himself, stating that he didn't know how it worked other than that the souls were repeatedly born into the same family and that sometimes the returning soul could be a brother, an auntie, a mother or a father. Lexi was more confused the more he tried to explain that souls didn't have genders or appearances; they just *were*.

'Wakey wakey, Rach, I have your favourite, banana and raisin pancakes with that nice maple syrup we got in Canada. We'll have to go again one day with Christopher, I'd like Nana G to meet him before, well, before she's too old.'

Rachel didn't really hear any of what Lexi had said besides the pancakes, which she could smell; rubbing her eyes, she tried to sit up a bit without disturbing their sleeping baby, who hadn't moved from Rachel's embrace all night.

'I'm sorry, I really am, I know I can be a pain sometimes. I was in two minds; I think I wanted him to be like me, so it wasn't so lonely, but it is better that he isn't. Do you fancy going to the park after breakfast?'

'Hopefully that creepy couple won't be there, it's twice now that we've seen them. Do you think they're reporters?'

'I doubt it, probably just scouting for somewhere nice to live. You're more paranoid than I am! We've been loads of times when they've not, so, nah, I don't think it's anything to worry about.'

*

Jess was dreaming about some far-flung holiday destination, all white sandy beaches and a turquoise ocean where she and Josh lay sunbathing with no worries at all. Then the ocean began to go very dark, almost inky blue, then to a velvety indigo which then began to get darker and darker, taking on a tenebrous hue; the waves began to rise too. In her dream she looked at the sand which was beginning to take on a terracotta colour before turning blood-red and she screamed.

'Whoa, Jess, you're OK, I was literally looking at you wondering whether to wake you up or not. I think I've found something.'

'Same dream, Josh, what do you think it means? Do you think we should stop talking about the "16/87s"? Is it a sign? We haven't even begun collating any info.'

'You're just a bit stressed, that's all. Your mum is stable at the moment, which is good. You saw your dad, so Gail didn't ruin anything, and today, if you forgot, is our one-month anniversary, well, a week late due to my shifts, but you get the picture!'

Jess laughed as she moved her newly dyed hair behind her ear and sat up. It had been a lovely five weeks getting to know each other. She felt safe with him in a way she hadn't ever felt before. Gail was right: he was loyal and lovable. At the moment he was behaving like an excited puppy, though, desperate to tell her what he'd found. He was waving the local newspaper around as Jess sipped the coffee that he'd brought back with him.

'Look, look!' He unfolded the newspaper to show her the headline and photograph.

'And?'

'Listen: *In the devastation of the snowstorm, Rachel Holby had to deliver her wife's baby single-handedly in the backseat of their broken-down car. The delighted parents named him Christopher after Lexi Holby's father, who tragically died on the night of her birth in the Great Storm of 1987. As a nod to the evening of his birth, they added the middle names Snow-Moon. The ambulance arrived shortly after, and mother and baby are both doing well.*

Jess was suddenly very wide awake, and it wasn't from the cappuccino Josh had given her. Her beautiful jet-black saucer eyes seemed even wider than usual. 'You think? It surely isn't going to be this easy, no, it can't be, this isn't some rom-com, these are our real lives.'

'Why not? If you believe everything happens for a reason, then maybe you're all supposed to find each other now. I mean, you'll all be thirty this October, maybe that has some relevance.'

Josh leant over and kissed Jess passionately. 'Well, there's your rom-com snog! Happy anniversary! Look, I've got to work this afternoon, but when I finish my shift I'll see if I can find out where they live. We'll figure out our next move after then.'

'Isn't that a misappropriation of your workplace, Detective Sergeant Holmes?'

Josh laughed, claiming that he didn't need to be a policeman to find out where someone lived in this day and age.

'I thought you were staying home today?'

'Rich called in sick, it's just for a few hours till someone else comes in to cover. I won't be too long then we'll have a nice dinner together, I'll grab something from Tesco Metro on my way back.'

'You old romantic!' She laughed. 'OK, I'll go check up on my mum while you're gone.'

*

'I think they've seen us, Josh! I'm not a great Watson to your Holmes, am I?'

Josh spun her around so she was no longer facing the park; looking into her eyes, he made a big gesture as if he were wiping tears from her eyes, before holding her tightly, cupping one hand around her head to snuggle into his grey overcoat.

'They'll think whatever they want to think, hopefully that'll distract them. Well, we know that's them now, come on, let's go.'

Jess bit her lip; she was feeling really confused. What did it matter if Lexi was one of the "16/87s"? It wasn't like she could just walk up to her and ask her outright, 'Excuse me, do you slip every full moon?'

'Well, you're top of the list. We'll add her as second and we'll see if we can cross-reference anyone on the spreadsheet I've made as to our next move.'

'You're enjoying this, aren't you?' Jess laughed.

'I love figuring things out. We know her dad Christopher Marks died the same night as yours and she was born the same day – she has to be one of you. The question is, where next?'

When they got back to the flat Josh pulled up the spreadsheet. He explained that he'd started with the girls born that night in the UK as it seemed a common denominator because the second one they'd found was also female, though he had to admit that was just a guess at the moment. Then he found out all the names of their fathers and whittled it down to those who had passed away that night. He had eight names, including Lexi Holby and Jess herself.

'See, not many. Originally, I thought there may be a lot more – obviously I can't be 100% sure, but I've discounted the boys because it's my birthday too and I don't disappear.'

'Just think, if you'd been born a girl, you could've been one of us!'

'True, but also my dad isn't dead, though bless him, he may as well be.'

'I think I might be ready to let you meet my mum. It's not that I've been avoiding it, just, well, I've told you what she's like and I don't want her getting upset for any reason – she seems to be on a fairly even keel at the moment.'

'Look, I'm off to visit my dad in the morning, come with me. If we're at the stage of meeting parents then that's a good place to start – after all, whatever you say, he'll forget it soon after.'

Even though he was laughing, Jess felt his pain. She was still thinking that Josh seemed too good to be true; judging by her previous relationships it wouldn't be too long before the façade slipped, she had thought. And yet, he was the only person who knew her secret and hadn't been scared off or suggested she should tell the world. The only thing she'd been concerned about was his drinking. She was allowing him some grace because he hadn't long buried his sister, but if it continued apace, she would need to say something.

'In vino veritas.'

'What?'

'Sorry, Josh, I didn't mean to say that out loud.'

'Evidently not – whether I'm drinking or not, I've promised you that your secret is safe with me. Do you honestly think I'm going to go out with the lads, get tanked up and tell my mates that my girlfriend disappears better than a magician's assistant?'

This was the first time she'd heard Josh talk like that; the irritation in his voice was obvious. Jess had felt so contented, a feeling she hadn't experienced in a long while. She didn't want anything to ruin it and yet she considered that it may be her default reaction, to sabotage any relationship before it could hurt her. She wished she could talk to someone; Viv didn't know the truth, no-one did, other than her mum and Josh. It was such an overwhelming secret to hold and now she had to believe that a guy she'd really only just met wasn't going to reveal something that she'd held clandestinely for nearly thirty years.

'Sorry, I just feel overwhelmed today. I'll come to meet your dad another time. I have to get ready for the presentation tomorrow afternoon anyway.'

It was a good excuse, and not actually a lie, though she could do these meetings standing on her head. The buzz of being in advertising had begun to wane before Josh came on the scene and she'd been seriously thinking of changing careers. After he'd left the flat, she pulled out her Moonology oracle cards. Shuffling them, she began to ask in her head whether she could trust Josh and then whether his drinking was a problem or not. Her friends thought it was just a load of "hocus pocus" and yet they soon came calling when a boyfriend had finished with them, or they couldn't make a decision that needed to be made, almost begging her to get them out. She kept shuffling until two cards fell out, one for each question.

'Full moon in Leo, don't let pride get in your way,' she said out loud. Interesting, she thought, and guessed this meant that she needed to let her guard down and trust in Leo's full moon.

Jess laughed as she turned the next one over.

'Full moon in Gemini, the answers you need are coming.'

Jess decided she needed to be patient. It didn't escape her notice that of the forty-four cards in the pack there were only ten "full moon" ones, which meant she only ever had less than a 25% chance of picking those ones, but every single time when picking for herself, that was what happened. It surely wasn't "hocus pocus", but her friends didn't have all the information that she held, and more to the point she knew she that she could read the cards as much as she could visit her papa. Maybe that might be a nice career change, though she doubted it would pay as well. She hadn't dared show the cards to Josh yet; he'd already had to take on board her biggest secret and she didn't want him to have to deal with anything else right now. She knew the answers would come.

*

'See, I told you they wouldn't be here, and besides, the last time we saw them she looked really upset, so I reckon they aren't reporters.'

'Me being paranoid, Lexi, I know, silly.'

Rachel had made Lexi feel uneasy, though, and the last thing she wanted right now was for Rachel's protective side to come out. She was like a "Mama Bear", and her defensive attitude often came across as aggressive. So, it was an especially nice trip when they didn't see the couple that day, Christopher was content and, most importantly, so was Rachel. Lexi felt her secret was safe and all was right with the world, for now. She knew that everything was transient and over the years had worked hard to remember that when things were tough. Now she was a mother she felt a responsibility that seemed to be more than just the *normal* duty. Would she ever tell Christopher the truth? What if Rachel wasn't there one night and he needed comforting after a nightmare and then saw his mum disappear? How would she cope with that? Lexi felt her chest tighten at the very thought of it all; she'd desperately wanted to be a mum and that hadn't been one of the considerations, but now, after his birth, that was all she could think of.

*

'So, we can confidently add Lexi Holby to our list of *suspects*.'

'Josh! *Suspects*, who do you think we are?'

'Sorry, wrong choice of words, force of habit!'

'I don't think that's funny. What now?'

Josh walked over to the kitchen counter to refill his glass; it didn't escape Jess's notice, but she held her tongue. She felt he was still grieving and was trying very hard to justify his actions. She wasn't a big drinker herself, so she couldn't actually determine if he was being excessive or not.

'For now, we'll tick her name off and look at our next susp… one, I didn't do them alphabetically but by location. It seemed most logical, but from my line of work I know that a numbered list is often done out of its order when new information comes in. Oh, I tried to speak to Anna again last night but still no joy. We're no nearer solving the Gail question than we are coming up with a plan as what to do when we've identified all of the "16/87s".'

Jess sighed but didn't respond verbally. She had no idea what Gail had meant; thankfully she hadn't seen her since that night but was sure she felt her presence when getting out of the shower this morning.

'Did Gail wear Daisy perfume?'

Josh took another gulp of his drink and looked at Jess square in the eyes. 'You've seen her! How else would you know?'

'No, Josh, I would've told you. I just smelt it when I got out of the shower, and I don't know anyone other than Viv that wears it. That's how I knew.'

'That must be a sign – maybe she wants to tell you something.'

Jess tried to explain that it wasn't unusual for loved ones to visit in this way but that it was all symbolic and it was up to the living to determine the meaning. She told him she couldn't *speak* to the dead – well, apart from her papa – but often felt their presence. The only advice she could give him was to maybe find a good clairvoyant to help them.

'How do we know a good one from a bad one?'

'You're the detective, you'll figure it out.'

But Josh didn't know where to begin, although he did remember a case he was working on once, years ago, where the detective spoke to various supposed clairvoyants to help find a missing person – maybe that was a good place to start.

THREE

WORM MOON

Joanna opened her laptop, her fingers hovering over the keypad, ready to write her suicide note.

Dear World...

No, she considered, she wasn't anyone special – why would the *world* care if she lived or died?

Dear Mum,

Yes, thought Joanna, she needed to write to her mum. By the time she came back from her holiday the nightmare would be over and she hoped that her mum would understand.

I can't take it anymore. I still see him in my dreams: there's no rhyme or reason to it, and no amount of therapy can make it go away. I wish you'd have prosecuted him, Mum, you must've known where he was. I'm not blaming you, I promise, but I just can't take it anymore. To know that your birth father is a rapist is the most heinous of situations. Ever since I saw that photo, I recognised him from my dreams – how is that even possible? Up until the time you told me I saw them as nice dreams, as if I'd formed a relationship with him. It must be like Stockholm syndrome. Then and from then on, my dreams turned to nightmares: the sand was no longer white, the sea no longer blue. I remember that dream the most. The sand turned blood-red and the sea obsidian-black, and I screamed, and continue to do so.

I stopped taking the medications – they zombify me and they don't stop the nightmares, so what's the point? It's getting worse, Mum, I try to kill him in my dreams, but he just laughs at me. Neither of us deserve this. I admire you. The way you managed to have a full life despite what happened. I cannot and this is the only way out.

Please look after Poppy – she's been the best cat (well, second best after Mallon, no-one could take his place) and she's my best friend. I don't want her to eat me, though, so I'm leaving the flat, but I left her plenty of food and water.

Oh, I'm waffling now, and what is the point of that? This is no reflection on you, and I am sorry, so sorry that I just can't cope.

I love you,

Joanna x

After she pressed print, she began to empty out all of the tablets from their containers. Joanna had been collecting them for some months now; she decided that there was no room for error, and just to make sure, she was going to walk up to the bridge and take them there before jumping. Filling up her water bottle with neat vodka was another assurance.

*

PC Adams walked towards the open office door at the back of the room. He coughed before knocking. Josh looked up and beckoned him in.

'Sorry to interrupt, Sarge, it's just that suicide at the bridge you asked me to look at. It's not as straight forward as I first thought. The girl's mum is away on holiday so we can't question her yet, but look at the suicide note.' He placed a photocopy of it in front of Josh.

'Firstly, *that girl* has a name, she's someone daughter at least.'

'Yes, sorry, it, err, it's Joanna Mulholland,' he said after looking upside down at the paper he'd placed in front of Josh.

'No worries, it's something I'm trying to remedy, my partner is always pulling me up about that – anyway, you were saying?'

'As you can see, she's accusing her biological father of rape. The girl – sorry, Joanna, is, was twenty-nine, so probably historical, but surely needs investigating, although I'm not sure if he raped her mum or he raped the girl, sorry, Joanna, or someone else.'

Josh was present but not entirely listening after he heard

her name. This was getting weirder by the day. Instantly he knew she *could* be one of the "16/87s". He'd memorised all the potential candidates on the original list before discounting ones whose fathers hadn't died. He remembered that her father had been listed as "unknown". However, it was what Joanna had written in her suicide note about the sea and the sand, the same as Jessica's dream, that shocked him. Weirder by the moment, he thought.

'Sarge, as I was saying—'

'Yes, sorry, mate, when's the mother back? Do you have her name? I'll take it from here.'

'I'll get the info to you ASAP.'

*

Miriam was cradling her baby in her left arm as she used the index finger on her right hand to trace around Joanna's face and over her thick black hair. She'd made up a song called "All Around the World" that she sang while outlining her baby's beautiful features. Joanna seemed to like it; she was very contented. Miriam thought that she should find her baby's appearance abhorrent, she looked so much like her father, but just as she loved her new-born, she also still loved Johan despite his cruel and brutal actions.

She remembered the first day she met him. Miriam had just started working as a PA on a South African Equity desk at major bank at the "Square Mile" in London. Instantly she'd known she had a crush on him. A year later he still hadn't apparently noticed her, nor did he seem to know her name. Most of the guys called her "Babs", as in Barbara Windsor, for the way she totted around in four-inch heels trying to make her four-foot-eleven-inch body appear taller. Her hair was a mass of blonde curls piled on top of her head to increase her height further. The tight mini skirt she always wore also added to their illusion of her as being a sixties sex kitten, despite it being 1986. Miriam thought it may well have been because of the antiquated behaviour of the guys, but she knew she couldn't complain.

Johan would often shout, 'Girl, get me a coffee,' and Miriam would always stop off at the toilet first to check her hair and make-up before taking his beverage to him. 'Black and strong, girl, *not* like my women, I hasten to add,' he'd say, before laughing and spinning his chair back to his desk.

Racist and sexist.

It wasn't just her; she knew that. If any of the other PAs walked past, he mostly shouted out some sexist comment to them or slapped their bottoms. Miriam didn't know how they felt about it. They all seemed to go to lunch together but never invited her and she didn't know why. At least they knew her name. There was a nice older guy, called John, who seemed different. He always asked her how her weekend had been, or asked how she was, with genuine interest.

He knew her name, but Johan didn't.

Miriam's twenty-first birthday was on 23rd January 1987. She'd taken a cake in to share with anyone who may be interested. She'd called out to Jeanette as she walked by that if she or any of the other PAs wanted some, she'd leave it on the side. Jeanette wished her happy birthday and carried on to her own desk.

At lunchtime Miriam took a walk over London Bridge; the loneliness had been engulfing her recently. Living a solitary life in her studio flat only added to that. Her elderly parents had sent a card. Her mum had written, "Happy 20th birthday, Miriam". It had made her laugh and cry at the same time. She needed to go home more often; it just seemed such a chore. Miriam had been what they called a "change baby". Her mum had three children in her twenties and thirties and then Miriam had unexpectedly come along as a gift for her mum's fiftieth birth year. Her older siblings looked after her parents as much as was necessary. Miriam left as soon as she could, but she felt lonely. Sometimes she wished she was at home with her dad shouting at the TV and the constant click-clack of her mum's knitting needles. She admired the way her mum seemed to be able to knit, chat and watch the TV at the same time. No, she considered, this was her big chance to make strides in the world, but after being in London for a year she felt as if she was just going round in circles.

On her return to the office, she could hear some of the staff starting to sing "Happy Birthday" – maybe she'd been wrong about being invisible; maybe Jeanette had told them.

But then she heard a loud South African voice behind her: '*Wankers!* I thought you'd forgotten!'

Johan pushed her out of the way as he shook the champagne bottle he had in his hand and then proceeded to pop the cork and spray the contents as he spun round. It hit Miriam square in the face and the fizzy liquid rolled down her glasses. It was times like these when she thought windscreen wipers should be invented for spectacles, then and when the foggy drizzle that seemed to be a constant theme in London's winters was falling.

She managed to shrink as much as she could as she made her way back to her desk to dry off her chest and her glasses.

Miriam's face flushed with embarrassment, and to add to her humiliation, she could now see Jeanette and John deep in conversation. He glanced over at her, smiling but in a pitying way. Miriam didn't want anyone's pity. She hadn't known they shared a birthday; strangely that delighted her, and she now knew he was thirty today. She knew his behaviour was wrong, but she couldn't help the butterflies she felt in her stomach.

Jeanette came over to Miriam's desk just as she'd finished wiping her glasses. 'I was just saying to John about it being your birthday too, and when the markets close, we're finishing early and going over to Lumbreras – would you like to come too?'

At last, thought Miriam, maybe after being here a year she was finally being accepted. Truth be told, John had convinced Jeanette to invite her to save face over the humiliating birthday debacle. Even if Miriam knew the real reason she still would've gone and realised this might be her first opportunity to get to speak to Johan out of the context of work.

The restaurant/nightclub had been opened early for Johan's party, and more and more guests were arriving as the evening wore on. Miriam couldn't believe he knew this many people but figured that a gregarious character like him must collect friends like other people collected Barbies. Well, OK, she thought, maybe she was the only adult still amassing a collection of Barbie dolls, but they would be worth money one day, she hoped.

Standing in a corner drinking a pineapple juice, she surveyed the party unfolding in front of her. They weren't even hiding their cocaine consumption. A skimpily dressed lady had a silver tray with a mound of white powder on it, offering it around like canapes. She'd seen Johan go up to the woman several times already, staggering around with a champagne bottle in his hand, again, but this time he wasn't spraying it. He didn't have a glass; he was swigging directly from the bottle. She'd also seen him kiss a few of the girls and wondered how many of them he'd slept with previously. Miriam felt weirdly jealous. She'd tried to catch his eye on several occasions, to no avail. She'd practised in front of the mirror so many times previously, so she wondered why it didn't work in real life.

John wandered over to her to enquire as to her wellbeing. 'I don't suppose this sort of party is your thing, Miriam? I'm over it now too. I'm heading for my fiftieth rather sharpish and I'm going to get out of the rat race and sail my yacht around the Med. I'm guessing you'd rather be curled up at home with a book and your cat?'

Miriam screwed up her face – did she look like one of those *cat ladies*? Was that the impression she gave everyone? Surely her clothes showed that she wasn't some meek librarian type. In her heart, though, she knew her outfits were uncomfortable, and she would love a cat but didn't think her landlord would allow it.

'Sorry, I didn't mean to offend. This lot, you know, it's all superficial and they'd all sell their grannies to meet their targets. You deserve better, so much better. My nephew, he's about your age, lovely lad, studying biomechanics or something like that. I could pair you up if you like?'

Miriam shook her head; John was well-meaning, but she wanted that superficial guy who could show her the bright lights of London, who'd take her out to fancy restaurants like this one. Shower her with expensive gifts, flying first class to exotic locations. She'd only ever been abroad once, to Benidorm with her parents when she was fifteen.

'I'm OK, John, no, thanks. I'm going to head home, though, see you on Monday?'

'OK, sweetie, I'll call you a cab. It'll go on expenses.'

Miriam nodded. He was very perceptive. She wondered if he'd been like the younger guys once. Had he managed to circumnavigate that? Or perhaps he'd just grown out of it. Perhaps they all did eventually. She could see out of the corner of her eye that Johan was involved in an embrace with not one but two girls. She felt the nausea beginning to rise in her mouth and told John that she'd wait outside for the cab.

The winter air hit her hard as she stepped onto the pavement; she hadn't realised how hot it was in the club. She pulled her coat tighter around her body and walked to the edge of the building where there was an alley, looking to keep out of the bitter wind. Miriam had only been there a few minutes when she heard footsteps along with a retching sound. Johan swung around the corner and proceeded to vomit. She rummaged in her handbag for a packet of tissues then went over to him.

He wiped his mouth on his shirt sleeve, catching his lip on his very expensive cufflink, and reached out to take the tissue.

'Is it bleeding? It feels like it is.'

'No, it's not, are you OK?'

'Oh, it's you! Coffee girl, or should I call you birthday stealer?'

'Miriam, my name is Miriam.'

'Well, Miriam, would you like a birthday kiss?'

He walked closer towards her and placed his hand around her waist. She could smell the weird mixture of vomit and champagne on his breath, but she didn't care. This was all her birthday wishes rolled into one. Johan began kissing her forcefully; this wasn't the fairy-tale scenario she'd played out so many times in her head, but he was kissing her.

Then he bit her lip.

'Ow!' She tried to step back from his embrace, but his grip got tighter.

'Come on, you like it a little rough.'

Miriam shook her head and tried to wrestle her way out of his grasp.

'I've seen the way you look at me – you're a little virgin, aren't you? I love virgin girls.'

Inside her head she began to scream, but when she opened her mouth no sound came out. She looked around, wondering where the taxi was, but unbeknown to her it had been and left. Desperately trying to wriggle herself free, she then swung her bag at his head.

'Oh, you want to play games, do you?' And he slapped her so hard she almost fell over; with that, he pushed her down to the floor as she was desperately trying to steady herself. He hit her again with one hand while his other was tearing at her clothes. Whatever he was doing now was hurting Miriam so bad and she managed to scream out, but then he struck her again and everything went black.

*

John's wife tooted her horn outside the club, and he signalled to her to reverse into the alley, and he began to walk that way. Then he banged on the bonnet of the car to get her to stop. In her rear lights he could see something on the floor and didn't want her to reverse over it and damage the car. She wasn't the best of drivers and was always more nervous when John was watching.

He walked up to the heap on the floor and bent down, realising it was a woman, but not any woman: it was Miriam, and she was beaten up badly. A low moan came from her as he took off his coat to roll up and place under her head. He shouted to his wife to get out of the car and help him; she was shocked by what she saw.

'I called her a cab an hour ago, what the hell?'

'You know her?'

'Yes, yes, she works in the office, come on, help me get her in the car and get her to hospital.'

Miriam never told a soul who had raped her. She knew she was supposed to hate Johan, but all she ever did was make excuses in her head as to why he had behaved like that. She never returned to the office; by the time she had recovered she realised she was pregnant. John and his wife had regularly visited her and had tried to convince her to have an abortion. That wasn't what she wanted. John placed his bonus in her bank account to tide her over and told her he would square it with the boss if she wanted to come back. He had no idea how little she earnt compared to the traders and his generous gift meant she didn't have to think about work for many years.

John and his wife never saw baby Joanna. He'd retired in the summer and had a heart attack on his yacht. At least his wife had told her; she didn't owe Miriam anything, but she never saw her again.

Here she was, still singing to the baby and still not

understanding why she had forgiven Johan, no matter how many times she ran the vicious event through her head. She would always have a part of him in Joanna and that seemed enough. Glancing at the clock, she noticed it was almost 3.30am and decided to put the now-sleeping baby back in her crib, but as she went to stand up from her own bed, Joanna disappeared from her arms. Miriam's mouth fell wide open and not for the first time in her life, no scream could be heard other than in her head, so loud it was deafening her.

She fell face down on her bed; was she being punished? Did Johan do that to so many other women that she had to be the one to be reprimanded for not speaking out and saving others? Her tears were free-flowing now and she managed to speak out loud between her sobs. 'Please bring her back to me – I will tell on him, just please bring her back!'

Miriam had no idea who she was speaking to, or if perhaps she was just dreaming. The last few weeks had been so demanding; she was exhausted. She hadn't watched the TV or even read a newspaper. Miriam didn't know how much time had elapsed until she heard a gentle thud at the foot end of her bed; as she looked up, she saw that not only was it 3.40am but Joanna was cooing contentedly.

'*Thank you*,' she said out loud, still not knowing who she'd been speaking to or who she was thanking. Holding Joanna tightly, she promised to go to the police and tell them about Johan.

But she didn't.

When Joanna disappeared and reappeared the following month, she made the same promise and continued to, month after month without ever getting the courage to do so.

Joanna was about six months old when Miriam was in town and bumped into Jeanette. The look of surprise on Jeanette's face at the presence of a baby in a pushchair didn't go unnoticed and Miriam decided to lie.

'Oh, this is Joanna. I'm a nanny now for a lovely family.'

'Oh right, we wondered what had happened after you left so abruptly. John had said you'd got a new job, but he didn't know where. So sad what happened to him and Johan.'

Miriam went to answer that she knew about John but stopped when she heard Johan's name.

'Johan? You said John and Johan? What happened?'

'John had a heart attack, and as for Johan, I reckon he got his comeuppance – in the big storm, he was apparently staggering home and a billboard fell and killed him instantly. He wasn't a nice guy, Miriam.'

Miriam knew that and more but stayed silent. After a few pleasantries the two women went in different directions. Miriam was attempting to unlatch the gate with one hand whilst holding the pushchair with the other. She lived on a slight hill and the pushchair's brake was broken so she didn't want to look like she was in some comedy sketch show chasing a pushchair as it careered away from her. With her hands full, she finally managed to get into the front garden, where she could hear a gentle little meow. Miriam wedged the pushchair against the back of the gate so she could safely let go and investigate. She moved towards the dustbin and the noise got closer. As she gently lifted the lid, she saw there, sitting on top of a bag of rubbish, was a tiny black kitten with a white streak on the top of his head.

'There, there, beautiful thing, you look like Joanna when she's back from her travels, though I don't think I'll be covering yours with mascara! Let's call you "Mallen", after the TV show!'

Miriam never told her landlord she had a cat, and she never told a soul that her baby kept disappearing.

*

'I'm telling you, Jess, these are just falling in my lap. There's got to be a bigger picture here.'

Josh downed his whisky in one go before pouring another.

'Do all you coppers drink so much?'

'Oh, don't go on. I wanted to tell you about meeting this Miriam woman. The mother of the suicide girl, Joanna. God, that's a sad one, no wonder she killed herself.'

Josh went on to tell Jess about visiting Miriam. She had admitted that she was raped and consequently Joanna was born; she said she would've tried to prosecute him but he died in the Great Storm, a freak billboard accident.

'That was all she would say, in between her tears. I asked as many questions as I dared without directly asking, but I think it's safe to say that Joanna was a "16/87". I wonder if we need to look at the list again – we can't assume anything.'

'It's this kind of thing that makes me want to find them all. We need to support them. They could all be struggling mentally.'

'But you don't, Jess, do you? Or is there something you aren't saying?'

'All I'm saying is that not everyone can cope. My mum took the brunt of it – I guess I was always so busy looking after her that I never had a chance to allow any negative feelings to come up. You have to remember that I love seeing my dad, but obviously that Joanna didn't. And that really is sad. Put your whisky down and let me make us a nice cuppa.'

*

Jess asked her father about the rapist on the worm moon, but he wouldn't elaborate. She wondered if he was being deliberately avoidant but couldn't understand why he would be. It was her and Josh's project, though, and she hadn't intended to involve her papa at all. She also asked him if he had met Gail. She'd been quiet of late; Jess knew she'd been around because of the aroma in the bathroom but there were no other clues. Josh had been pressing Jess, especially after another evening of booze, that surely she must know something – after all, she had that "foresight" gift. Tomorrow he was meeting with a clairvoyant; maybe Jess was too close to him to be able to tune in.

*

The room where Josh was meeting Mary Jane was dimly lit. He immediately thought he'd made a mistake. There were so many charlatans out there; looking around it was like some funfair caravan mystic's home. There were silks draped over a circular table. Incense was burning and low chanting sounds were coming from the stereo in the corner. On top of the table were a pack of cards. Josh hoped his detective skills would weed out any frauds and he absentmindedly picked up the tarot cards.

'Starting without me, my lovely?'

Josh jumped; he hadn't seen that she was already in the room. He had a bit of a hangover after arguing with Jess. He knew he was drinking even more than usual, but he didn't really see it as a problem. So much for his skills, he thought, if he hadn't noticed her. Maybe she'd only just materialised; after all, this year had been the strangest in his whole life and nothing would surprise him now.

'Carry on,' she nodded, 'give them a good shuffle.'

'My girlfriend has cards, not like these, though.'

'And we aren't here to talk about her, lovely girl, though, Jem? Jen? Jess! Yes, lovely girl, Jess, you mustn't lose her.'

In the space of less than two minutes Josh knew she was the real deal, and he didn't need to be a detective to know that. He quickly racked his brains to make sure she could never have found out on social media who he was. He hadn't even given her his real mobile number or surname. Josh had used a "burner phone" – he wasn't taking any chances.

'Why would I lose her?'

'Not my words, they're Gail's. She has regrets – does that make sense?'

Josh meekly nodded.

'This card here indicates that you are struggling with a problem.'

'Is that a question?'

'No, no, it's a statement. Gail says she's no longer in pain and she really appreciated that you looked after her to the end.'

'Is she my mum?'

'Now she's laughing – no, you already know that.'

'So, what's the secret?'

'I don't actually think that's relevant – my words, not hers. She says you have an important job to do, and you should focus on that.'

'But I need to know! That's why I'm here!'

Mary Jane turned over another card. 'I don't really need to use these, let's just chat.' She swooped up all the cards and put them to one side.

'No! What did you see? Was it something bad?'

Mary Jane shook her head and told Josh that she only really needed the cards when she was finding it hard to connect with the spirit world but that Gail had been with her all morning and Josh being open helped, even though he'd initially been sceptical. Mary Jane went on to give him more evidence that she really was gifted. Little things, really, like his favourite childhood toy, but she still didn't give him the answer he wanted.

Josh stood up; he'd heard enough.

'You still have ten minutes; you don't have to leave.'

'If Gail isn't going to tell you what I need to know there's no point, is there?'

'Maybe not now, but I know she will when the time is right. She keeps saying "patience" and that you mustn't ruin your relationship with Jess. Can you think why she would say that?'

Josh lied by saying no, but he gathered it had something to do with the argument. The only disagreements they'd had were to do with his excessive drinking.

'She says that you need Jess as much as she needs you; her exact words are – and please excuse my language – but she says, *Don't fuck this one up!*'

Josh knew that was the sort of expression Gail would use, but he didn't feel that it was his fault his ex-girlfriend cheated on him.

'Infidelity is not the reason for break-ups; they are a symptom of a bad relationship, and Josh, you know in your heart why that happened.'

Josh was momentarily stunned. He believed everything this woman had said to him so far, but that sentence was like she was reading his mind.

'I'm just a vessel for communication between the spirit world and this world. It is *all-seeing*, and I just report what *I* see. Listen, we all have *work* we have to do on ourselves and that doesn't make us bad people, but it's easy to fall down into an abyss and that's not what Gail wants for you. She tells me that it is Jess who will eventually give you the answers you want, but have patience – you need to help her first without pushing her away forever.'

As Josh walked back to his car, he was replaying everything back to himself. It was a trick he'd learnt at Hendon, to make sure that he didn't forget even the most minor, mundane detail that could be the key that unlocked a case.

He knew that tonight was the full moon. He wanted to make things up with Jess before she disappeared. He knew what he had to do, but was he ready? He sat in his car with his hands on the steering wheel; he hadn't even turned the ignition on. Once again, he replayed the events with Mary Jane. He didn't think he had a problem; it wasn't something he'd even considered. He allowed his mind to wander back to Lucinda, his ex. He started with when things were good and then thought about how the fights had started, each and every one of them. He remembered when he'd caught her in bed with the guy from the gym. Personal trainer who got too personal, such a cliché, but yep, that guy had obviously been listening when he hadn't. What was the last thing she'd said to him? Take *blank* and get out of my house? Take your *blank* and get out of my house? Josh was banging the steering wheel trying to remember. Jack! Why had she brought his mate into the conversation? He and Jack had been working on a case up in Liverpool and had come back early; Josh invited Jack for a takeaway with him and Lucinda. Jack had restrained Josh from punching out the PT guy instead of helping him. What did Jack know that he didn't? He needed to figure it out. Starting the car, he reversed away from Mary Jane's house and towards Jess's home, or *their* home now since she'd invited him to stay. He hated going back to Gail's, too many memories, and Jess had suggested that he took some time out to think about what to do with the house and that she was happy for him to move in.

He really needed a hug.

However, he arrived at the flat to find a note saying she'd gone for a run. At least she didn't have a PT, he mused. He poured himself a drink and began scrolling through his phone. As he idly went through Facebook, he saw a post from Jack, who had moved to Liverpool a couple of years ago. He shook his head; he felt this was way too much of a coincidence, but since the start of the year, nothing surprised him anymore. Jack had posted a photo of his new-born, Connor, and Liverpudlian wife, Holly. He hit the like button and went into his contacts, easily finding Jack's number; he pressed dial.

'Yo! How are you, *Daddy*? You kept that one quiet!'

'Mate, I've rung you loads, don't you ever listen to your voicemails?'

'Sorry, Jack, I did, I just wasn't ready to talk about Gail.'

They then began to chat, Josh playing his cards close to his chest. He wanted to ask him about that day at Lucinda's but didn't want to seem as if he'd only called for that information.

Eventually Jack intimated that he needed to go, so Josh took a deep breath. 'Listen, before you go, can I ask you about Lucinda?'

'I told you, mate: she shacked up with that PT. I think they're married now – no kids, though. What about you? Heard from one of the guys that you've got a new girl.'

'Yeah, she's great, but I don't want to fuck this one up. You know, I think back to that day, and you didn't man up with me; you weren't on my side. That cuts, mate, and she told me to leave and take you with me – don't you think that's weird?'

Jack took a deep breath. 'She wasn't referring to me. Jack as in "Jack Daniels", man. You were getting out of hand – you weren't there whenever she needed you and he was. That's the bottom line.'

Josh looked at his empty glass. 'Cheers, mate, I'll let you get on.' He ended the call before Jack had the chance to say goodbye.

Walking towards the sink with the bottle in his hand, he poured it down the drain. Then he went underneath the sink and fiddled about in the back, beyond all the reusable carrier bags, before pulling out another bottle disguised as detergent and pouring the liquid away.

He went into their bedroom. Jess had given him one wardrobe and three of the drawers in the tall chest. Opening the wardrobe, he began pulling out his shoes; tucked into the toe of each of them were miniature bottles of alcohol. Once they were all out and on the carpet, he began to cry. How had he got here? He obviously had a problem if he had to hide the evidence. What made him do that? To stop Jess nagging him like Lucinda always had. The penny had finally dropped, but he didn't think he could do this alone.

Getting up, he went into the bathroom to wash his face, just as Jess arrived back home. She called out to him as she wandered in the direction of the bedroom. She stopped in her tracks when she saw the collection of bottles on the floor, and he came out of the bathroom.

They both stood staring at each other in silence which seemed to Josh like the longest time; he spoke first: 'I need help.'

Jess didn't reply but instead walked over and held him tightly, and he began to sob again.

FOUR

PINK MOON

The only way Storm knew that it was almost the full moon was when she got her period. OK, so that wasn't the most reliable data she could have, but she didn't want to draw any attention to herself, such as getting a lunar calendar like she had at home. Since her incarceration she had been determined to stay in the shadows, just as she had done throughout her whole life. That also meant always having a supply of mascara to cover the white streak that appeared after she returned from her travels.

When she'd first been sentenced, she'd asked to be put in solitary confinement, but those in authority couldn't justify that. She then decided that she'd be better off if she were in the bottom bunk so that the bulge of her body disappearing wouldn't be seen if her cellmate was awake.

Her last one, Marina, was such a heavy sleeper and snored so loudly that it was never an issue. However, she had now been replaced by Jodie, who was a live wire and wanted to talk for as long as she could rather than go to sleep. In the end, Storm told Jodie why she was there, in a deliberately aggressive way as if to warn the girl that she'd end up the same way if she didn't go to sleep. Storm didn't mean it, just as she didn't mean to kill Jason; he'd just been in the wrong place at the wrong time.

It had been the weekend after freshers' week; the two of them had previously hooked up but that still didn't give him the right to sneak into her room. They'd all been at the local pub and carried on drinking in the shared kitchen of their student flat. The only reason her mum had let her live at a uni away from home was if Storm promised to lock herself in on every full moon. Her mum had personally put three locks on the inside of her bedroom; she'd always been self-sufficient. It had always been just the two of them. Storm's father had died of an overdose the night she was born, and her mum was determined to lead Storm to a totally different lifestyle. She'd studied and got herself a good job, managed to get Storm into a good school and encouraged her academically. Not once did she ever question why her daughter vanished every month; when Storm was old enough, her mum would just say, 'Ours is not to question why, ours is just to do and die.' But she didn't want Storm to die, just to live her life as fully as possible, unlike her father. It comforted her mother to know that Will had all traces of addiction leave his body at the time of his death. Storm used to talk a lot about how regretful he was and that he felt he had a relationship with his daughter which wouldn't have happened if he were alive.

Jason should be alive, thought Storm. No matter how many times she replayed that night in her head, there was just no justification for the actions she'd taken. The first full moon after his death she hoped she would see him, but only her dad, Will, was there on the beach. When Storm was with Will the tortuous self-loathing never was. That was something she didn't understand.

Storm could replay every last moment prior to Jason's death, which she often did as a form of self-punishment. She remembered the smell of his Burberry aftershave, what he'd been wearing, the jeans with a belt, buckling under the strain of his belly; he'd tucked his shirt inside of them. Storm had laughed and untucked the shirt that he hoped would hide his puppy-fat belly. She told him that as the shirt was square at the bottom it was OK to have it out over his jeans. She'd also joked with him that while he was slightly overweight, he wasn't fat enough to warrant his own documentary series. He'd used his one and only chat-up line requesting that she felt his hair as it was as soft as a chinchilla but that his hair was the only soft thing about him. Storm had laughed and reminded him that his belly was in competition with his hair. They'd been singing and sort of dancing to Rhianna's "Umbrella" and her other three flatmates had been laughing so hard in the kitchen when they tried to deny any romantic notions between them.

Jason had excused himself and they all thought he'd gone to bed. Storm had glanced at her watch – 3.20am – and knew she too had to go. After entering her room, she locked each one of the three bolts and then finally the Chubb lock. She wandered over to the sink in the corner of the room to clean her teeth, not knowing that Jason was hiding in her wardrobe.

He was going to play a prank on her, hoping to make her laugh, hoping he was going to laugh her into bed. His father had always said that his comedic retorts would get him all the girls. He told Luke, one of the other flatmates, who had also thought it was a good idea.

Storm was too tired to even change into her nightwear; she turned the lights off and just flopped on her bed face down. Jason was biding his time, waiting for the right moment; he'd been listening for ten minutes now. It was all quiet and he suddenly began to think that this prank hadn't been such a good idea, but how to get out of it? He started deliberately coughing in the hope she would call out; she didn't. Then he started calling her name, to no avail. Finally, he stepped out of the wardrobe, called her name and simultaneously turned on the light. The bed was empty; he initially thought that she'd sussed him out and was hiding under the bed to prank him back. She wasn't there and he spun around 360°; she definitely wasn't anywhere in the room.

And then she was back, face down on the bed.

Instantly she knew she wasn't alone, even though Jason was stunned into silence. Storm instinctively reached down for the baseball bat. Her uncle Marcus had made it at school in woodwork and metalwork class. The wood exterior of it belied its lead insert; it looked fairly standard. Her mum had remarked at the time that she wished she could've taken that class instead of cooking and sewing and how that had never helped her in any way when she'd lived in the squat. The truncheon was always just under her bed on the right-hand side, and without thinking she jumped up and swung as hard as she could without even opening her eyes.

Jason hit the floor with a heavy thud.

No amount of pleading that it was self-defence made any difference. She couldn't prove he'd attacked her; she didn't have a mark on her. Luke took to the stand and said that he thought she was a "bit strange", but in the few weeks that he'd known her he had no reason to think she was violent.

Manslaughter, that was the final verdict.

Storm had served nearly a decade when her first chance at parole came up in 2017. She had been a model inmate and had never caused any trouble.

*

'You can't go! You just can't.'

'Jess, it's my best mate's stag weekend, Rich ain't going to forgive me if I don't go.'

'You're a recovering alcoholic, you can't swan off to Scotland this early on in your sobriety.'

'I'll tell them I'm on antibiotics.'

'Like they're going to take any notice of that. How about you tell them the truth, Josh?'

*

Storm's mum Lizzie had a distrust of the internet ever since its inception with the old analogue dial-up service. It took several years before the young teenage Storm had convinced her to have it installed. The night before she sat her daughter down and said, with amazing prescience, that one day it would be a listening-in device and consequently they must never speak about her affliction when it was turned on. In later years, when it did indeed seem as if everything they spoke about was shuffled in an algorithm, she made Storm yet again promise not to ask Google if there was anyone like her. Lizzie explained that she feared that Storm would be taken away by some shady government officials and become a "lab rat".

She also explained as soon as she felt Storm was old enough to comprehend what living with addiction was like. She wanted the rot to stop with Storm. It didn't have to be a foregone conclusion that just because her father was a drug addict and that both sets of grandparents were alcoholics that it was inevitable. Lizzie had swerved that, though she was often intoxicated by the fumes of marijuana that some of the other guys in the squat smoked.

The squat. A time that Lizzie often looked back on as a reminder of how far she had come. The only addiction she ever had was towards Storm's father. She thought she could fix Will. He often said all the right things only for it to amount to nothing. Lizzie dreamt of them living rurally, in a beach-type house overlooking a loch away from all the bad influences. In the end she had to admit that the only thing he truly loved was heroin.

When she was thirty weeks pregnant the council finally gave them a one-bedroom flat. It had no heating apart from a gas fire in the living room. The windows used to ice on the inside, and she wore three jumpers to keep her warm, stretching them over her ever-expanding belly. Will used to break into the gas and electric meters whenever he was desperate.

The flat was a bus ride away from the squat, but Will used to walk. Anyone with working legs and an overriding desire could save the bus fare. When she was in labour, he met her at the hospital, saying all the right things about getting clean. For a few minutes she actually believed him. Will said he was going to get them both a coffee and Lizzie had given him the only thing in her purse, a ten-pound note.

He didn't return.

It was no surprise to her when two days later the police came into the maternity ward. Lizzie knew that they were visiting her and not to just admire her beautiful baby in the cot beside her bed. When they left, she tried to contain her emotions, but the tears seeped out of her eyes. She hauled herself out of the bed and pulled the curtains open. The policemen had drawn them around her bed when they'd arrived, but she couldn't see the point. The other three new mums in her ward had clearly overheard. She met the eye contact of one of them and despite the overwhelming sadness that was creeping up from the soles of her feet to the top of her head, she stayed defiant. Staring back at the new mum, she said one word: 'And?'

It was at that moment that she decided enough was enough and that she would do everything in her power to stop the cycle. She wanted to help others in her situation and went to college, eventually becoming a Family Liaison Officer for relatives of the addicted. Lizzie felt it was the least she could do, because if anyone understood the pain of loving someone who loved a drug more than life itself, it was her.

*

Jess was playing with her food. Josh's plate sat opposite hers, his meal congealing as it got colder and colder. She understood his "FOMO" but it was done now. He'd returned from work and gave it to Jess with "both barrels". She took his vitriol; he'd thrown something wrapped in a newspaper into the overflowing bin in the kitchen. She didn't even ask what it was. He'd slammed the door on his way out, saying that he was going to an AA meeting. Jess was used to her mother's mood swings; she'd never expected the same from her boyfriend.

She flaked her fish like she was flicking through her phone, wondering what her next move should be. As nice as the "dine in for two" was, she was in no mood to eat. She pushed her chair away from the table; it caught the threadbare rug and nearly toppled her over. Josh would've laughed at that, but no-one had been in the mood for laughing.

Jess put her plate on the kitchen drainer. She needed to empty the bin before throwing away both plates of food. As she hauled the bin liner out of its container it spilt its contents all over the kitchen floor. The rolled-up newspaper unravelled itself to reveal a haggis. Josh's friends had obviously given him a souvenir from their stag weekend. She got it. Recovery was a long process and no amount of support from her was going to change that. Opening the cupboard under the sink, she took out a black bag to place the contents of the bin in. She left the haggis till last; the sheep offal had started to smell. It was only as she was using the newspaper it came in to pick it up that she saw the headline:

STORM MCDONALD RELEASED FROM PRISON.

Had it been any other first name she probably would've just discarded it. Jess stood up and pulled a couple of sheets of kitchen roll from its holder to pick up the haggis with and wiped the newspaper with the remaining sheet.

> *University killer released from prison on parole after almost ten years. Twenty-nine-year-old Storm McDonald always claimed it was self-defence when she attacked her flatmate within her locked bedroom door. Jason Mullaney, nineteen, had his head caved in by a truncheon that had been made by Storm's uncle. It was of wooden construction but had been bored out to put a piece of lead inside of it.*
>
> *Storm McDonald was brought up by her single mother after her heroin-addict father overdosed and died the night she was born on the Great Storm, 16th October 1987...*

Jess didn't need to read any further. Even in her mother's more lucid moments she had told her that if ever she was in a situation where her secret was revealed she should kill the person. When Josh had discovered what happened to her the last thing that she wanted to do was commit murder. It had actually been a relief. But this happened ten years ago. When Jess was nineteen, maybe she would've taken the same action as Storm.

She thought about Josh; he seemed to think that all these coincidences meant they were on the right path. Jess didn't believe in coincidences; everything happened for a reason. She agreed with Josh, though, that they knew they had a higher purpose and they needed to see it to its conclusion, whatever that was.

When he came back from his AA meeting she would make things right, whatever that meant. Jess was glad that he'd not gone to Scotland and was proud of him for telling the boys what the real reason was. To her it denoted that he really did want to stay in recovery, and that needed applauding.

*

Storm was becoming impatient; today was Freedom Day and she couldn't wait to sleep in her own bed. She wondered if her mum had redecorated, doubtful, and at least she wasn't going back to a young teenage room – there'd be no Take That posters on her wall. Storm was daydreaming and had to be woken out of the stupor by one of the officers.

'Storm, are you listening? I said you are to go home and tomorrow someone will come and put a tag on your ankle. You're out on licence, so no disappearing, do you hear me?'

Storm nodded in agreement but felt goosebumps on her arms; the word "disappear" caught her attention. She realised that she hadn't thought about visiting Will until now. Would her tag go off when she vanished next? Storm didn't think she could ask how much time would pass before the alarm went off; her mum had instilled in her not to raise any suspicions at any time. She could've asked her cellmate Jodie; she knew she'd had one before and probably knew how to circumnavigate it.

Lizzie was waiting for her daughter, hoping that her incarceration hadn't taken too much of a toll on her, but more importantly, she prayed that Storm hadn't picked up any bad habits. She berated herself. *Bad habits* – that was an understatement; it was more that she worried Storm had become a drug addict. Prison was supposed to rehabilitate whilst taking away liberty when she felt that it often corrupted those previously of good character. Lizzie's clients included several families who'd claimed their offspring hadn't touched drugs until going into prison. She'd loved one drug addict; she didn't know if she had the energy to love another.

Lizzie's other consideration while she was waiting at the prison gates was whether or not Storm would get on with Malcolm. It was one thing listening to her mum gush about her new boyfriend, it would be quite another when she realised that he'd moved into the family home. Lizzie hadn't been lonely. She was used to being on her own; she sat well with herself, but her heart ached for companionship of a romantic kind. Telling Malcolm to go away for a few days was the best decision whilst Storm was settling back in.

Except it wasn't.

It was then that Lizzie realised that there were a couple of guys a few metres away from her, one with a camera around his neck. She hadn't figured that Storm's release would be of interest to anyone but herself. Glancing at her watch, she saw it was nearly time. She had a large red scarf loosely slung around her neck; she slipped it off and edged herself closer to the gates. As they opened and Storm came towards her, Lizzie ran as fast as she could and threw the scarf over Storm's face.

'*WTF, Mum?*'

'Shush, keep walking, I'll guide you; they're taking photos!'

One of the men then began shouting, 'Storm, Storm, do you have anything to say to Jason's family? Do you think it's fair that you have your freedom and they never will? Storm, do you have anything to say to the family of the boy you murdered?'

Storm could feel the tears beginning to form at the inner corners of her eyes. She wanted to say so much. She wanted to speak to Jason's family, but no matter what she said she couldn't tell them the truth, and besides, nothing would be of any consolation to them. She'd just have to learn to live with it on the outside world.

Lizzie pushed Storm's head down and shoved her in the Toyota Yaris. She'd bought the car when Storm had passed her driving test just before uni, but her daughter had only driven it twice.

'Stay down, I don't think they're following us – just let me get on the dual carriageway first.'

Was this how it was always going to be? Suddenly home didn't feel like a place of safety either.

'I think I might move to London once I'm off licence.'

'London? You've never been and it's so far away.'

'Exactly, and that's the best reason for going.'

'It'll calm down, and as they used to say, today's news is tomorrow's chip paper.'

'It's not *for* them, Mum, I need to get away from all the constant reminders.'

The rest of the journey was spent in silence apart from the sound of the radio and Storm fiddling with the knob, scanning through the stations. Rhianna's "Umbrella" came on and instantly Storm felt herself transported back to that night. She turned the radio off; would she never be happy to hear music just in case it came on? No, just as she was sure that Jason's family didn't need any reminders to feel their grief, neither did she.

Guilt not grief.

Within half an hour of Storm being home, she realised that Malcolm had moved in. Selfishly, she had a tantrum like a toddler. It was *their* home not his, and how many times when she was growing up did her mum say that they could never have anyone living with them? Lizzie tried to placate her and speak to her like the adult she was, telling her that she needed love in her life just as much as anyone and that between the two of them they would make sure Malcolm never found out.

Storm ran up to her bedroom and slammed the door. Nothing had been touched since she'd left for university. It was clean, but the bed linen was exactly the same, now slightly discoloured from where the sun had caught it through the bedroom window. She opened her wardrobe; clothes that were ten years old had no appeal, but the shoebox underneath did. Storm gingerly opened it; she wasn't entirely sure of its contents, but she knew she'd written on the lid with a Sharpie "sentimental stuff".

The stub from a concert she'd been to with Woody and the love letters he'd written her. A few knick-knacks he'd given to her, a cuddly toy they'd won at the fair and his gold ring that she used to wear. She naturally wondered what he was up to now – probably married with kids; he'd always loved them. They used to speak about how one day they would have their own. Only they didn't and that was her fault. They'd been celebrating their exam results, drinking too much, and she'd kissed another boy from their class, in full view of Woody. To add to his humiliation, when he grabbed the lad, she broke up the fight and inadvertently punched Woody so hard he fell over. He never spoke to her again and Storm, full of regrets, went off to uni.

Storm put the box away and surveyed her surroundings. On her wall, still stuck on with Blu-Tack, was her lunar calendar from 2006. If only time had stood still. If only she hadn't hooked up with Jason; if only he hadn't decided to prank her. No, she thought, she caused this, just as she'd caused Woody's heartache, and she would just have to learn to live with it.

Somehow.

*

Things were already strained between Storm and Malcolm, despite her looking to be as cordial as possible, but today was the full moon and Storm showed her anxieties with stroppy petulance. Lizzie had already warned her to behave and tried to reassure her that he would be none the wiser during the night. She'd spent many of them in prison, but before that they always had a special supper and chatted about Will on those nights. Storm knew they couldn't, and although she'd craved normality – well, her normality – all the time she'd been in prison, she couldn't even have that now. The takeaway Chinese food did nothing to pacify her. Both women had the same fear about the ankle tag, and they were right.

The telephone began to ring about seven minutes after Storm had disappeared. Lizzie answered it and Malcolm lay there listening. Yes, of course Storm was at home, she'd told the official. Then Lizzie knew she had to keep them talking just for another couple of minutes. Malcolm got up and put his dressing gown on, proclaiming he was going to Storm's room. Damn, thought Lizzie as she proceeded to waffle on the telephone, of course she knew her daughter was home, she told them, and yes, she would fetch her for them to talk to. She also stalled them by asking questions – was it normal for the tags to have the odd malfunction? Malcolm was shouting out to Storm and rattling her door which was locked from the inside. Then he began to call out to Lizzie, so she placed her hand over the mouthpiece and glanced at her watch, 3.39am. She asked the caller to hold while she fetched Storm.

Malcolm was becoming irate, still banging the door and calling her name loudly. Then he heard it being unlocked. Storm was rubbing her eyes as if she had just awoken and now Lizzie was standing there too, holding the phone out to her. Once she'd finished the call, Malcolm was incensed that she hadn't answered him. She replied by saying that she was a deep sleeper and then slammed the door in his face.

Over breakfast, Storm announced that she still wanted to move to London, with Malcolm retorting that it would be a good idea, to broaden her horizons, he added. Any hope of them getting along seemed to be long forgotten. Lizzie felt like "piggy in the middle". They both seemed to resent each other's presence and were only tolerating each other because of the love they had for Lizzie. Storm didn't know if she could go anywhere, at least until she had her tag removed; she would still ask her parole officer, though.

*

The parole officer was going through her notes. Three times now, Storm McDonald's tag had gone off, almost the same day each month. A weird anomaly; she needed to call the company and find out if they had glitches like this on any of the other tags, and could it perhaps be a bad batch? She'd met with Storm earlier that day and asked her outright whether she knew the reason. Storm had shrugged her shoulders and asked how the hell should she know? But now the tag was off, and it was her time to get her life back together.

Lizzie was right: she knew nothing about London, but it was almost as if there was some sort of invisible force field drawing her to the place. Storm knew that London wasn't paved with gold, nor did the so-called "bright lights" hold any enticement for her, but she knew she *had* to go. It wasn't long before she was on the train, London-bound. Lizzie had pulled a few strings to find her some accommodation and an interview for a job. The rest was up to Storm. As much as Lizzie hated to admit it, she was glad. The enormity of keeping up the façade for nearly thirty years was totally draining. At least the decade she spent in prison gave Lizzie some respite – well, it didn't stop her worrying that one of Storm's cellmates may reveal her secret, but she had slept better than she'd ever done since 1987. Out of sight, out of mind? Yes, in a way Lizzie did think that. It reminded her of when her daughter went out clubbing in her youth. If Storm was coming home, Lizzie would pace the rooms in the house until she was safely in bed. However, if Storm was staying over at a friend's house, Lizzie slept soundly. Of course, going out on full moons was forbidden. Lizzie had made that abundantly clear when Storm was young. She figured it was a small price to pay for the secrecy.

*

'Hey, Josh, a young woman came in today for an interview. I saw her waiting outside the HR office. Her face seemed a bit familiar.'

'And?'

'She looked like the girl from the haggis paper!'

Jess went on to tell him that she'd heard the woman's voice as she was on her way to use the loo and it had been then when she'd heard the Scottish accent and had put two and two together. Consequently, she asked Hannah, the receptionist, what her name was. Hannah had then replied in hushed tones that it was that Scottish lass, Storm McDonald, who'd murdered her boyfriend. It wasn't common knowledge in London and Hannah had asked Jess for advice as to whether to tell the HR manager.

Jess told Josh that she'd persuaded her not to, insisting that they probably knew anyway.

'We need them where we can keep tabs on them, for sure, and you'll be able to find out her address. This is getting crazy, isn't it?'

'Wasn't it always?'

Josh laughed and then enquired as to how Jess's mum was. He knew she'd been over there after work and got used to being able to read Jess's face, but today she wasn't giving away any clues. A small tear formed and gently fell down her face, bringing her mascara with it.

'Worse, not the worst I've seen her, but I still sometimes think she'd be better off dead and I hate myself for thinking like that.'

'You aren't alone, I'm here for you, and besides which, all these "16/87s" have mothers, which is more than I've ever had.'

Jess had started to notice that he always managed to turn the conversation around to himself. Was that a red flag? They'd only been together four months; the alcoholism was enough to deal with, but his knack of "turning tables" was becoming more evident. Can leopards change their spots? Was this just because he was still grieving? Jess began to get a headache, and all these thoughts were just compounding this. She forgave her mum for everything because of her grief. Could she do the same for Josh?

*

'Maw! Maw! I got the job!'

'That is great news.' Lizzie called out to Malcolm to let him know too and he shouted back his congratulations.

Storm huffed, 'He's probably glad I'm not coming back.'

'Don't be like that, Storm, he is genuinely happy for you.'

'Happy that I'm not there, more like!'

They spoke for a few more minutes before hanging up. Storm threw her phone onto the sofa and surveyed her surroundings. The flat was a bit pokey but at least it wasn't like the squat her parents had lived in. Lizzie had often talked of those times; this was a world away from that. Storm admired her mum so much for all that she had done, and miraculously avoiding the addictions of her partner and her own parents. Storm did love the taste of alcohol, though she hadn't had many opportunities in her life to drink it, but when she had, she always over did it. Which was why she'd betrayed Woody and why, ultimately, she'd killed Jason, or rather she had under the influence. Storm didn't really blame the alcohol for either of those tragedies. She blamed herself, and there was nothing worse. Her parole officer had suggested she attend counselling, but Storm had refused. Now, here in London, she was beginning to think it might not be such a bad idea. She wandered into the kitchenette which overlooked her sofa bed, such was the tiny size of this studio flat, and unscrewed a bottle of cheap wine. Before the evening was over, she had popped to the off-licence on the high street and now there were three empty bottles in the overflowing rubbish bin along with empty takeaway cartons.

In the morning Storm decided that was enough. No more drinking alone – what purpose did that serve? She could see how easy it might be to fall into an abyss she may never get out of. Storm considered as to whether it was just a forgone conclusion, an inherited addictive personality. However, if her mum could break the chain, and knowing that Lizzie did that specifically for her, then surely she owed that much to her mum.

The walls of the studio flat seemed to be closing in on her further; a tightness of her chest made breathing difficult. The enormity of being an adult hit Storm for the first time.

She suddenly felt her world was caving in and had no idea how to pilot it.

*

'I did my cards again today.'

'And? I always thought you sort of people couldn't do your own. Do you fancy doing mine? Why is it that you never have? Are you afraid of what you might see?'

Typical Josh, question after question, she thought. Maybe he deserved that much. She began shuffling as she continued to talk.

'*You sort of people?* Come on, Josh, what's that supposed to mean?'

'It wasn't derogatory, honest, you can be so sensitive.'

'They didn't say a lot actually, but I know we're on the right path, but I don't know how it pans out. Here, take one.'

Josh reached over to where Jess was holding the cards, spread out in a fan shape; he went to the middle.

'*Frog?* Thought these were Moonology cards not animals!'

'It's all connected, Josh, those ones are called "Moon Totems". It says that the path has been cleared for you to make a change that previously seemed unachievable. Well, that's true, isn't it?'

'I've been doing that for several months now, so nothing new, and you could've deliberately engineered that, couldn't you?'

Jess sighed; she knew when he was behaving like this that there was no talking to him. What she hadn't said was that she'd pulled a card every month for him since they met. It was always the Frog. He still had a lot of work to do on himself and Jess questioned whether she had the energy to help him through it. She still wanted that "Prince Charming", but was she doomed to be forever kissing frogs?

FIVE

FLOWER MOON

'My name is Emilie and I'm an alcoholic.'

A chorus of 'Welcome, Emilie' ran around the dusty church hall. She'd already noticed that the room was obviously used as a children's nursery too. Brightly coloured artwork was everywhere; counting and alphabet charts were scattered on the doors and available wall space. What shocked Emilie was how dirty the floor was. She hoped that was a one-off, and besides which, she may not even come back here. She hadn't decided yet.

'I know exactly when it started, I was four years old.'

Emilie laughed nervously before continuing, 'I don't mean that I started drinking then. That was when my mum killed my baby sister in front of me. I was in and out of the care system, with various foster parents, and, well, it wasn't an easy time. I started drinking when I was twelve, when my so-called foster dad…' Emilie hesitated and only realised she was crying when a tear fell off her face and onto her hand.

'You're doing great, Emilie, there's no judgement here.'

Emilie nodded but sat back down; she didn't want to say any more. She'd already said far more than she intended. She couldn't stay; the revelation was too much. Not only could she not stop the tears from flowing but she felt like everyone was staring at her. If they were, it was with empathy, but it was too much for her.

*

'Emilie! Emilie! Come here now! The devil is using her again.'

Emilie rubbed her eyes as she wandered into her parents' bedroom, where she peered into her baby sister's cot; it was empty. She looked under her mum's bed. Emilie thought the baby was playing hide and seek. Four-year-old Emilie couldn't understand.

Her mum started some sort of incantation and was flicking water over the crib. Her voice was getting louder and louder. '*This child has gone again and when she is back, I will stop the devil in his tracks! He leaves his mark with a white streak in her hair!*'

Emilie had no idea what her mum meant or where her baby sister Adele had gone. Her mum pushed past her and ran down the stairs, telling Emilie not to move.

'Adele! Adele! Where are you?'

Little Emilie spun around and then heard her mum coming back up the stairs, an axe in her hand.

'*Watch, Emilie!* She will be back soon, you must see this – sit in that chair.'

Emilie did as she was told, then her mum started rummaging around in her dad's chest of drawers, pulling out various neck ties. She then proceeded to tie both Emilie's hands and feet to the chair.

'Do not turn away! The devil needs to know we will not have him in this house, and this is his final warning. I shall stop him coming through Adele and he will know not to come near you, or the same thing will happen!'

Emilie could taste last night's dinner in her mouth, and she swallowed hard to make the vomit go away. Everything that was happening was beyond her comprehension. She had no idea how long she'd been tied to the chair; it seemed like forever, but it was less than ten minutes. Her mother then started to sway and talk "in tongues". Every other sentence in her thick Kenyan accent was directed at Emilie: 'Look at the crib! Do not turn your head!'

The last time Emilie's mum said that Adele reappeared in her cot. With one swift blow the mum wielded the axe and instantly killed baby Adele.

The nightmares began then and never left, only to be supplanted by different ones when she was fostered by Mr and Mrs Potter. By now Emilie was twelve years old. It started with verbal abuse, calling her "the killer's daughter", which then turned into racial abuse; Mr Potter called her "the ni**er's daughter". This was usually followed up with an off-the-cuff remark about how at least there was one less of "them" in the world.

Emilie had decided that there was no God. How could she have been placed in their care? Surely there must've been some *auntie* she could've gone to? Why wasn't anyone checking up on her? The only thing she liked was school and she always wished the day there was longer. After school she would walk as slowly as she could home – anything to delay the inevitable.

Mr Potter had taken to visiting her during the night.

At some point she realised that she didn't have to go *home* – that was something she never had after Adele died. All she needed now was a plan. She knew that Mr Potter hid money in the back of the kitchen cupboard that held the coffee mugs. Emilie wasn't going to take it until the very last moment. She'd considered sneaking out the odd ten-pound note to try to slowly build up a stash, but she was so afraid of being found out and what Mr Potter might do if he did. Emilie had taken a peek on Sunday night and there was a big bundle of cash in there. Deciding to wait until Friday when they both went down the pub the week seemed endless. The only reason she wanted to wait was because on Friday she would get the results of a science test they'd taken. If only she wasn't bothered about school; she may well have stolen a few hundred pounds.

When Mr and Mrs Potter went to the pub as usual, she waited thirty minutes, just to be sure. Emilie had gathered up her meagre belongings and stuffed them in her school backpack along with her science books. She'd deserved the 97% on that test; she had wished it was full marks, but that was OK, she guessed. Emilie pulled out the kitchen stool to climb up to the cupboard and stood on her tiptoes, rummaging around trying to *see* with her hands – nothing. She climbed onto the kitchen countertop, nearly losing her balance, stupidly hanging onto the cupboard door, which pulled off one of the hinges. Normally she would've been terrified of the repercussions, but she laughed; she wasn't hanging around to find out. She methodically took one mug out after another until she got to the money one. It was an old mug with the slogan "I spent most of my money on beer and women, the rest I wasted". Emilie picked it up – nothing, so she threw it on the floor. Pieces of ceramic scattered everywhere. She then began to systemically take them all out, turning them upside down in the hope that it would reveal some cash like a magic trick, all to no avail. She gleefully smashed each one on the floor until the kitchen resembled a Greek wedding. Emilie was just about to close the cupboard when she glimpsed what she thought was a corner of a note, perhaps a twenty-pound one. It had slipped between the back board of the cupboard and the wall behind it. Only a tiny corner was visible, and she very carefully tried to prise the purple paper out with her fingernails. Emilie felt like she was performing an operation – one false move and it would be all over. How she hoped that one day she would be a surgeon and people would address her as Ms Akinyi and hold her in high esteem.

Twenty pounds and a school bag of belongings were all she had to her name – well, apart from her library card. She'd go there tomorrow, she thought, it was always nice and warm in there. Where to sleep tonight, though? Emilie had no clue, though she did feel an overwhelming desire to taste cider again. One of the boys at school had secretly smuggled some in recently and they'd passed it around in the field behind the science block. The trouble was she was only twelve and the second problem was that she also looked young for her age.

She would never be able to convince Mr Ahmed to sell her some from his little shop; he was used to seeing her in school uniform. Emilie thought better of it and continued walking along the high street to Tesco, stopping once she arrived at the magazine aisle to browse through a comic but really to observe the cashiers, all of them, but she decided they would never serve her. There was only one thing to do and that was to steal it.

Emilie was reluctant to do anything immediately; she was enjoying the warmth in there too – well, apart from the freezer aisles and even the fruit and vegetable section was chillier than the rest of the store. She wandered down the alcohol aisle and stopped about halfway down. She dropped her bag to the floor, deliberately letting its contents spill out before starting to repack it, slipping a bottle of cider from the bottom shelf into the central part of her bag, stuffing clothes back in and zipping it up to hide her contraband. She put her science books under her arm and strode out of the store.

She wanted to run but decided on brisk walking, not turning around in case she was being followed, though she soon made it to the park. The butterflies in her stomach were not fear, even though it was dark; freedom overrode everything. She couldn't recall a time when she had experienced these feelings other than once when she'd attained 100% on a maths test. That was her only comparison.

Emilie managed to find the swings and sat on one. Her mum used to take her there; they were vague memories, but she remembered the sensations of being swung higher and higher, so exhilarating. The young girl hadn't noticed that she'd put the cider in her bag upside down and the fizzy liquid exploded like a volcano when she opened it. As she placed her mouth over its top in the hope that she could stop the flow of alcohol being lost to the ground, it was then that she heard laughter behind her. Emilie recognised the lads; they were a couple of years above her at school.

'Want a hand with that?' asked a lad whom she knew as Ashley.

She let him have a mouthful; he passed it on to his other two friends and within a couple of rounds it was empty. Emilie wanted more. Ashley assured her that he could get served in the off-licence, so she gave him the only money she had, the twenty-pound note. They told her to wait on the swings and they would be back, proclaiming that if Emilie was with them the store owner wouldn't serve them as he would guess.

In her naivety she let them go and never saw them or the money again. That night she stayed in the bandstand to sleep. It was cold but at least it kept her out of the wind.

*

Auntie Adele was everything the Potters were not and best of all she shared a name with Emilie's sister. Her carer had wondered if that would be a problem and had suggested she called her "Auntie Addie", but Emilie declined. The warmth this woman exuded was such that Emilie felt she was being swaddled in a huge duvet in her big embraces. This home was definitely going to be OK. Adele had gently tried to cajole Emilie into speaking about her sister and the Potters without success, and again, that was OK. Best of all, thought Emilie, was that Auntie Adele knew how to plait her hair. Just that one kindness helped so much.

The rest of Emilie's schooldays were filled with laughter and studying. Auntie Adele helped her decide where her education was going and was supportive when Emilie decided not to go into medicine but to be a lawyer instead. When she heard that her mother could potentially be paroled, that was the third time she tasted alcohol. She had walked to the off-licence, easily passing for an adult now, to buy some cider. Emilie knew she wanted to fight in the future to make "life mean life" and to make sure that children, not only those in foster care, would be able to speak up about abuse knowing they would be taken seriously. For now, though, she sat in the same bandstand she had when she'd run away and drank the whole two litres within minutes.

Emilie wanted to block out the nightmares that often purveyed her sleep. Auntie Adele, on more occasions than Emilie could remember, came into her room after hearing the night terrors and comforted her, rocking her back to sleep, always saying, 'My child, everything always unfolds as it should.' But now? It was easier to be soothed knowing her mum was under lock and key; however, now, potentially she could be on the streets. She may even want to take Emilie away from Auntie Adele. Sixteen-year-old Emilie knew that her mum could request that she spent at least the next two years living with her. She squeezed the empty plastic bottle with every bit of energy she had. No, she thought, surely the parole board wouldn't release her, and surely they wouldn't make Emilie go back to the woman who'd murdered her sister. The woman didn't deserve the "mum" title, in no way, shape or form.

*

The mother was finally released when Emilie was taking her bar exams. She was a fully-fledged adult entering the working world and could make her own decisions. Adele sent on the letters that Emilie's mum wrote; she never opened them, chucking them into the open fireplace in her ground-floor garden flat. It was a sparse home, neat with little furniture apart from the bulging bookcase. On the mantelpiece, sat proudly in the centre, was the only photo she had of baby Adele, sitting on Emilie's lap when she was just hours old. Whilst technology could have reproduced the photo in pristine condition, Emilie didn't want to do this. The Polaroid didn't fit its frame properly, was creased in places and a coffee stain was on the top right-hand corner, but to her it was perfect. She slipped it into her handbag for luck with her exams, silently swearing to Adele that she would make sure anyone she prosecuted for heinous crimes wouldn't get away with a lighter sentence. If she could have, she would've brought back capital punishment. Languishing in prison was not suitable retribution, not at all, according to Emilie.

*

Her breakthrough came in 2014 when Jimmy Savile was finally convicted of historical crimes, albeit posthumously. She didn't remember much about that weekend; she could afford much stronger drinks than cider, drinking them neat and at speed. Emilie was desperate, wanting to blur all the horrific memories that this case had reopened from the box in her mind that she'd shut tightly many years previously.

When she ignored her morning alarm, finally waking up at midday realising she didn't know what day it was, her bed was sodden, her mouth dry. Looking in the mirror, she didn't recognise the person staring back at her. She picked up her phone to see what day it was, noticing the missed calls from work. It dawned on her that she should've been in court that day. Listening to the voicemails, she was glad that her colleague had been sent on ahead to the court; if she hurried, she could make the afternoon session. She just had to think of a plausible excuse.

Emilie's boss, Clive, had a motto: "hire the best, be the best". Ruling the department with the charisma of a warthog, he stomped around, often yelling at them for the most minor misdemeanour. Glimpses of his kinder nature sometimes slipped in, especially if he saw someone struggling, but they were few and far between. When he realised he'd overstepped the mark, he would apologise, but always with the caveat that he was a hard taskmaster because he wanted to bring out the potential he knew they all had.

She ran from the train station in her trainers; as she entered the courthouse, she was attempting to put on her lucky black court shoes – literally not only the shoes she always wore in court but the smart heeled leather ones of the same name. Emilie stumbled and fell at the feet of Clive. He helped her up and she was just about to launch a diatribe of excuses when he interrupted her. 'Go home, Emilie, I can smell the alcohol on your breath. I will see you in my office at 8.30 in the morning to discuss your future.'

Sheepishly hanging her head in shame, she left, with tears in her eyes, and decided to walk home to sober up. Emilie sat on the courthouse steps to change her footwear once again. Mr Potter was still ruining her life even in his absence. She knew she had two choices: lie through her teeth and hope Clive believed her or tell him the truth and maybe convince him that they should go after Mr Potter to make him pay for his crimes. She decided on the latter and made a promise to herself that she wouldn't touch another drop of alcohol.

*

She spent three years diligently following every lead she could find, cajoling and empathising with each of the victims she found, promising them that she would get the justice they all deserved. Seeing him on the stand sickened Emilie to the very core. When asked his full name he said, 'Art Potter.' It put her in mind of the Artful Dodger – quite apt, she thought before the judge insisted he gave his full name, "Arthur Horatio Potter". Little man syndrome, decided Emilie. She wanted to be on the prosecution team, but Clive dismissed her due to the conflict of interest. Many of the witnesses had dropped out before the trial started. Emilie didn't blame them; she understood their reticence, and some were afraid of being publicly revealed and having to explain themselves to the people in the lives they had carefully constructed. Rebecca was wavering before the trial even began. Emilie had spent a lot of time coaching her, one of the few victims who was prepared to go to court, but in the end she crumbled. The defence lawyer argued that she was still of dubious character and had only come forward in the hope of securing a financial gain. When he asked Rebecca that directly, she didn't deny it.

Emilie had lost count of the times she had slammed the door of her garden flat behind her, pissed off that someone had got away with their crimes due to a *technicality*.

Emilie had lost count of the times she had slammed the door of her garden flat behind her and poured a quadruple vodka, then another and then another.

Today, she wanted to die when she slammed the door behind her. She couldn't keep her mum behind bars and now she couldn't get Mr Potter behind bars. What was the point of it all?

After pouring herself a large vodka she looked in the drawer beside the cooker, scrambling around, searching for as many painkillers as she could find. Twenty-four – would that be enough? She had about three quarters of a litre bottle of vodka left. Would that be enough? There was only one way to find out.

When the last of the tablets had been swallowed, she began to think about Adele, both of them. Baby Adele didn't stand a chance. Emilie wondered what her life would've been like had she been alive. Even though she'd only been four years old she clearly remembered the moment when Adele reappeared in her crib. Not for the first time she wondered if her mum was right; was that the devil at work? Sometimes that seemed the most logical explanation for the most illogical event that had occurred. Emilie had previously, when very drunk, searched Google to see if there was some other phenomenon that could've caused it. Nothing, but she'd got side-tracked by her dating app notifications. She rarely went on dates and wondered why she even bothered most of the time.

Auntie Adele – how Emilie wished she was with her, to wrap her up in her huge embrace and tell her everything would be OK and, as she always said, "everything always unfolds as it should". But it wasn't OK and if this was how things were supposed to happen there was something very wrong with Auntie Adele's thought processes. Now she had nowhere to go with her feelings other than deeper into the abyss. Auntie Adele would be furious that she hadn't confided in her. Emilie laughed; there was no way Auntie Adele would be *furious*. The most angry Emilie had ever seen her was being slightly annoyed, never furious. Then she started to cry; she'd promised that she would call after the court hearing but couldn't bring herself to. Her phone had been beeping for the last hour, but she'd ignored it.

Emilie could feel herself drifting in and out of consciousness; she actually liked the feeling. Nothing was hurting now. She wished Arthur Horatio Potter was dying, not her. She wished she had killed him and then killed herself. Why hadn't she thought of that before? Why had she taken the tablets…? 'I need to live,' she said out loud. As she tried to stand up she looked like a new-born donkey taking its first steps. Her fingernails slipped off the worktop she was trying to cling on to in an effort to stand and she slumped back to the floor. 'OK, I'll stay here, at least I'll meet baby Adele,' she hoped. Talking out loud to herself was a habit she'd always had; she wondered if everyone who lived alone did the same. So many questions were running through her head. Was there a God? Was there a Heaven and a Hell? Where would she go? 'Doesn't matter now,' she slurred. Emilie thought she heard someone banging on the door but decided it was in her head, and either way, she couldn't get up to answer it.

'*Emilie! Emilie!* Open the door!'

Adele was beside herself; she'd been trying to get hold of Emilie since the trial had finished but to no avail. She managed to find out the result so she knew Emilie would be in a terrible state. Adele didn't have the money to get an Uber; she'd never told Emilie that she'd been basically living in poverty for the last few years. Adele knew Emilie was having a problem with alcohol. She understood addiction, not just because of the many children she had fostered but because of her own addiction to food. Adele would rather have a cake and eat away her feelings, a family-sized cake all to herself, instead of having the heating on. The three buses to get to Emilie's home were at least free, as she had her bus pass, but slow. Adele had half an idea of what may have taken place, but her fear was so deep that she didn't want to explore that scenario; she just knew she had to get there.

Adele took a deep breath and barged her gargantuan shoulder against the door, but it didn't budge. Two more attempts, and the last one was successful, and that was when she saw Emilie unconscious on the kitchen floor.

*

'Ooh, I caaan't come to the phone as Josh and I are… OK, leave a message and I'll get back to you!'

Josh laughed at Jess's voicemail message; he hadn't heard it before and loved the sexy voice she put on. He then responded, 'Wish I was there! Hey, Jess, I'm stuck in West London and I'll be late – I've found a meeting nearby and after the day I've had I need to go. I'll be home as soon as I can.'

He then popped his phone on silent and put it in his pocket. Locking the car, he began to walk towards the entrance of the church hall. He sat down just as Emilie stood up. Listening to her short story was heartbreaking; he wanted to hug her and tried to make eye contact, but she was staring at her shoes. Emilie stood up without looking around and ran for the exit, with Josh immediately following.

Her eyes were so totally blurred by tears that she misjudged the door frame as she ran and slammed into it. Her handbag caught on the door handle, relieving it of its contents, sending them all over the floor. Josh took hold of her. 'Breathe, Emilie, it's OK, just breathe.'

Emilie did as she was told, initially taking large gasps before following Josh as instructed; gradually her breathing normalised. She then knelt down to retrieve her belongings from the floor, noticing a tampon had rolled underneath a car. She decided she'd ignore that and continued on with Josh's help. Emilie was soon apologising profusely as she got into her car.

Josh sat on the concrete steps after she left, taking in all he had heard. Here he was, looking to take the edge off his need to give in to his addiction, and Emilie had the most tragic story; he felt himself shrinking at how insignificant he felt. It hadn't escaped his notice that she had a semi-colon tattooed on her wrist. Josh had been to some dark places but had never thought of or attempted suicide. He still didn't understand why he was an alcoholic; there was no one defining episode that he could pinpoint which had started it off, instead a gradual increase over the years. Jess thought it was because of losing Gail; Josh hadn't told her that he'd been much worse in the years before they'd met.

He didn't want to go back in; he no longer wanted a drink. Walking to his car, he could see something in a puddle being illuminated by the moon. Jess had told him that today was the "flower moon". He didn't know what the significance was, apart from the obvious for Jess, but he remembered her saying something about Native Americans naming it for the May blooming of flora.

Picking the card up off the floor, he could see it was Emilie's driving licence. He knew her flat wasn't far. Having been in West London frequently on a case, he'd got to know the area. He was investigating a local Jehovah's Witness suspected of being a pervert. Josh had nicknamed him a "pervicrite" – a pervert who proclaimed to be a man of God but was such a hypocrite. They were ready to arrest him tomorrow; the evidence was now overwhelming. However, now the question Josh was asking himself was whether to post the licence back to her anonymously or drop it off at her home. He glanced at his watch and decided on the latter.

Finding a parking space proved to take longer than the actual journey; he glanced at his watch again, hoping that Jess wouldn't be sitting at the table across a dinner that was getting cold. He felt her patience with him recently was waning; he didn't blame her. He thought it took a very special person to take on a policeman as a partner, especially one who came with baggage that weighed more than the rigours of the job.

There were just a few steps down to Emilie Akinyi's garden flat once he'd parked up and pressed the doorbell. Josh wished he'd just posted it through the letterbox now; technically, there was no reason for him to see or speak to her, but he did want to make sure she was OK.

'So much for AA being anonymous!' were the first words out of her mouth on opening the door. At least she was laughing.

'I know, I know, and I'm sorry, I should've just posted it, but it seemed like fate after I'd been wondering if you were OK.'

'Would you like to come in?'

Josh looked at his watch again. He should've let Jess know what was going on. Being very late and not checking in with her was becoming a habit. He knew he should leave; he could see Emilie was fine. But was she really?

'OK, but just for five minutes, I need to get home.' He was going to say "get home to my girlfriend" but omitted the last part and didn't know why.

Walking into the living room, he was surprised at the spaciousness of it. A large, open fireplace dominated the room despite the high ceilings. The full moon was shining through the French doors to the garden, illuminating the space which had only a two-seater sofa, a bookcase and a coffee table in it. Jess, he thought of Jess; he needed to – no, not needed. He wanted to go home.

'I've gotta go, girlfriend waiting,' he said as he rolled his eyes, trying to make light of the situation. 'That group is not my usual, so I doubt I'll see you again.'

'I was going to offer you a drink.'

'Double whiskey?' he joked. 'I wanted one, that's why I was there.'

'Vodka was my nemesis and my best friend all rolled into one.'

Josh moved over towards the fireplace and picked up the photo from the mantelpiece.

'You and your sister?'

Emilie nodded. 'It's the only one I have of Adele.'

The "lightbulb moment" dropped there and then for Josh. He seemed to have been steered here by some unknown source.

'My *mum*, and I say that loosely, thought she was possessed by the devil. It's not unusual in our culture, but the action she took was heinous, unforgivable.'

'I'm sorry for your loss,' he blurted out before remembering that Jess had said that once the night he met her, and he had criticised her for it. 'I know people say that without thinking, but I'm sorry, it was automatic.'

'No apologies necessary – you better get home to your girlfriend.'

Emilie thanked him again for returning her driving licence as he walked back to his car.

Josh quickly texted Jess to tell her that he was on his way home and that he had news. He had studied and memorised the spreadsheets intently, even the one with the discounted people on. Adele Akinyi – she was near the top of the alphabetical list of the "non-starters", having died before she reached her third month on this Earth. He guessed that's why Emilie's mum had murdered her. What must she have thought when her baby kept disappearing? If her culture believed in the devil that would have been the answer she'd reached, but her solution was definitely not. He began to cry, feeling overwhelmed by the knowledge, and for the first time he thought about all the mums in that same situation. Jess's mum couldn't hold on to her sanity and Emilie's mum had resorted to murder. Finding the "16/87s" had seemed like an adventure, but now he knew that the trauma had destroyed at least two mothers. He needed to speak to Jess and figure out how they could help the remaining mums. Their initial decision was to let the "16/87s" know that they weren't alone, that they weren't weird, odd or abhorrent. Now they needed to find a way that was more inclusive to all family members – who knew how many siblings were also holding the secret? They needed a club like the AA.

At that moment he understood why he'd ended up in West London. The "pervicrite" was a diversion tactic, though he was glad to be taking that sort of person off the streets, but it had led him to Emilie. Even though he'd told her she wouldn't see him again, he had a feeling that the meeting wasn't going to be their last.

SIX

STRAWBERRY MOON

Everyone in the ward was talking about the storm, or "the Great Storm", as people had started to call it. All Dawn could think of was how long it would be before her baby slept so she could go along to the smoking room. When she'd finished feeding her baby she asked the nurse if she could put her in the nursery for a break.

The door seemed really heavy to push, not as hard as pushing the baby out, but she was so exhausted. She thought that no-one who hadn't experienced it could know what it felt like, it was certainly worse than she'd ever imagined, and Terry still hadn't visited yet. God knows what he was up to; Dawn could imagine that but chose not to. He provided and that was enough; she didn't need to know the details.

Pouring herself a cup of coffee, she eased herself onto the armchair, putting her feet up on the table and lighting her first cigarette of the day. Another lady was standing, complaining that she wished she could sit but it was too painful. Dawn looked around for an ashtray, but it was out of her reach. The woman now had her back to Dawn; obviously she didn't want to talk. Without thinking she flicked the ash in the plastic cup on the table; the lady turned to pick her cup up and Dawn realised what she'd done.

'Stop! Sorry, but I was using that as an ashtray.'

The woman then gingerly walked to retrieve the ashtray from a table further away and gave it to Dawn before leaving the room. 'Miserable sod,' Dawn uttered under her breath. Beside her in another chair was a folded newspaper; picking it up, she flicked it out to see the whole front page: "Mother of three still missing". Dawn scan-read it through, not really taking in any details, and turned to the cartoon section – she could do with a laugh, she thought.

'Hello, you OK, pet?'

Dawn looked up to see what she thought was a heavily pregnant woman standing in front of her. 'Great, thanks, I'm Dawn, would you like a ciggie? Haven't they induced you yet?'

The larger lady started laughing. 'I've had my baby! I'd love one, ta, I'm Helen.'

Dawn could feel her face flushing; she decided that Helen probably looked that size, pregnant or not. She was desperately trying to think of something to say to deflect her embarrassment.

'Did you have that weird feeling, almost like the baby

wasn't there? I had a little girl; I haven't named her yet cos my fella hasn't even been to visit.'

'Yep, that must be normal, I guess. Mine hasn't been either – they say it's bad out there. I named mine Kylie; I don't wait for no-one.'

'Could be worse, look at this.' Dawn held up the tabloid newspaper to show her.

'Bet it's the husband! Always is.'

Dawn nodded in agreement, though she didn't actually agree. Helen was intimidating; her presence loomed large in the room, just like her body. She sounded like a character out of *Emmerdale Farm*. Dawn hadn't met anyone from the north before, though her husband often went. Whenever he came back, he would make her laugh doing his version of their accents.

The two new mums shared another coffee and cigarette before a nurse popped her head around the door. Little Kylie needed feeding.

'Same time tomorrow?'

'More like later today if we're lucky.' Helen laughed.

Dawn sat for a few more minutes contemplating her new friend. Helen didn't seem to be fazed by anything, certainly not her missing husband. That made Dawn ponder on whether "Tez", as Helen had called him, was her husband, partner or boyfriend. Sounded like a Turkish name, or maybe Maltese, Dawn decided. Either way both of their other halves had yet to show. Tez was probably still stuck up north with a genuine reason for not being able to visit. Although Dawn remembered that Helen had said that he was working down here and she'd come to surprise him, not thinking for a moment she would go into labour, which debunked that theory. Terry, well, he was like a bad penny and would eventually show up, giving Dawn even the flimsiest excuse because he knew how to get round her. Her mum had asked why she let him treat her like a doormat. Dawn's only reason was always that she loved him. Sometimes she allowed herself to think of what life would be like without him. For a few moments she acknowledged that it would be less stressful.

No more worrying that the police would turn up to raid their flat.

No more worrying phone calls from him saying he'd been arrested and would she send his brother to pick him up?

No more worrying that he'd cheated on her again and brought her cheap flowers from the petrol station.

Dawn knew, she'd always known, but now she had their baby girl to think about. Maybe it was time to change. She had an urge to go and hold her baby, hold her tight and tell her she would always protect her. She wished she was like Helen. In that one long conversation Dawn deduced that no-one pushed her around; she was her own woman, no-one else's. What surprised Dawn was that Helen didn't come across as cold – intimidating, yes, but then everyone was to Dawn. Her mum had told her on many occasions that "the only person who can make you feel inferior is yourself".

She ached for her mum.

It hadn't even been a year yet.

How she wished her mum had met her granddaughter.

She'd died not even knowing she was going to be a nan.

Things have to change, thought Dawn as she waddled back to the nursery.

Helen was passing. 'Done my duty, I'll give you an hour

and meet you back for a ciggie.' It wasn't a question or an invitation. Helen demanded it of Dawn, but she was happy to comply. She needed a friend right now.

*

The two women soon became "ciggie buddies", meeting at any possible chance. Dawn had written her address down on a paper napkin, telling Helen she could visit whenever she was in London. Helen made her laugh telling her stories about people she bumped into and the antics that she got up to. Dawn had originally thought she sounded like someone from a soap opera, but knowing quite a bit about her life now, it seemed that she did indeed live like she was in one too.

They were just finishing their third cup of coffee of the day when in walked in two policemen.

'What's he gone and done now?' enquired Dawn with a look of resignation which belied her inner anxiety.

'Mrs Baldwin? Mrs Terence Baldwin?'

'Yes, you know who I am – as I said, what's he gone and done now?'

'May we speak to you in private?'

'Anything you need to say you can say in front of Helen, I've already told her what he's like.'

Helen didn't say anything but was starting to get a sinking feeling.

'Mrs Baldwin, if you're sure?'

Dawn nodded as the policeman continued, 'I regret to inform you that Terry was involved in a fatal accident. He'd stolen a car and was involved in a high-speed chase. We now think that he was on his way to visit you. In the back of the car were two teddy bears and two bunches of flowers.'

A single tear fell from Dawn's face, hitting her chest as she nodded her head. Helen moved over to embrace her, holding tightly to her new friend, knowing that she was going to potentially cause Dawn even further heartbreak. The hug gave her the release she needed, and the tears began in a tsunami. After the police had finished their formalities and left, Helen asked if she could call anyone for her. Between her sniffles she cried that she wanted her mum. Helen knew that was impossible. In one of their chats Dawn had spoken about the sadness she felt without her mum in her life.

'Dawn, I always think that once you've had bad news, anything else is less important. They also say that bad things come in threes.'

Puzzled, Dawn looked up at Helen, blowing her nose hard and pulling another tissue from the box on the coffee table.

'What do you mean? My mum, then Terry, who's next?'

'No, not your mum. Terry – well, *Tez* – me, and Kylie.'

Dawn took a moment and then quickly understood.

This friend whom she'd confided in, whose stories she'd laughed at, was telling her that her husband was also Kylie's dad. Dawn's mind was spinning like a roller coaster. She tried to remember if there were any clues she'd missed. All Helen had said about Tez was that she'd met him at a nightclub in Leeds and she'd fallen pregnant pretty much straightaway. Helen had never spoken about him with love; she'd just said he had moved in with her but worked away a lot.

Taking stock and with a deep breath, Dawn began to realise that she was free. Despite loving Terry with all her heart, his behaviour was something she'd never have to worry about ever again. She couldn't have him now, but then neither could anyone else. It wasn't Helen's fault; she hadn't known. Dawn felt confident that Helen would never have dated a married man. She was wild but Dawn knew she had morals. Amazing what you can learn in a short space of time, she thought, and then instead of the tears there was a tsunami of laughter.

'Dawn, it's OK. You can hate me if you want. I seriously didn't know; I'll leave now, and you'll never have to see me again. Me and Kylie will be fine. I'm sorry, I'm so sorry, pet.'

With that, Helen got up and moved towards the door, but as she reached the handle, Dawn spoke. 'No, don't go. None of this is your fault and definitely not Kylie or Jade's fault.'

'Jade?'

'Yes, Jade. I've always loved that name and it's better than anything Terry was coming up with. He kept saying he wanted to name the baby Chardonnay or Chelsea for a girl and Axl or Foley for a boy!'

'Jade is much better. God, he really loved *Beverley Hills Cop*, didn't he!'

The two women laughed and hugged each other. Weirdly, everything felt OK, thought Dawn.

*

Helen hadn't decided 100% until she was facing the registrar, squirming in her seat as the lady asked for the father's name.

'Unknown.'

Helen bit her lip. She didn't want to tell the truth nor garner any sympathy. That should be reserved for Dawn. She'd invited Helen to the funeral, but she definitely didn't want to go, and besides, one of the cleaning ladies must've thrown away the paper serviette with Dawn's address and phone number on and she had no way of contacting her.

'Miss White, Miss White, we're done now.' The registrar handed Helen baby Kylie's birth certificate.

'Sorry, I was miles away. Don't suppose you know how I could find where somebody lives, do you?'

'The father?'

'No, a friend I met in hospital.'

'Have you any idea what area she lives in?'

'I remember her saying something about the Kidbrooke Estate, that's all. I'll take the bus and ask around, someone might know.'

The registrar was shaking her head. 'I wouldn't advise that; it can be a bit rough around there and you'll certainly find that Londoners are not forthcoming or as friendly as they could be. They'll be suspicious, if anything, and won't tell you even if they know. I was born in Yorkshire too – took me a long time to remember not to randomly start speaking to people on the tube!'

'OK, it was just a thought, thanks anyway.'

Helen stood up; her arms were aching holding Kylie. She had no pushchair nor baby clothes. The hospital had given her a few bits to tide her over, but she'd have to get back home to all the stuff she'd bought.

'Hang on, just a thought, but if you go to the library nearest where you think she lives you can look on the electoral register. It's free – there's a bus stop about two hundred yards from here that'll take you straight there. Ask the driver where you need to get off.'

'Cool, I'll definitely think about it, thanks again.'

Helen had extended her stay at the B&B and had reluctantly paid for the week she'd been unexpectedly in hospital for. Tez had met her there the first night; he hadn't seemed overly pleased about her surprise visit and reminded her to only use his mum's phone number in emergencies. It had been an emergency when she'd suddenly gone into labour. Tez's mum came across as irritated when Helen asked her to urgently tell him she was having the baby and definitely shocked at the news.

Helen now knew why.

*

The next day she found the library and consequently where Dawn lived. It didn't surprise her that Terry wasn't listed as living there – from the sounds of things, he preferred to live in the shadows. Helen had written to Dawn asking about the funeral and casually said she would visit if she ever came down to London.

She was surprised that Dawn had replied by return post. Her handwriting was almost child like in its illegibility and filled with spelling mistakes, for which she'd apologised, saying she'd never gone to school much as she was too busy hanging out with Terry. Dawn had underlined the words *please come and visit soon, you're the only one who understands how I feel.* Helen thought that she would sit for a while in her kitchen deliberating what her next move would be. As impulsive as ever, she immediately started packing some things, grabbed Kylie and was on her way to the train station.

*

Helen had to drag the pushchair up two flights of stairs, a carrier bag full of booze clinking in the basket below the baby. The air smelt of urine and weed; the lift was out of order. She understood what the registrar had meant about the estate. She thought it was so badly designed: too many dark alleyways and bridges connecting the various different blocks of flats. Helen wasn't afraid, though; that was an emotion she rarely felt.

Dawn's smile widened as she opened the door and hugged her new friend as if her life depended on it. She couldn't stop thanking Helen for coming and was backing away to let Helen in as if she were meeting the Queen and couldn't stop bowing. Helen quickly scanned the room. The first thing she honed in on was the four-strip of black and white photobooth pictures on top of the gas fire. They weren't in a frame, just sellotaped to the wall, though what was unmistakeable was that Dawn was wearing school uniform. Helen looked up at her in real life; without the hospital gown she could see now just how young she really was, that and the clothes she was now wearing.

'How old are you? How old was Terry?'

Helen held her breath; Terry certainly hadn't acted or behaved like a schoolboy, but he could've been. He'd told her he was twenty-eight, same age as her, but then he seemed adept at distorting the truth.

'I'm sixteen, nearly seventeen. Terry just missed his twenty-second.'

OK, not quite so bad, Helen thought. She couldn't see any photos of their wedding day – maybe they couldn't afford them. The flat was sparsely decorated and smelt a bit damp.

'Did you marry on the day you were sixteen?' joked Helen.

Dawn was shaking her head; she wasn't really married. Terry had come home once and had given her a driving licence stating that she was "Dawn Baldwin" and was two years older than she really was. She remembered saying to him that she couldn't even drive, and whose licence was it? Hers, that was all she'd needed to know from then on.

After explaining to Helen, it seemed she had more questions. It was beginning to feel like she was at the police station again. It had only happened once; they were trying to find out what she knew of Terry's misdemeanours and informed her that she was living in "a den of iniquity". She'd had to ask what that meant, and it wasn't long before they let her go. Under the copper's breath she heard him say, 'Dumb blonde.' That was OK by her; she was just pleased to be out of there without breaking Terry's confidence. Not that she knew a lot, but she often eavesdropped when he was with his friends and she was, he thought, asleep in bed. She would put a glass to the wall to help her hear better.

'I met him because he used to sell gear on the estate. He lived with his brothers, but when my mum passed away, he came to live here with me. My mum knew she was ill and put my name on the tenancy agreement, so they couldn't kick me out.'

'You're all flushed, you don't have to tell me anything. Let's crack open this bottle of Pink Lady – it was only 98p at the offy, so I got four bottles.'

'I-I-I've never drunk before and I'm feeding the baby myself, midwife said you can't.'

Helen laughed. 'You may not be legally allowed to drink, but you are an adult, and a mum to boot – no-one can tell you what to do! I had chocolate for breakfast, and no-one can tell me off!'

'But the bab—' Dawn began, but Helen shushed her.

'This,' she said, holding up a tub of SMA, 'means you can do what the hell you want! I didn't like feeding; the only person I want sucking my titties is definitely not a baby! And what's with that bucket of shitty nappies? It's 1987 not 1967!'

'The midwife—'

'Let me tell you about midwives. Mine came over, older than my gran, never had a baby in her life, and promptly put the disposable nappy on back to front! Now, have you got any glasses?'

Dawn produced a pint glass and a plastic beaker as Helen proceeded to show her how to make up the powdered baby milk.

The young girl downed the alcohol in one and nearly choked. 'Is this champagne? The bubbles have gone up my nose.'

Helen was laughing so much. 'Whoops, think I may have peed myself a little bit.'

The two of them both started laughing.

'I don't know what it actually is, just fizzy sweet booze.'

Dawn held her beaker out for more, then downed that one too.

'Whoa! Slow down – it may taste harmless, but it's far from that.'

'I want you to stay, Helen, I like you.'

'Well, I'm not exactly going home to Leeds tonight, am I?'

'No, I mean, I want you to live here.'

'Two glasses of plonk and you're off your head.'

The inevitable came around quicker than Helen thought, and she found herself holding Dawn's hair back whilst she puked in the loo, simultaneously trying to placate two babies.

'You southerners can't hold your drink! Look, I've made you a coffee – you need to sober up, and we need to get some sleep before the night shift. Are you feeding on demand or every four?'

Dawn didn't answer; she found herself still staring down the toilet bowl alternating between puking and crying. When the careers officer had asked her what she would like to do for work she'd said, 'Mum,' but this wasn't what she'd imagined. She did have a job for a while in the bakery on the high street, but when she was pregnant, they looked for any excuse to fire her. Apparently licking your fingers when displaying the fresh cream cakes was a sackable offence. It suited Dawn just fine.

She had insisted that Helen sleep in her bed rather than the couch. The flat was a two bedroom but the spare one was Terry's "office" and was locked. Dawn continued to chat despite Helen repeatedly telling her to be quiet. She felt so sorry for this, well, schoolgirl. To lose her mum and her so-called husband within the space of a year – apparently she was all alone in the world now. It seemed grossly unfair.

'I don't think I'm going to make a good mum, Hels.'

'Don't be silly. Look, I'm one of nine. My mum never had a clue – some of us aren't even sure who our dads are, but we mostly turned out OK.'

'Do you see her?'

'Come on, Dawn, sleep time! So long as one of us pops in and gives her a tenner every week, she's grand. It means we all only have to see her every couple of months, so it's a win-win. Now, go to sleep.'

'You're so clever, Hels.'

'Is that what you're calling me from now on?'

Helen laughed as Dawn nodded; she'd been called worse. One of the babies started to cry, which set the other one off; they'd both looked so cosy in the crib together.

'Come on, if we feed them both now, they may sleep through till seven. It's nearly half three already.'

Dawn looked over to where Helen was feeding Kylie on the edge of the bed. She thought Helen was a gift from her mum. She was big and cuddly, like Mrs Claus, strong like Geoff Capes and clever like Margaret Thatcher, but Dawn decided not to tell her all that, in case it upset her and she turned into the Hulk.

Jade seemed to like the bottled milk, which was handy as Dawn thought her breast milk was probably still over the limit, despite the amount of vomit earlier on. The two women were winding their babies and joking who'd get a burp first when Jade and Kylie disappeared.

It was Dawn who spoke first; she jumped up off the bed. 'Are you a witch?' she screamed. 'Did you come to steal my baby? Is Terry really dead? Did you both plan this to steal my baby?'

Helen stood up and moved towards the hysterical Dawn, slapping her hard around the face.

'Get a fucking grip, Dawn! Kylie's gone too, I dunno what the hell is happening, but I sure as hell didn't have anything to do with this, and you're the one who buried Terry, not me!'

Between her sobs Dawn managed to say that they needed to call the police.

'And say what? Both our babies disappeared while in our arms? They'll think we got rid of them!'

'So, what should we do? You're the brainy one.'

'*I don't know!* Let's make a cuppa and talk, you need to calm down.'

'Why are you so calm? *Help* me, please!'

Helen wasn't calm, not in the least, but she'd be damned if she let Dawn or anyone else see her drop the façade she'd used since she was a girl. Being the oldest of nine, she'd learnt how to hide her emotions as one uncle turned into another, another baby being born, another uncle coming along. It was all she could do to keep her siblings safe and that meant having her wits about her at all times. Forgoing any emotions that would reveal any chink in her armour was always tough, but this was another level.

She handed Dawn a cup of coffee and looked her directly in the eyes.

'I have absolutely no idea, but I don't think we should call the police yet – we need to get our stories straight.'

'Now you sound like Terry. There is *no* story but the truth.'

Just then, they heard a little cooing sound and both ran to the bedroom. Kylie and Jade were on the bed; it looked like they were holding hands, contented, happy. Dawn picked Jade up and held her close. Helen just stood, shocked, and her carefully constructed veneer dropped as quick as the tears that were falling from her face.

'Pick her up, Helen!'

'Look at their hair,' was all Helen could say.

'What are we going to do?'

'Nothing, absolutely nothing. No-one would believe us anyway. They'll say we were drunk and incapable of looking after our babies; they'll take them away from us. This is our secret, right?'

Dawn was touching the white streak now visible in Jade's hair and noticed Kylie's was the same. 'I don't even know how to deal with her hair, let alone now like this.'

After what seemed like an eternity, Helen picked up her baby and smothered her in her voluptuous bosom. 'You're OK, kiddo, where you been?'

The two young women looked at one another, knowing this would be a secret they'd be prepared to take to their graves.

Helen wasn't going back to Leeds; she knew that now.

'Look, when I got off the bus there was a barber – they specialise in afros. We'll ask them, and if they don't know, well, one of their women will. It'll be OK. The streak, it's called poliosis, I don't know if I'm pronouncing that right, but did you ever watch that TV show *The Mallens*? They all had it. I'd read the books before they made the show.'

'You're so clever, Hels.'

'I read; I learn by reading, which is why I don't always get the pronunciation right. There was no way I was going to be able to go to university, but I will get a job and help you support Jade.'

Helen sighed; would she ever be able to have her own life? Maybe being the provider for everyone was why she was put on this Earth; deep down she thought she must secretly like it or what was the point?

In that moment she walked over to Dawn and kissed her on the lips. 'We'll be OK, we'll stick together, we'll figure this out together.'

*

'Kylie! Kylie! Slow down, you're scaring me.'

'*You* need to slow down; you're going back on our pact. We always agreed, no live-in boyfriends.'

'But Felix is different, and we're in love.'

Kylie started to drive even faster. It wasn't that she didn't like Felix – far from it, he was a lovely guy and stayed most weekends – but no, no moving in; it wasn't allowed. She gripped the steering wheel even tighter, and her right foot got heavier on the accelerator.

'*You need to shut the fuck up. What do you think he'll do when he finds out we disappear every month? Are you insane?*'

'You're the insane one. Stop the car *now*, I want to go home.'

But Kylie wasn't listening; she was banging on the steering wheel trying to get Jade to see things her way. She didn't think she was driving too fast, definitely well over the speed limit but not like Lewis Hamilton-fast; besides, her little Micra wasn't exactly a racing car. Kylie didn't see Jade reach for the handbrake until she yanked it up and the car began to spin.

Everything started to go in slow motion. Kylie thought that sort of thing only happened in the movies. Luckily there were no other cars around when they came to a stop facing the way they were previously coming from.

'WTF, Jade? Trying to kill us both now? We'll be permanently with Dad then, is that what you want? Thought you wanted to be with Felix?'

'I was in control; I knew what I was doing.'

'Not the point! Just because that prick of an ex of yours used to take you to Asda car park to spin his car in doughnuts doesn't mean you knew what you were doing. Even if you thought you did you had absolutely no idea what I would do, did you?'

Jade dropped her head as Kylie restarted the car which had stalled in the incident. A driver of a van was now tooting his horn because they were blocking the road. He swore at Kylie, and she made a hand gesture back while she deftly turned the car around.

'Well, I didn't think you'd spin the car—'

'Exactly! Look, we're going to be late to set the cakes up, that's assuming they're still in one piece. We'll talk about this later and I expect a full apology – *you* are in the wrong, Jade.'

The two girls didn't speak to each other for the rest of the journey. Kylie turned up the radio and Jade began to sing, badly. It normally made Kylie laugh.

'Shut up, J. Look, we're here now, we're representing Mum's bakery, so put on a smile and act like nothing's happened. I'll deal with you later!'

In her head Jade repeated Kylie's last sentence in a silly kid's voice. Kylie always acted like the older sibling but technically she wasn't. Just like their mums – Mum Helen always was the boss. When they were young, Jade used to say, 'OK, Dad,' in a sarcastic voice if Helen told her off. The girls were the only ones in school who had "two mummies", but no matter how hard they vehemently denied that their mums were a couple, no-one believed them. In the end it was easier to let them think what they wanted. By the time they were in their mid-teens they almost deliberately dropped it into the conversation, thinking it made them look cool. They also used to joke that every full moon they turned into Lily Munster – only to themselves, though. Their mums used to make them dye the white streaks away and no-one ever saw it.

*

Moonpie had begun as a home-baking business. Dawn found she had a flair for making cakes and definitely didn't lick her fingers when baking. Helen was a natural businesswoman and took care of that side. It helped that when they broke into the spare room, they found piles of money that Terry had stashed away. By the late nineties they'd opened their one and only shop. It was a disused premises on the high street; apparently a hoarder had rented it because his house was too full. The landlord hadn't minded as he'd always paid the rent, but when the guy died, he knew he'd have a lot of work to do. Helen persuaded him to let them have it free for a few months if they did all the work.

It was when they'd been clearing out that they found piles of newspapers, all in date order. Many of them were discoloured with age, some almost sepia in appearance. As Dawn went to pick one of the piles up it fell, spreading it all over the shop floor – well, at least where they assumed the floor was; it was all still covered in so much stuff. The first headline she saw was from 1997: a missing girl had been found. Dawn remembered that well, as she had been the same age as their children. She left that pile to look at the front page of one dated in 1987; it was another missing mum and Dawn recognised her instantly as being the woman whose coffee cup Dawn had used as an ashtray – maybe she was as miserable as she'd appeared that day. They knew the other missing mum had been found after the storm, but she didn't remember this one and she considered not mentioning it to Helen as she knew she'd blame the husband – well, if the woman had one. She had then sat and started to flick through them, looking to see if anyone was reporting back then that they too had children that disappeared.

Helen had found her sobbing, tearing at the papers like a banshee. Helen had told her that she was sure their kids were the only ones, joking, 'Come on, moonpie, dry your eyes.' And that was how they named the shop. Dawn always wanted to expand and open more bakeries, but Helen insisted that the niche market they had was because they were a small family business, and it would lose its ethos once they expanded. She was also concerned at having to put their trust in others when they weren't around.

Helen tried to lighten the moment by saying that she should apply to go on the game show *Going for Gold* as she had such a detailed memory. Dawn reminded her that the programme had stopped in 1996.

'Proves my point, Dawnie!'

*

The village fete was a charity event that Moonpie always supported. They had let the girls run the stall since they were teenagers. Kylie and Jade knew the routine and managed to get everything just so despite not talking to each other.

'I'm going for a walk.'

'Fine by me, just be back to help me pack up. I can run it myself.'

'What if you need the loo?'

'Jade, I don't give a fuck, whatever.'

Jade decided she'd just have a wander around the other stalls until she could think of a way to appease Kylie. She knew she'd flip when she found out Felix wanted to move in, but were they supposed to put their lives on hold forever just because of twelve days in the year? Jade wanted it all; she wanted to marry Felix and have his children. She couldn't be like Kylie with her "use them and lose them" attitude. Jade had already decided that she would make sure Felix never found out, but Kylie never gave her a chance to explain her idea.

She stopped to tie the shoelace of her Converses, and as she stood up, she found herself in front of a stall called "Moonology"; intrigued, she read the sign outside – tarot readings with a difference, fifteen minutes for ten pounds.

'Hi, you interested? It's just a bit of fun and I'm donating the money to the church fund.'

'I-I-I don't know, I've never done anything like that.'

The woman extended her hand to Jade. 'I'm Jess, come in, just a bit of fun.'

Jade thought Jess's hand was cold, eerily so; everyone used to say the same about her and her sister too. Intrigued, she followed Jess into the little tent.

The two women sat down, and Jess passed Jade two sets of cards to shuffle.

'So, all I need is your first name and date of birth, then we can start.'

Jess began to write on the paper with a pencil, but as she got to Jade's date of birth, she snapped the tip. '16th October 1987?'

'Yes, what's wrong?'

'No, nothing.' Jess was racking her brains. It was at a time like this that she wished she had Josh's memory. This Jade must be on the list – well, only if her dad had died; she pondered as to how she could engineer that question.

'There's been sadness in your life.'

'Hasn't everyone? It's a bit vague.'

Kylie had taught Jade to be cynical about everything and everyone. She often said Jade was gullible. It wasn't that; Jade just believed that everyone was good and just, despite being proven wrong on many occasions.

Jess turned over the first card. Full moon in Gemini. Great, she thought, this girl is a twin and there were definitely no twins on Josh's spreadsheet.

'I see twins, does that make sense?'

'No.'

'OK, let's have a look at the next card. The answers you need are coming, but you've been under a lot of stress lately. Does that make sense?'

Jade nodded and fidgeted in her seat.

'Still seeing the twins, though.'

No-one ever thought Kylie and Jade were twins; they shared a birthday and a father, but that was the only commonality. Jess turned the next card over.

'I'm sorry, it's another Gemini one. I've never seen those three times on the trot unless there are twins involved. As I said, it's just a bit of fun, so maybe we shouldn't focus on that. Either way, this card represents communication – maybe there's someone you need to have better communication with, does that make sense?'

'Look, yes, it's my sister – well, half-sister. We share the same dad and weirdly the same birthday.'

As soon as Jade started talking, she could hear Kylie's words in her head about how she always needed to be on her guard as she tended to get "verbal diarrhoea" once she started talking.

'I've said enough – we had an argument over my boyfriend, but we'll figure it out. I need to go. If you come to our stall we'll give you a free cake, it's Moonpie, our mums own the bakery on the high street.'

Jess knew she was running out of time. 'I feel a fatherly presence around you, does that make sense?'

'I need to go.' Jade stood up to leave before finishing with, 'We never knew our dad; he died the day we were born. I have to get back to Kylie, I'm sorry.'

Jess didn't know how she kept the disbelief from her face. She followed Jade out of the tent just as Josh was coming towards her.

'Jess, you look like you've seen a ghost.'

'You, you're too astute, but you are never going to believe what just happened. Is there a Jade on the list?'

'Yep, Jade Baldwin, father – Terence.'

'You need to look for a Kylie too.'

'Defo no-one with that name.'

'No, maybe not on the spreadsheet, but they have the same dad, so they were told. Maybe we need to look a little further afield. Their mums own Moonpie – how many times have we been past there? Not once did we see a connection.'

'Not until now, but that's the point, isn't it? We're drawing them in towards us, or rather, something is. It's pronoia.'

'It's what?'

'Pronoia, the belief that everything in the universe is conspiring to *support* you, like the opposite of paranoia.'

SEVEN

THUNDER MOON

It seemed to Josie as if the country had responded to her grief, as if the sky had fallen in. Just like the "Chicken Licken" story she hoped to read to Daisy one day. This wasn't an acorn that had fallen from the sky, though, more like an oak. In actual fact, they said that Sevenoaks turned that day into "one-oak".

This lovely commuter village just outside the town, that Tom had convinced her to move to, promising a better life, air quality and a sense of community and space that London didn't seem to provide – it was supposed to be their "forever family home".

Now he had gone.

Josie had stayed in the hospital for five days; when she returned home, the power was still off and the oak tree that had fallen on the conservatory, hitting and killing her husband Tom, was still there, but he wasn't.

Tentatively she stepped inside, assisted by the cab driver, who carried her bags whilst she carried her baby. She could see the fridge freezer had leaked all over the Amtico kitchen flooring. The house smelt weird, she thought, lifeless, she decided. She paid the driver. Daisy was still asleep, so she left her in the living room and went to sit in the conservatory.

Tom had only come home to change his clothes. How Josie wished she'd made him stay at the hospital with her.

But she hadn't and now he was gone.

She touched the oak tree, the last thing that had touched Tom. Looking on the floor she could see one of his blood-stained trainers, discarded. Josie held the shoe to her heart. It hurt so bad; her heart was physically hurting. She wondered if that was the true meaning of being heartbroken.

Literally, your heart hurts.

She looked at a pane of glass beside the broken ones; it was misty, the seal broken. It had been like that since they'd bought the house. She allowed herself a little laugh, thinking it would've been better if the oak tree had hit that one.

The sound of the chainsaws reverberated across the fields. Sevenoaks was indeed reduced to one oak now, thought Josie. In their small hamlet they'd been without electricity for six days. Why was the world still turning? Didn't anyone know Tom was dead? Josie thought everything should stop. 'Fuck you! Fucking chainsaws!' she screamed.

Baby Daisy responded with her own scream. Only a week old and Josie had learnt that loud noises perturbed her daughter. It didn't surprise her. When the doctors had told her that Daisy was completely and utterly blind, with not even the slightest chance of vision now or in the future, Josie had been totally calm. She decided that the loss of her husband was the cause.

It wasn't.

Josie hadn't told her mum yet; she couldn't face her hypercritical comments, her un-filtered views on everything and everyone. She knew her mum would say something about the drugs she and Tom used to take, using that as an acceptable reason for Daisy's blindness.

It wasn't.

Tom and Josie used to take recreational drugs. It was just the "done thing" in the social circles of their financial world. The money was flowing, abundantly. Everyone was looking for the same *high* they got at the end of a successful day; cocaine was the drug of choice. They weren't addicted – well, Josie wasn't 100% sure about Tom, but she definitely wasn't. That was irrelevant, though. Josie had to navigate bereavement, so maybe she did need something right now. Something to make her world seem bearable.

Josie scrambled in the lower drawer of the drinks cabinet. She was hoping to find a little packet of the white stuff. Bemoaning as to why she and Tom would leave empty packets in there, she split each of the three to lick any residue there might be.

Taking a large glass from the cabinet, she proceeded to put a dash of every alcohol that they had into it and downed it in one, not thinking for a moment that Daisy needed her to be alert and not to taint her breast milk. The baby was still crying, and Josie was pouring another cocktail.

'I'm coming, I'm coming.'

Daisy immediately responded to Josie's voice; she stopped crying as if she was waiting for the inevitable physical comfort of her mum.

Josie picked her up and held her close; Daisy turned her head away from the alcohol-stained breath of her mum. She'd already noticed that her baby's other senses seemed to be on hyper-alert; she definitely wasn't nose-blind.

'I'm sorry, my little Chicken Licken, I don't know what to do or where to turn. Our sky has fallen in, and I have no clue what comes next. I will be your eyes, always, I promise you that.'

*

The funeral had taken place. It had to be done. Josie's mum thought she shouldn't have brought Daisy, but there was no way the new mum would leave her. Everyone had been at their home for the wake; the only person left was George, Tom's younger brother. Josie had the oak tree removed; she'd scrubbed the floor of Tom's blood and had a glazier replace the damaged parts of the conservatory, including the pane with the broken seal. It looked brand-new again, but it didn't feel it; the imagined images of Tom lying dead remained.

'George, I should call you a cab.'

He wasn't listening; he was just staring into space. Josie understood his grief but was still reeling from a comment he'd made earlier. She'd always known he had a crush on her ever since Tom had taken her to meet his family. George was only sixteen at the time, while both Josie and Tom were twenty-one.

'You know, I could be your replacement husband.'

That was what he had said; it wasn't in jest.

Vino veritas.

Josie didn't want a replacement husband. She wanted hers back. She wanted the arcadian, idyllic lifestyle that Tom had promised and delivered.

Until he didn't.

'Sit with me, Jo, I'm sorry, I didn't mean what I said earlier.'

He did.

'I think I want you to leave now.'

'You only *think*, so you're not sure.'

'I am sure, George. If you're going to say crazy things like that when I am grieving, then you definitely should go.'

George started to cry.

Josie had always hated his arrogance. He played rugby and was always afraid to be, in his words, "a softie poofter". Tom was never homophobic. She didn't actually think George was either, it was just the locker-room banter, but that was definitely no excuse. He'd often say racial slurs too. Josie remembered her wedding; David had been the only black guy there, and George, after he'd imbibed more alcohol than one would think possible, made a comment directly to their friend. As soon as they'd come back from their honeymoon, they took David and his girlfriend out to dinner to apologise on George's behalf. Tom had said that George was too embarrassed to speak directly to David.

It wasn't true.

He'd chosen not to.

Josie was brought out of her daydream by Daisy crying.

'Mummy's coming!'

'How do you do that, Jo? I've noticed that every time she cries, she stops as soon as she hears your voice.'

'Oh, you aren't that drunk then. I don't know why, but it sure makes my life easier.'

'I want to talk to you seriously.'

'I'm going to feed Daisy – look, make us both a coffee and then we can talk.'

George duly did as he was told while he tried to gather his thoughts. He had no idea what he was going to say; it was after twelve already, not that the time was relevant. He wondered how long it took to feed a baby. He was fully aware that he couldn't replace Tom in Josie's affections. He'd held a torch for her for so long, yet he was realistic. He missed his big brother so much, and the only person he felt would understand was Josie.

They spent the next few hours talking, really talking, for perhaps the first time in their lives. George's idea was that he moved in – not in her bedroom; she lived in a five-bedroom house, so there was plenty of space. He promised that he wouldn't make any advances on her, that he understood Tom was the love of her life and he would never seek to replace him.

He was very convincing.

In Josie's grief-stricken state she almost said, 'Yes.' Then Daisy started crying.

'Look, let me feed her again, it's gone 3am. You can stay over; we'll talk in the morning.'

George was still sitting on the sofa when Josie returned with Daisy over her shoulder, gently winding her.

'Think we all need to sleep now, don't you agree, George?'

'I just wanted to say one more thing…'

He didn't get the chance; Daisy disappeared right in front of their eyes.

Josie opened her mouth to speak, but George spoke first. 'I'll call the police!'

'And say what exactly, George?'

'Well, we can't do nothing, I-I-I just don't know.'

Josie started to hyperventilate.

'Look at me, take some deep breaths, come on – one, two, three, one, two, three.'

It wasn't working. George ran into the kitchen and rummaged through the drawers, looking for and finding a paper bag.

'Here, sit, breathe into this.'

Josie's breath started to normalise after a few blows into the bag. She stared into thin air, hugging herself with her own arms, rocking backwards and forwards. Then the tears started flowing. George put his arm around her; Josie didn't feel threatened, but she pulled away from his embrace, and as she did Daisy reappeared back on her shoulder.

'Did we just imagine that?'

George never left.

*

George loosened his tie as he opened the door leading to the kitchen. He hadn't had a great day at work. He wanted to kick off his shoes and lounge on the sofa with a nice cold glass of Sancerre. Josie obviously had other ideas. Daisy was content with being in her playpen despite her mum's obvious manic behaviour.

She'd had the oak tree that had killed Tom made into a beautiful kitchen table. She often caressed it to feel closer to him, but now strewn across it was the wall calendar in pieces. Each of the previous months were torn off and put in order.

'Josie, what's going on?'

'Wait, wait, don't talk, I think I've got it! Just give me a mo…'

George shook his head as he went to the fridge to get his wine. He hadn't noticed that the now-empty bottle was on the kitchen table along with the calendar. Fortunately, he always made sure they never ran out, but it wasn't going to be cold. He went into the drinks cabinet and took a new bottle, proceeding to pop it in the freezer to help chill it quicker. Sitting at the table, he picked up Josie's half-empty glass and began drinking it.

'Are you going to tell me what's going on now?'

'OK, OK, yes, yes. So, when my periods came back, we made a connection that was when Daisy disappeared, wasn't it?'

'Yes, yes, and what are you saying now?'

'That I never realised we'd got it wrong. I mark it on the calendar, every month, and also when Daisy goes on her travels. They're often out by a couple of days. It's the white dots.'

'Now you are confusing me! You use red stars for your monthlies and blue for when Daisy goes. I didn't put the white dots on there.'

'I know, I'm not saying that!'

'What the hell are you saying then?'

'The white dots are… they are circles, indicating the full moons. The calendar company put them on, just as they put black circles on the new moon dates. It fell off the back of the door this afternoon, and when I went to stick it back it was open to the list of abbreviations. I've looked at them all. Whenever I put a blue star there is a white dot. Just like my red stars are either just before or just after the blue ones. It's not my period she coincides with – it's the *full moon*! And, you know the first time her hair had the white streak in it? We didn't colour it and after about two weeks she woke up without it – that was on the *new moon*! The black circle.'

'And that is going to help us? How?'

Josie stood up, took the wine glass from George's hand and drank the dregs from the bottom, shrugging her shoulders as she went to pick Daisy up. 'I think it just means that at least now we'll know exactly when she's going. I wish finding out where she goes was as easy.'

'Da-da.'

'*George!* She said "Da-da", did you hear that?'

'All babies say that first – it's not like you'd ever let her call me that.'

'Too bloody right, I appreciate what you do, but no, you'll never be her dad. Do you think that's where she goes?'

'Don't be a twat, Jo.'

'Shut up – if she's starting to talk, I don't want her picking up words like that and remember, you're only here by my good grace. You just don't think, do you?'

'You'll never stop reminding me of that. When are you going to treat me as an equal?'

Josie didn't want to argue. Maybe it was wrong of her to always rub George's nose in it. She did appreciate his help, but it had still only been nine months since Tom had passed away.

She looked at Daisy and smiled. 'Where do you go, my little Chicken Licken?'

'Da-da.'

That was all the confirmation Josie needed, and George's life wasn't going to get any easier.

*

'No, George, Tom always put the windbreaker in the top box last. We're never going to get to the beach the way you're faffing about!'

'Beach.'

'Yes, chicken, we're going to the beach.'

Daisy's smile got wider as George started to frown. He'd grown up in the shadow of his brother and nothing had changed. He didn't have to be there; Josie treated him with disdain most of the time, but he loved her. Today was, hopefully, going to be the best day of his life. He'd deliberately put the windbreaker in first because he had hidden a sign in there asking Josie to marry him and didn't want her to see it before the big reveal.

'Can't help who you fall in love with…'

'What's that, George? What are you muttering under your breath?'

'Nothing, just thinking that she repeats every word you say now.'

'That's how kids learn and why you have to keep your swearing in check.'

George continued to load the car for their day trip to the Kent coast. Josie hoped Daisy would enjoy the sandy beach and an ice cream for the first time. She didn't talk to George until they'd finally parked up. The seagulls were particularly loud, but that, surprisingly, didn't seem to bother Daisy. It was unexpected because usually Josie had to be aware of sudden or different sounds which could agitate Daisy.

By now Josie had got used to speaking a running commentary on what was happening around Daisy to help her learn about the world without being able to see it. Sitting her on the beach near the water's edge, she took hold of Daisy's hand.

'I'm going to put your hand in the sand now, Daisy, the colour of sand is…'

'Lello.' Daisy giggled.

Josie took a sharp intake of breath. She never knew why she told Daisy the colours, it was irrelevant, really, but she was absolutely sure she hadn't spoken about yellow sand before. She beckoned George to come over but put her finger to her lips to indicate that he shouldn't say anything. She patted the blanket to get him to sit down.

'George is here now, Daisy. What colour did you say the sand was?'

'Lello.' Daisy giggled again.

'Fluke, what's it matter anyway? We need to move back; the tide is coming in.'

Just as he said that the water touched Daisy's little toes. 'Sea, blue,' Daisy announced before pointing in the air. 'Sky, blue.'

Josie and George stared at each other.

'Sun, hot, lello.'

'Who told you that, Daisy?'

'Da-da.'

Josie always harboured the thought that perhaps Daisy was with her dad when she disappeared but dismissed her feelings as grief, which she knew was the ultimate price for love. This hadn't been the first time recently that Daisy had said something only a sighted person would, and Josie was beginning to think her notion had been correct in the first place. Her heart ached; if only she could see Tom too, but at least she had her memories. A tear began to form in the inner corner of her eye, and she sniffed to stifle it. Daisy reached up to her mum's face.

'No tear, Da-da love.'

'I want to go home, George.'

'We've only just got here, what's the matter with you?'

'Everything,' she sobbed.

George knew he would be wasting his time with the homemade sign; it wasn't going to happen today. They'd never even shared a bed. Not today, but maybe one day, George hoped.

*

Daisy had been invited on to Lucy Edwards' podcast. She was excited, as they'd briefly met at a fundraiser. Daisy loved podcasts and Audible books, which she thought were one of the greatest inventions of the twenty-first century. When she was little her mum had bought her a toy Mother Goose who told stories when you put a cassette tape in it. Apparently, her mouth lip-synced the words while playing; Daisy was unaware apart from the clacking sound of the toy's beak, but she loved falling asleep listening to the fairy tales. She was apprehensive on the subject matter of the podcast. Just a Q&A session, Lucy had told her. The topic was "Do blind people dream, and if they do can they 'see' when they dream?".

It should have been straight forward. Daisy had been blind since birth – of course she dreamt, but ordinarily it would've been just the other senses without images. How someone smelt, sounded, felt and even tasted. Except Daisy *did* know what it was like to see. If ever she wanted to know what something looked like, a vision would appear on the beach courtesy of her dad. She knew Lucy was beautiful; on the last full moon she'd asked him to show an image of her. Daisy just needed to be careful not to say anything that a sighted person would.

It went really well – after all, she thought, there were only roughly twelve days a year when she could actually see. Before she knew it, she and her guide dog, Tilly, were on their way to meet her mum at a restaurant close by. She'd said goodbye to Mo, her mum had been insistent that Daisy's boyfriend mustn't be present, and found herself, as usual, waiting. Daisy wondered what was so important that it couldn't involve her boyfriend of five years. Mo worked nights, so it was fairly easy to navigate the secret-keeping. If he was ever off on a full moon, she made excuses for him not to stay over. Recently he'd been talking about them making their commitment permanent. He didn't outright ask her to marry him, but that was the general gist of it. Daisy was coming around to the idea and even considered telling him the truth. In the early days of their relationship, she'd felt the features on his face and asked him to describe himself. She chuckled at the memory; when her dad had showed her what Mo looked like, she knew he'd been a bit more flattering about himself. What shone through the image of him was his kindness. Her dad agreed.

She smelt her mum's perfume and the scraping of the chair on the pavement.

'So, what's up, Mum? Why are we having lunch on a Wednesday?'

'Can't I treat my daughter once in a while? And I wanted to see how your podcast went. Your make-up looks nice too.'

'Well, I wouldn't know, would I? It feels nice; Lucy did it. Anyway, go on, spit it out!'

'George and I are splitting up.'

'About bloody time – he's overstayed his welcome for nearly thirty years! You've been arguing all my life. I'm blind, not deaf!'

'I just think, well, the reason it's taken me so long is because unlike other grieving people, I *know* there is life after death. Even people who believe can never be 100% sure, but because of you, I know he's there. Maybe that's made it harder.'

'So, it's all my fault then.'

'No, no.'

Josie took a deep breath; trying to make light of the situation she joked that whilst Mummy and George were breaking up, it wasn't her fault and they loved her as much as they'd always done, just as she would've said if Daisy had been a child.

Except she hadn't been brave enough, until now.

Josie wasn't sure if it was because Daisy was nearly thirty or whether she'd just finally found the courage to put herself first for once. Either way, it was a huge weight off her shoulders. She wanted to move house and take Daisy with her. Whilst George hadn't had to pay the mortgage, it had been paid off by Tom's life insurance at the bank, he'd still contributed financially for the last twenty-nine years. Josie had decided to split the proceeds of the house sale. Two thirds to her and Daisy, which left enough for George to buy himself a small property with his third. Josie had always thought that she would never want to leave the house that Tom had died in, but she was, after twenty-nine years, finally ready to move on.

It wasn't that George was a bad guy; he just wasn't Tom. He knew it too, always playing second fiddle to his dead brother. Josie wouldn't marry him despite the number of times he had asked. She knew that the only reason they'd got together was because of a shared grief. There was a common thread running through the bereavement, but that's where it ended. Josie definitely wasn't strong enough in the early days; she could barely meet Daisy's needs. As the months turned into years it became easier to let him stay rather than face the truth. George had been such a great help with Daisy, not least because of her blindness but also because of her habit of disappearing every month. It was a huge secret that had held them together. If there was one certainty in Josie's life it was that George would never betray Daisy or reveal her secret. They had made a pact the first time she reappeared.

'Did you say, "It's not you, it's me?".' Daisy laughed.

'Well, that wouldn't be true now, would it? Do you think Dad will be pleased?'

'I've told you before, Mum, over there it's different. There's none of those seven deadly sins. He harbours no resentment. I think he was glad George stepped in; besides which, he knows you could never love anyone like you love him.'

'I wish I could see him…'

Josie had spent all of Daisy's life wishing for that. There was no explanation either way. In her heart she was glad it was Daisy, not her. She knew what Tom looked like; she knew what it felt to be in his embrace; she knew him. If it weren't for the disappearances Daisy would never have known her father. Maybe then she would've called George "Dad", but that was never in the equation.

'Lucy's really great, Mum, we're so alike, apart from her doing the marathon back in April.' Daisy laughed. 'I couldn't run to save my life! Olga, her guide dog, got on with Tilly too. She's invited me to a gala she's attending, something to do with that socialite Lady Charlotte Fortescue-whatshername.'

'Fortescue-Thornville, your grandad knew her dad, they were Freemasons. It was their lodge that paid for your schooling.'

'Well, at least I'll have something to talk about to her.'

'Do you remember when you were at Dorton House?'

'I can hardly forget my schooldays now, can I?' Daisy laughed.

'You know what I meant; it only shut down about four years ago. I was so worried for you, but I knew it was the right thing to do. At least you didn't have to board, we couldn't have chanced that. Luckily it was only around the corner. A lot of the kids around the UK had to board, but it was worth it as it was such a highly regarded blind school.'

'Think you're supposed to say "visually impaired" nowadays.'

'Either way, I just meant that we've coped with every upheaval we've had, so moving house shouldn't be any more difficult.'

Daisy ignored her mum's last announcement. 'How many times did George ask you to marry him?'

'I lost count, to be honest, but at least once a year.'

'And he never slept in your bed, did he? I remember the proposal after the film *Love Actually* had come out. He tried to copy the signs like the scene with that guy from *The Walking Dead* – what was his name? And Kiera Knightley. Andrew Lincoln, that's it! Thank God for audio descriptions! Do you think he hoped I wouldn't get it because I couldn't see them?'

'He was put off by your laughter, as I remember.'

'It was the Christmas carol playing and his silence that made me guess.'

'He's not a bad guy, Daisy. If anything, I've prepared him to be a good husband and father. He's nothing like he was when your dad died – he was a real arrogant turd before. If you think about it, he's fifty this year and hasn't had a girlfriend since his brother died.'

'His choice.'

'True, which is why we need to sell up and give him a chance to find reciprocated love. Would you prefer it if you and I bought a bungalow, seeing as you've always had the downstairs bedroom?'

'You're forgetting one thing, Mum, have you ever considered that I might not want to live with you anymore?'

*

'Do you fancy a cuppa, Josh?'

'I'd rather a whiskey, the day I've had, but yeah, a cuppa will have to do. What about you? How was your day?'

Jess was excited to tell Josh that she'd had lunch with Storm again. Both of them had decided that if they could befriend any of the "16/87s" it would make their lives easier for when the time came.

Jess said they had been joking about her being the second famous Scottish woman called Storm. Josh didn't know what she was talking about; he had never seen *The Matthew Wright Show*. Jess filled him in about how the young TV presenter was also born in 1987 but in April. There was no confusion, though, as Storm McDonald was the only one of the two who'd been in prison. She never shied away from her past, telling Jess that she felt she had to leave Scotland, though, because she believed Jason's parents deserved not to be in the same country as her. She decided not to lie to anyone as the truth would always come out.

'Well, not quite the whole truth, eh, Jess?'

'She wasn't exactly going to tell me that now, was she? I lied about my birthday month, though. I'm not ready for that. She was a bit shifty when I said you were a detective sergeant. Actually, she'd joked that you were an older guy cos of your status at work and didn't believe me when I said you were also born in 1987.'

'Fast track for the geniuses.' Josh laughed.

'Bet the Met regrets that now,' she countered.

'Very funny, so, what next? What are we thinking in regard to the blind girl?'

'*Josh!* She has a name, you know. Daisy, it's a cute name.'

'Be funny if she was named after Gail's favourite perfume.'

'You're just looking for connections that aren't there. It wasn't even out then.'

Jess moved back to the kettle that had now boiled before pouring them both a cup of tea.

'Can you read tea leaves, Jess?'

'Well, not in a tea bag I can't! Never tried, to be honest. I don't think we need to be worried about what happens next – seems like everything is unfolding itself.'

'Heard she is going to be on that Lucy Edwards podcast.'

'And? She's not exactly going to do a tell-all on there. Pretty sure it'll all fall into place.'

Josh took a sip of his tea. It often felt to him that they were so consumed with solving her situation that Jess seemed to have forgotten her promise to help him find out what his secret was. As if she was reading his mind, she picked up the conversation.

'Your sister has asked me to be friends on Facebook. What do you think? Shall I accept her?'

Josh shrugged his shoulders. 'Entirely up to you, but she'll either try to sell you some old jollop she's pedalling or unfriend you as soon as you say something she doesn't like. She's always blocking and unblocking me. She's styling herself as some *healer* now, doing coffee enemas and Yoni massages – whatever they are. Might try that, though, I love a good massage.'

Jess spluttered her tea over the kitchen table with laughter. 'You don't have the right equipment for one of those! It's a sensual massage for women's bits.'

Now Josh was laughing too. '*Women's bits?* Can't you just say *tits and fannies*?'

'Whatever – either way, I don't want her seeing my *bits*. I will friend her – maybe I can gradually get her talking about Gail. I don't think we're getting very far with that project.'

Josh nodded; he was glad she hadn't forgotten that he too had a mystery that needed solving. He'd been sober for 154 days. He needed to feel like it was all for a good reason. Life was definitely better having Jess in it, but he still missed his friend Jack Daniels. Keeping busy, not only at work but on their side-line, was the key, and he'd started running with Jess too. He couldn't give up the cigarettes, though, and could never keep up with her. He told Jess he could only deal with one addiction at a time. His boss had called him in recently to praise him, saying his productivity was better since his sobriety. Josh told her about that, stating that he hadn't said *a lot better*, just better. He'd been so good at his job and disguising his problem that he didn't think it was that noticeable, apart from in his heart. He no longer needed to use any subterfuge and consequently slept well, with a clear conscience, which was the best sleeping pill ever.

EIGHT

STURGEON MOON

Charlotte opened her laptop, waited for it to fire up then poised her fingers on the f and j keys.

> *My name is Charlotte Fortescue-Thornville, and I am going to die.*

Backspace, backspace, delete, delete.

Everyone is going to die eventually, just some sooner than others. There wasn't 100% certainty of her imminent demise, but if you were to place your bets, it was about odds-on.

Who wrote their memoirs before the age of thirty? mused Charlotte. Only Z-list celebrities wringing out their last five minutes of fame, their books ending up in Poundland. She only knew this because she and her friends had been in the store once for a laugh.

Who wrote their memoirs before the age of thirty?

People who were going to die.

My father died the day I was born from a heart attack because he was old enough to be my great-grandpa.

Backspace, backspace, delete, delete.

No-one would be interested in that; it's probably more common than people think. She decided to find out from Google later.

My mother was a bunny girl who wanted to snare Hugh Hefner, but she couldn't get anywhere near him so pounced on one of his old, white, super-rich UK friends.

Backspace, backspace, delete, delete.

Yes, factually true, thought Charlotte, but her mum didn't deserve all that being dragged up in 2017. She'd taken enough flak from the media in the 1980s when she'd married him. Back then when Charlotte was born, the award-winning tabloid headline was "Charlie Inherits the Chocolate Factory".

Again, factually true – her father, Albert Fortescue-Thornville, owned the oldest and largest chocolate manufacturer in the world, and had never had any other children.

I am an ordinary girl in an extraordinary world.

Backspace, backspace, delete, delete.

Charlotte thought that it sounded like song lyrics; besides which, it wasn't the world that was extraordinary – it was *her*.

I am an extraordinary girl in an ordinary world.

Backspace, backspace, delete, delete.

Still like song lyrics.

My name is Charlotte Fortescue-Thornville and I disappear every full moon. I meet my dad; he likes it there because he isn't old and decrepit.

Backspace, backspace… no, thought Charlotte, this *was* the story she wanted to tell, but not until after her death. She had already decided to ask her consultant to put a number on it. She figured if she had three months left and wrote one thousand words a day, give or take, she would get it written and filed away safely to only be read after her demise.

To find out I had breast cancer at twenty-eight is obviously something that is… fucking shit.

Backspace, backspace, delete, delete.

Her mum hated swearing, claiming that only people who had a lack of vocabulary swore and that she didn't spend all those thousands and thousands of pounds sending her to the best private school in the country to end up swearing like some delinquent.

Charlotte didn't realise it would be so difficult to put pen to paper, or rather fingers to keyboard, to lay her soul bare. Not only about the illness but the biggest secret of all time.

I carry the biggest secret of all time. I sit in my ivory tower overlooking Regents Park, not wanting for anything…

Backspace, backspace, delete, delete.

She didn't want everyone to think she was just some rich girl making up fanciful stories. The rich bit was true, she didn't know any other life, but would people think she was making all the rest up? Did it matter if they did or didn't? After all, she was going to ensure it was published posthumously, so she wouldn't know what was happening. Or would she? Charlotte thought that she of all people should know the answer to that. Her dad always knew everything, so, assuming she would be with him after death, then it would make sense that she would see the fallout from her memoir but would be unable to do anything to change what people thought or believed.

An hour had gone past. Charlotte was tired; she had only written one sentence. She deleted that too. A thousand words a day? She'd only managed to write twenty-six. Chuckling to herself, she shut the lid of the laptop. She had thought that she would write the words, print them off to place in the safe then delete the document. It was the only way she could be sure that no-one would see it until she was ready. No chance of a cyber-attack in the safe.

She looked at her reflection in the mirror, her head bereft of hair. Never did she think she would miss the white streak that she dyed away every month.

She did.

Her dad was always reassuring her that she would get well, that she would be free of the disease, but that didn't correspond to what the doctors said. Was he lying to her? Charlotte remembered asking him a question when she was about six years old, so desperate was she for a pony. Her mum had steadfastly said no, but her dad had told her she would get one. He was right and his answer to that was, 'It's impossible for me to lie over here.'

He could've been lying then; maybe that was just luck. Her head was aching – too many thoughts and not enough energy to deal with all of those and the constant nagging that her life was ending.

There was a gentle tapping on her bedroom door before her mum asked to come in.

'You OK, sweetie? It's been a long day – here, take your meds and I'll get you something to eat. Come on, what do you fancy?'

'You mean you'll get Chef to make me something.' Charlotte chuckled.

'Or we could order in?'

'Ice cream, that's what I fancy. Ben and Jerry's Caramel Chew-Chew.'

Lilian picked up the phone by Charlotte's bed and pressed for the kitchen. 'Please send up Charlotte's favourite ice cream and two spoons.' Lilian stroked the top of her daughter's head.

'Mummy! You know I don't like that.'

'You always used to love me stroking your hair.'

'*Exactly!* Stroking my *hair*, not my fucking bald head!' Charlotte picked up the phone. '*One* spoon, please bring just one fucking spoon!'

'Charlotte, come on now, you're not some filthy navvy, are you?'

'Well, you weren't exactly on the right tracks of life before Daddy, were you? All poshed up and erased now, *Lilian*.'

Once when Charlotte was younger, she'd found out her mum's name was actually Lisa. Lilian had thought she'd airbrushed out her previous life when she met Albert, but it didn't deter the tabloids.

Lilian sighed; she didn't think it fair to argue about something that was long buried. She understood her daughter's need to take it all out on someone, so she let herself be Charlotte's punching bag.

Charlotte turned away from her mum, drew her knees up towards her chest, lay on her side and pulled the bed cover over her head.

The ice cream was duly delivered only to sit all afternoon until it had turned into a warm milkshake. Just like every other time she'd asked for it recently.

*

Dear Journal,

I spoke to my nurse who said it might help to write down my thoughts, so here I am. I think that's probably better than trying to write a memoir. What do you think, Journal? And why don't you call yourself a "diary" anymore?

Do you like this green ink? I pinched the idea from my consultant. He always uses a Mont Blanc fountain pen filled with green ink. And what do you think of your cover? "Follow Your Dreams" – that's a joke. If I followed my dreams, I'd be dead and living with my father.

I'm twenty-nine and three quarter years old and desperately want to get to my thirtieth in October. I was at the hospital today having my last chemo before the blood tests to see if it's working. If it wasn't for Ricky, I think the paps would've got the photo. As I went to walk towards the back entrance, he texted me saying they were on the lookout for Bruce Forsyth but would get double if I were spotted. Mummy pays him well. He's a pap himself, but he's on our payroll, so it's all on our terms. He took over when his dad retired. I actually fancy him, Journal, you didn't know that, did you? No-one does! I think he is thirty-five. Mummy wouldn't be best pleased. She still hopes I'll end up with Henry Schweppes-Brown, but he is so goddamn awful – besides which, Camilla says he has a small dick.

Speaking of Camilla, she was on at me to make a guest appearance on that reality show she's on. I said no twice. Once because I can't stand the way it portrays us and secondly because my cancer isn't in the public domain. I'm sure she just wants more followers and to show a softer side to her character, they really had it in for her when she dumped Rupert on air.

Wow! Journal, how comes you're so much easier to talk to than Memoir? LOL! He was never going anywhere.

Charlotte was interrupted by her phone beeping. It was the rock star's son. He was back in the UK and wanted to meet up – well, he actually texted to say he was on her street, and could he come up? She adored him; they were kind of kindred spirits. Both incredibly rich but neither had done an honest day's work in their lives. It wasn't their fault – happenstance, that's all. She thought she'd tell Journal about him later.

Picking up the phone, she called down to say they should let him in when he arrived but not to send him up to her suite. Texting him back, she said she would be ready in about an hour. He didn't know about the cancer, but she also knew that he wouldn't blab to the papers. Charlotte looked over to her dressing table: four wigs sat on stands, each of varying length, matching her original hair exactly. Her mum had called in a wig maker who specialised in imperceptible hair pieces, but they still made her head hot and itchy. As soon as she came home, she'd tear it off, along with the glue residue and some of her own skin. Charlotte always put her make-up on first before finally drawing on her eyebrows.

'An hour and ten, Chaz, that's early for you! Come on, give us a hug, been a long time.'

'Well, I wasn't doing anything else. How long you here for?' Without a break in her sentence, she lifted the receiver of the phone to ask for champagne to be sent in and turned back to her friend. 'LP, OK?'

He nodded and they continued their conversation.

'Only two weeks – Pops is promoting again. They're having a bit of a renaissance. Should've seen his new wife's face when he announced he was going on a world tour last year! She couldn't leave the country cos she was preggers.'

'I know, I read it in the paper, Scorp.'

'You of all people should know not to believe everything you read. How come you aren't calling me by my new name?' He laughed.

'I read that too, Scott, but you'll always be Scorpion Lovedream to me!'

'It was getting old, bit like us!'

'Speak for yourself – we're technically still in our twenties!'

'I've heard rumours, Chaz, and I hate to tell you, but looking at you it seems they're true – you're a bag of bones.'

'Just been running around, busy, at the gym – I may've lost a pound or too. I'm great, though, honest.'

'And you shaved your eyebrows for fun? You can't kid a kidder, Chaz.'

Charlotte's hands moved up towards her forehead. Crap, she thought, how did she forget to draw them on? Her mum had suggested she had them tattooed, but Charlotte had decided against it. She took a deep breath and began to tell him. An hour or so and two empty bottles of Laurent Perrier later, they were still crying in each other's arms. She loved him like a brother – hell, she thought, if he was straight, she'd marry him.

*

Dear Journo,

See, we must be friends if I've already shortened your name! Soz it's been a while. I was rushed into hospital – something to do with my haemoglobin or something. Well, I do know but can't be bothered to write about it – basically I had to have a blood transfusion.

I couldn't find you when I came home. Mummy had put you in the safe. She said I shouldn't leave you lying around as someone might read you, which means she read you. So now you have a new home in the safe – well, as we know Memoir was never going to live there.

Mummy says we were lucky as the haemoglobin dropped the day after the full moon. That would've been ghastly, especially as the night nurse used to stay too long in my room, chatting about stuff I have no interest in. She was so excited, thinking Camilla would visit, which she had but obviously not in the middle of the night! One of the other nurses had probably told her.

Daddy told me I would go in but said I must have faith that everything will unfold as it should, whatever that means. It's weird because when I'm there I can feel my hair. Daddy says that's because it's how he chooses to see me.

I have been thinking about dying a lot, a lot.

I'm not afraid, but…

I don't want to.

Scorp came to visit – he'd extended his stay as he'd hooked up with a Premiership footballer. I told him it would go nowhere, and the secrecy would drive him mad. He maintained it was just for fun, but we all know how he falls instantly in love with anyone who comes on to him – don't you dare do that, Journo, LOL.

Back in five minutes, Mother is calling…

OK, so maybe it was half an hour! Lucky you weren't hanging by your fingernails, Journo!

Had another debate with Lilian – yes, I know who she is, pointless, absolutely pointless. Before the chemo she encouraged me to freeze my eggs and I said no. Why are we even talking about it? I can't change it now. I never wanted children anyway. Can you imagine looking after a decrepit old lady who disappears every month? What would the carers do? Lilian was going on about adoption and retaining the Fortescue-Thornville name in perpetuity. If I outlive Mother – I know, a long shot, but if I do, I will be leaving all the money to children's charities. Rich kids... well, we know the cost of everything but the value of nothing. Not wishing to generalise, but Henry and Oscar do nothing to alter that stereotype. So entitled, and they think everyone is beneath them and treat them less well than their dogs – maybe it's ingrained in them at prep school. That's not fair. I do know lots of moneyed people who aren't like that, so maybe it's me who's stereotyping. I don't know, I'm getting tired.

OK, I'm going to make a pact with you, Journo. If I do make it, I'm not going to hang around – I will set up those charity foundations ASAP. Are you God, Journo? Been thinking about Him for a while now, but I don't get it. Maybe He is everywhere (hopefully not in the lav when Cami and I are on one!). It's OK, Journo/God, the only drugs I've been taking since I've been ill are prescription ones.

I'm getting tired now, but just wanted to let you know I haven't died yet.

Charlotte liked being in love, but it had been a long time. She wondered if it would've been better or worse to share her illness with a boyfriend. She'd been dating a lot but when she became ill decided it would be better if it were just her and her mum facing it together. It was hard enough having to hear her mum crying; if it was a boyfriend as well that would be too hard to bear. What if he ran at the first sign of malaise? Or became so stifling and suffocating? Charlotte thought she'd made the right decision. All she had to do now was get better and then maybe a knight in shining armour would come along, or Ricky, she laughed.

*

'Lady Charlotte Fortescue-Thornville.'

'What's that, Josh?'

'Next on our list – how are we ever going to get close enough to her?'

'Well, if we've been learning anything it's that we haven't exactly had to try to gravitate them towards us.'

'She's not been seen for a long time now, nothing in the papers or trashy mags.'

'She comes across as less of a bitch than that Camilla – maybe she's had enough of the limelight, especially if she's one of us.'

'You mean one of the "16/87s", not *me*, remember. What do you fancy for dinner?'

'Not fussed. I did find out Kylie's surname, at least her mum's, assuming she took the same, White.'

Josh scanned down his spreadsheet, shaking his head. A "Kylie White" wasn't on the list. 'Give me five minutes, I'll check births and deaths again.'

'It's already August, Josh – do you think we're going to find them all by my birthday?'

'I don't think we're on a timescale, or is that what you've set your heart on?'

Jess shook her head and began to look in the fridge for something that grabbed her fancy. Cream cheese, a half-eaten pork pie, a couple of squishy tomatoes.

'Do you fancy Nando's?'

'Uh-uh.'

'Josh, I said do you want to go out to eat?'

'Sorry, yes, sure, and now I know why Kylie wasn't on the list – her birth certificate says "father unknown".'

'So, we're to assume that Kylie has the same dad as Jade, so she is one?'

'Not necessarily, but probably – either way, we've already decided to get all the family members of the *slippers* together, so it's kinda irrelevant.'

'Come on, I'm starving. How's Emilie? Have you seen her again?'

'Let's talk in the car.'

Josh had been seeing Emilie, quite a lot. He knew he shouldn't, but she understood him in a way Jess couldn't. No chemistry or flirting, just the commonality of alcoholism. If it was as innocent as he thought, why couldn't he bring himself to tell Jess? He was struggling with that one – maybe over dinner tonight would be the right time, he thought.

*

Hey, Journo!

Bet you thought I'd forgotten about you; you won't believe what's been happening… I am cancer-free! No-one could believe it, not least the doctors. The only person who it didn't surprise was Daddy – he actually said, 'I told you so.' We have been partying non-stop.

I think you are God – should I call you Jod? Or Gourno? LOL, probably not, that'd be blasphemy. Maybe He is working through you, because I don't know if I would be here if I hadn't started writing to you.

When I bumped into Oscar, he was going on about how Henry really wanted to reconnect with me (think his parents have been talking to my mother!). Anyway, I said that I'd rather kiss him than Henry, so I did! Life feels alive, it feels… I just can't describe it. The air seems fresh (even in London), the skies seem bluer, the grass greener – oh wow, Journo, this is unbelievable.

On top of that Ricky is coming to tea this afternoon. He'll be here soon so I need to finish getting ready. He told Mummy it was urgent. I mentally ran through my behaviour recently and am pretty sure I haven't done anything to cause any consternation – I hope, LOL. I just heard Martha, the PR woman, arriving. She comes through the front door, while poor Ricky has to use the tradesmen's entrance.

The funniest thing was when Mummy told me, she finished with, 'He's a rather attractive chap, isn't it?' So, I definitely know she read that I fancy him. What should I do with that information, Journo?

Thank you for listening to all these thousands upon thousands of words I have written to you – you've been an absolute trooper! This isn't the end of us, Journo, it's just the beginning! Mwah, mwah, mwah.

Charlotte took one final look in her full-length mirror. She'd had to buy new clothes – not that she minded, but her size eight ones were hanging off of her. She smiled: hair on, check; make-up exquisite, check; and eyebrows, double check. Her hair had started to sprout randomly on her head but there was no way she'd be seen without a wig. As the meeting was with those that knew, she just put a Chanel scarf around her head like a turban. She'd been rubbing vitamin E into her scalp and the sore patches were healing.

As she walked into the drawing room she could see that

Martha, her mum and Ricky were seated. It felt like she'd walked into her own wake.

Martha spoke first. 'Ricky has told us that Murdoch's lot have proof of your cancer and are going to run a two-page spread tomorrow.'

'I don't care anymore,' countered Charlotte.

'If we let them, they'll say whatever they like. You'll have no control.'

'Martha,' began her mum, 'are you suggesting what I think you are?'

'It worked for you back in the day, didn't it?'

'Eventually, but they all still think I'm a gold-digger. I don't think I would've been accepted into society were it not for Charlotte.'

Ricky then chipped in. 'Get in there first. Martha can get you full approval for the copy and then it'll be a huge coup for them as an exclusive.'

'Have we got time?'

'*Mummy!* You're all talking as if I'm not here. What about what *I* want?'

'What *do* you want then? You want them to drag up your ex-boyfriends, your ex-friends, who will all be ready to dish the dirt and make up lies for a payday?'

'Of course not! What would I have to do, Martha?'

Martha explained that she would call the editor and arrange for them to come over for an "at-home interview" shortly and a photographer would take some shots. She then said that it was up to Charlotte if she wanted to reveal her hair, or rather lack of it, but she thought that that would make for more sympathetic copy.

'I'm not after sympathy, I just don't want Mummy's name being dragged through the mud over this.'

'Look, Charlotte,' Martha was getting frustrated at the lack of decision-making between them all, 'the online comments will happen regardless, but I think in general you will be viewed favourably. We'll donate the fee to Cancer Research and you can set up a small charitable foundation to continue a cash flow. It'll only take a couple of hours – let me call them.'

Charlotte nodded; her day had started off all sunshine and rainbows, but now the taste in her mouth wasn't sweet, it wasn't sweet at all.

'Whatever am I letting myself in for?'

'A solution, Charlotte, it's the only way,' replied her mum.

*

The headline this time was "Charlie gets a Golden Ticket". She thought they could've been more original, especially because of all the other cancer patients who weren't doing well. It looked like she was health-privileged due to her wealth. She had to concede that yes, she did have the best doctors and was treated at the new state-of-the-art cancer hospital by Harley Street, but apart from the speed of diagnosis, everyone, surely, was treated the same.

She hoped.

When Charlotte thought about it, she decided that the only real difference was that she had her own room, satellite TV and a decent chef to prepare her meals. Not that she ever ate much in there.

One sentence at the end of the interview said she was donating her fee, but they didn't make as much of her new charity foundation as she would've wanted. That was OK, she decided. Martha had told her she was working to get her an appearance on *Lorraine* where they would solely focus on the charity. Martha was also putting together a celebrity event but couldn't yet decide on the angle. Charlotte insisted there wasn't an *angle*; however, Martha reminded her that it wasn't enough to just be cancer-free. It incensed her that she had to trade her life for a fame she did not want. It was Martha who'd persuaded her to help Camilla on the show.

Camilla's PR was also Martha.

*

Dear Journo,

It's true what they say, Lorraine Kelly is just as nice in person as on the TV. How I wanted to confide in her – she seemed like she would understand.

But I stopped myself.

I told her that when I thought I was going to die I wasn't afraid. I wish I could've said that I know where you go, and it is the most peaceful place on Earth that you could ever imagine. Well, I'm guessing not the Earth – not sure where it is. I finished that part by declaring that I had made my peace with death.

She also wanted some gossip, asking if the rumours were true that I was joining the cast of Hoity-Toity. Two episodes, that's all, and everyone needed to know I wasn't doing any more than that. It's a good excuse to say I would be too busy with my charity foundation. That is true but if it weren't I would've found another justification.

I spoke about you, Journo, and how it was one of the nurses who suggested it. I made a point of getting in my joke about why we don't call you "diaries" anymore. She did laugh. Then she suggested I could turn them into a book for other young sufferers of cancer. Can you imagine that, Journo? LOL. It would be too much editing to take out the stories about my father.

I may moan at Mummy a lot. OK, more than a lot, but when I think about it, she has had to keep the secret for nearly thirty years too. I didn't understand when I was a little girl; I still don't understand now. What would happen if everyone knew? If that was the exclusive, I think they'd sell an awful lot more newspapers. We've had some near-misses in the past, like when I was rushed into hospital to have my appendix out. And that time when Josephine from prep school stayed the night. I pretended to play hide and seek. I could go on, but I think you know all of this anyway, Journo. Am I going mad? Why now?

When I spoke to Daddy about it, he gave his usual answer: 'Everything will unfold exactly as it should.' Though he added a caveat that I mustn't be tempted to tell anyone or it could create a paradox.

Off for drinkies with Cami and the gang shortly. Henry found out about me kissing Oscar. He made a big drama about how he didn't care because of Harriet. I thought that was just a "showmance". I don't care, I'm not going to hook up with Oscar anyway. I want to ask Ricky to take me out for dinner. Not sure where. I don't want him to feel uncomfortable, but that's assuming he agrees. I won't offer to pay the whole bill, but I'll make sure he accepts half.

I guess I need to just carry on and be grateful that I am well.

Mwah, mwah, Journoly (new name for you, LOL!).

*

Josh didn't know why Jack had chosen a coffee shop on Marylebone High Street. He didn't care; he was just glad that his friend agreed to the meeting. It was an important part of his recovery, number nine on the twelve steps at AA: "Make direct amends to such people wherever possible, except when to do so would injure them or others".

He'd decided he couldn't meet Lucinda. He slotted her into the category of "it would injure", not her but himself, classing himself as "others". Too much water under the bridge and he didn't want to rehash that part of his life at the moment; she was at the bottom of the list, and maybe another time, but not yet. Jess was everything he could hope for. Even when he told her he had been secretly seeing Emilie, she wasn't fazed. She understood and, more to the point, she trusted him.

Josh had started to get impatient with the lateness of his friend and had to remind himself that it was a privilege that Jack was meeting him. Draining his coffee cup, he signalled to the waiter to bring him another. He lit his fifteenth cigarette of the day, drawing deeply as he surveyed the pedestrians from his pavement table front-row seat. Theatre, he thought, all of these people unknowingly playing a bit part in the movie of his life. They all looked very privileged; he was sure he could see a TV camera crew further down the road. As it neared towards him, he could see the two women that were being filmed. Camilla Magnussen-Smythe and Charlotte Fortescue-Thornville.

Jackpot.

He had read recently that Lady Charlotte was in remission from a cancer no-one had known she had and that she would be joining the reality series *Hoity-Toity* for two episodes.

Jackpot.

But how on Earth was that going to help him? He was still lost in his thoughts when he was startled by Jack slapping him on the back.

'Your eyes popping out of your head, Josh?'

'Whoa! Nah, mate, all good.'

Josh called the waiter again to refill his cup and get Jack a fresh one. He stood up to hug his old friend, and maybe held on for a little too long, prompting Jack to pull back and ask if Josh was dying and saying farewell. He assured Jack he was fine and began to speak his overly rehearsed but truthful apology. Josh felt the tears pricking his eyes and tried to stifle them.

His friend smacked him on the thigh. 'It's OK, mate, no need for that. I can see you're well and that Jess seems to have done wonders with you.'

The two old friends laughed and began to reminisce about their single days, deliberately omitting the worst drunken episodes. After his second and Josh's fourth coffees were finished, he stood up to leave.

'You never told me what's brought you back to London.'

Josh knew from an earlier conversation that he'd left the police force but hadn't said what he was doing now.

Jack pointed to Lady Charlotte, who was now only about a hundred metres from the men.

'Security detail for the Chocolate Heiress – I start tomorrow.'

Josh smiled. 'Serendipity shining its light again.'

'What's that, mate?'

'Nothing, give my love to Holly and Connor.'

NINE

HARVEST MOON

Josh looked at the two candidates' profiles. His boss had asked him to sit in the room for the final round of interviews. He knew that the Asian guy was the most suitable and would also meet the inclusivity quota. He thought his boss was leaning towards him; Josh disagreed, for all the wrong reasons. Hilda Bartholomew was the other candidate and Josh knew he had to have her in his sights. Her father Patrick was a hero. He had been Margaret Thatcher's personal protection officer. Patrick had been there at the time of the Brighton bombing in 1984 and was instrumental in getting the then-Prime Minister to safety.

That wasn't what Patrick was famous for.

In the Great Storm of 1987, Margaret was taking an early flight for a meeting with François Mitterrand in Paris and was keen to go, so sleep wasn't high on her priority list. As the first female Prime Minister left No. 10 Downing Street a lone gunman, assumed to be an IRA supporter, took a shot at her. Patrick used his body as a barricade and lost his life, just as his first child was born.

In the interview she told Josh that she preferred to be called Hils. Her mum had named her after Margaret's middle name, Hilda. It was in a show of respect that her parents supposedly held for the Prime Minister. Hils joked that it just got her teased at school because she had a name like an "old granny".

Josh managed to engage far more with Hils without even trying and his boss had to agree by the end of the interview that she would be a good fit for the department. He couldn't wait to get home and tell Jess.

*

Hils slung her coat over the back of the sofa which then slid on the floor, then called out to her partner Martin, 'I'm going to shower, and we've got reason to celebrate!'

Martin came out from the kitchen; he could already hear Hils singing in the bathroom and saw the bottle of champagne on the coffee table. As he picked up her coat from the floor, something fell out and slid underneath the sofa. He bent down and tried to retrieve whatever it was. No joy – he'd need a longer arm. Standing up, he walked over to the cupboard under the stairs to find the feather duster to use as an extractor.

There was £2.47 in fluff-covered coins, a sticky rhubarb and custard boiled sweet, not his, they were Hils' favourite and… a positive pregnancy test. He sat on the sofa staring at the plastic with the two blue lines. Martin was going to become a father. A huge smile came across his face. No, they weren't trying; they hadn't even had "the conversation". Having only dated for just coming up to eighteen months, it hadn't seemed necessary. That didn't matter.

Hils was rubbing her hair with a microfibre towel as she walked back in the room. She was still singing and didn't notice what Martin was doing; picking up the bottle of fizz, she started to open it.

'Whoa! *Mummy*, don't think that's a good idea!'

'WTF?' She then saw what Martin had in his hands and continued to open the bottle, deliberately aiming the cork at his face before taking a swig. Pointing at the test Martin was holding, she took another swig. '*No*, the good news is I got my promotion, I'll deal with *that* tomorrow.'

'It's *our* baby, you can't do that!'

'It's just a collection of cells, not a baby, and it's *my* body, not yours.'

'You callous bitch…' As soon as the words fell out of his mouth he cowered in the corner of the sofa as she approached him. She hit him with the champagne bottle, then tipped the rest of the contents over his head before slamming the door and going to their bedroom.

Martin was a bit livelier than her other boyfriends. Her friends called them all "wimps" and she thought he was of a similar ilk. He was, but sometimes he couldn't help but say what he was thinking, and Hils metered out the punishment accordingly.

She hated and liked herself in equal measure. Justification was her favourite word. He had no idea how she felt; he didn't know she vanished every month and was scared to bring a baby into the world. Of all her previous boyfriends, she liked Martin the best, but now he would have to go too. Hils had always made him sleep in the spare room around the full moons. She told him from the beginning that she liked to sleep alone when she had a period. Martin thought that a bit quirky, but he was so enamoured by Hils that he would've agreed to leave the country every month if she'd demanded it.

She regretted wasting the champagne.

He regretted calling her a bitch; he would be sleeping in the spare room. He had her cycle memorised, but this was for an added reason.

Martin showered and settled himself into bed, playing video games. Hils only let him play them when he had to sleep in the spare room. He usually enjoyed "period week", but he just felt sick. He was sure he would be a good father. Sometimes he felt like telling his dad what she was like.

He never did.

Martin grew up with an overbearing mother. Both he and his dad were afraid of her. It looked like history was repeating itself. He decided that there was no point in having that conversation; his dad had never attempted to leave or stand up for himself.

Martin probably wouldn't either.

He loved Hils but often just felt like her lapdog, as if he had to be grateful for the small scraps of love that she threw his way occasionally.

Martin couldn't concentrate on his game and kept getting *killed*. He scoured the internet looking for photos of early pregnancy to see if Hils was right. Was it really just a "collection of cells", as she'd said? That depended on your belief, according to Google. At what moment is a foetus an actual human being? That depended on your belief. He read some appalling stories which just generated more and more of the same.

'Thanks, algorithm,' he said out loud.

Looking at the clock he could see it was nearly 3.30am. Six and half hours since he'd been smashed in the head by a bottle-wielding Hils. The pain had subsided; his heart would take a little longer to heal. She was right: it was her body to do as she pleased with; it had just upset him. Martin was glad she'd got the promotion; he knew how much it meant to her. Suddenly, he got up, as if he was in a cartoon and the lightbulb emoji had appeared above his head. He would offer to be a house husband. His job in IT, whilst well paid, wasn't a happy environment. His colleagues weren't his friends, even the so-called "nerdy" ones. Martin was bullied at work and at home. He would much rather only have to deal with one set of problems, and he would be delighted to stay at home with a baby. He needed to tell Hils, and now. Martin knew he wasn't allowed to go in their bedroom, but this couldn't wait. He'd been practising breathing techniques for a few months now; after one of Hils' "episodes" he'd looked it up online. Martin hated that his heart would beat as fast as a Formula One car at speed anytime he needed to tell her something she may not like. Sometimes when lying in bed it was so audible that she would comment. It was her who'd likened it to a racing car in the first place. He began talking to himself, begging himself to be calm, to breathe, to know exactly what he was going to say and to choose his words wisely.

'Hils, Hils, wake up, I'm sorry, but I have to tell you something.'

No reply.

Dare he try again? Yes, he didn't think he was loud enough, so he banged a little harder on the bedroom door and raised his voice, albeit in a polite way. '*Hils, Hils, I'm sorry, but I know you don't have work tomorrow so please forgive me for waking you but I need to talk to you!*'

No reply.

Oh crap, he thought, this wasn't going well. He knew she was a light sleeper, so her silence spoke volumes.

His heart started doing overtime again.

Very gingerly, he turned the handle to see if she'd locked herself in. A pointless exercise, he thought, as she always locked the door when sleeping alone. Except… except it swung open; however, she wasn't in bed. Martin thought he must've dozed off and not heard her leave the house. He was sure he hadn't, but Hils often made him doubt himself. She was always so convincing whenever she spoke that he was never sure if he was right at any given moment.

Turning the light on, now he knew he couldn't irritate her, he looked around. This was supposed to be their "love nest". A place of romance, of sleep and, yes, of eventually making babies. He looked at the single stem rose in the test-tube vase on her side of the bed. Hils never said thank you, or offered any acknowledgement, but every Friday he bought a new one. It was a small gesture that he hoped conveyed his love. The photo frame on his side was of the two of them on holiday. Behind the smiles he remembered the barbed words she'd thrown at him just before it was taken. She had demanded they took the photo for her social media and commanded him to smile, so she wouldn't look like she was dating, in her words, "a miserable fuck".

He picked up her pillow and smelt it. Hils always smelt good. As he went to put it back, just as she liked it, she appeared on the bed.

'You know I'm going to have to kill you now, don't you?'

Martin moved to the corner of the room and slid down the wall with his knees to his chest, hugging himself, rocking his body and nodding in her direction.

'Don't be a twat! I *should* kill you, but I won't. My dad says I need to go easy on you.'

'Y-y-y-your dad is d-d-dead,' stuttered Martin, his eyes now wide and not blinking.

'Yes, true, but aren't you pleased he talked some sense into me?'

Martin could do no more than nod his head. Words were forming, but nothing was coming out of his mouth. He thought he was dating *Satan*; he thought that explained everything. Her hair now had a strange white streak through it – maybe that was the mark of Lucifer or maybe she was a vampire. That would explain a lot, he thought. He'd seen so many films featuring vampires and devils that would seem to justify her behaviour.

'I actually love you, Marty. My life has been, well, strange doesn't even begin to explain it. I'm actually sorry I hit you now.'

Martin realised that he could now blink, and not only that but his heartbeat had regulated. He pressed a button on his watch – 88bpm, best it'd been all evening.

'I'll get you an ice pack – that cork hit your eye good and proper.'

Martin could do no more than nod again.

She returned, laughing. 'OK, so frozen peas will have to do. So, ask me what you like, you'll never get another opportunity.'

'Why can't we have the baby?'

'Not that question! I mean, how come I vanish, how come I get to see my dad every month… actually, no point in asking that because I don't know the answers, but this is why I can't have a baby.'

'What does that matter?'

'I can't take the chance. I saw what it did to my mum. I – or rather *we* – can't take a chance that the baby might vanish too.'

'Don't you see? You'd be able to help it because you know what it's like and you wouldn't have to give up work. I will – I'll look after it.'

'*No*, that's not going to happen.'

'If you don't have the baby, I will—'

'You will what, Marty? Tell on me? No-one will believe you.' She picked up the photo frame and threw it at him. 'See, you're making me angry again. *You*, you are going to promise me that you won't *ever* tell a soul, and if you do, you'll face the consequences. Besides which, no fucker will believe you anyway.'

*

Hils surveyed the waiting room, profiling everyone she could see. It was a skill that had always come in handy in the police force. There was a scared young girl, about fifteen, clinging on to her mum as if her life depended on it.

She was that girl once, but she wasn't scared.

There was a couple in the corner, talking in hushed tones, never once breaking eye contact.

She'd been a part of that couple once.

Hils had let her then boyfriend come with her. It wasn't his baby, so he went along with her choice.

There was a woman alone, maybe in her early twenties. She looked terrified.

Hils was that woman once, but terror was an emotion she'd never felt.

The older woman reading her book would also probably be Hils, some day in the future. At fifteen she had decided that she would never have children. It was just her luck that no matter what precautions she took, she felt like the most fertile woman in the world. Hils wondered if any of the other patients were profiling too. Just at that moment she was called in.

'Ms Bartholomew, this is the sixth time we've seen you. It's about time you considered being more responsible. Terminations are not a method of birth control, no more than the morning-after pill is. I dread to think how many of them you've taken.'

'Whoa, hang on a minute, Doc, I have asked you and my GP so many times to sterilise me, but you won't. I *am* careful, always.'

'Then maybe someone somewhere thinks you need to have a baby?'

'I'm not the fucking *Virgin Mary* – are you going to do it or not? Cos if you don't, I will find someone who will.'

With that, Hils stood up to leave.

'Ms Bartholomew, we can't sterilise a woman who isn't even thirty yet, unless there are extreme valid reasons. We'll terminate on this occasion, but I strongly advise you to perhaps seek out some counselling to perhaps understand why this keeps happening.'

'*Perhaps* I don't want to.'

*

'What's up, Josh?'

'Not sure – Hils is settling in the team, but I've seen a few questionable comments she's made to others. It's just not sitting well with me. At the interview she never showed even an iota of anything other than sweetness and light.'

Jess started laughing. 'Everyone's on their best behaviour in an interview.'

'Nah, it's not that – something is jarring. I even wondered if she wasn't one of the "16/87s".'

'So, you think we're all going to be *good people*? We already have one murderer in the mix!'

'Mitigating circumstances. Storm was young and in a situation that she handled the wrong way. I'm not condoning what she did, but we have to look at the bigger picture. Who knows what you might've done if you were in that situation as a teenager?'

Jess shook her head; she couldn't imagine that, but Josh was right – who knew? He then went on to explain that he'd looked at her shift patterns in the three months since she'd been there, her probation period was ending and her appraisal was next week. He needed to know before then; if she wasn't a "16/87", he wasn't going to view her favourably. Josh acknowledged that he wasn't exactly being ethical but felt that to their personal ends it was.

Josh announced that he was almost 100% sure she was as she had managed to clock off before 2am on the first full moon, and the second one she'd got cover for, declaring that she had a "family emergency". The next one was in a couple of days; Hils was due on a night shift and he decided to take her out in the patrol car, making any excuse he could think of. Most likely he would say it was part of her appraisal.

*

An eight-year-old Hils was being her usual defiant self.

'I don't want to wear that dress,' she declared.

'It's Auntie Margaret's seventieth birthday and we're going to a posh hotel called Claridge's in London.'

'She's not my auntie, Daddy said she wasn't. Are you even my real mother?'

Beth despaired; she didn't expect it to be this difficult, raising a child as a widowed mother, but Hils had other ideas. This hadn't been the first altercation this week and Beth knew it wouldn't be her last. Bribery was her last recourse, but of course Hils knew that and was waiting, tapping her foot on the floor.

'Let me read you Aun… Margaret's letter. They come from the House of Lords now and you know they always contain a cheque. Sit down, we'll talk about the dress later.'

A sullen Hils sat on the floor rather than the sofa her mum had pointed to. Her arms were folded. 'Well, get on with it then.'

Beth coughed and took a sip of her wine.

Dear One,

How fast our birthdays come around. I shall be seventy just three days before your eighth birthday, and of course this will be still tinged with sadness at the anniversary of your father's passing. I am having a party on your birthday at Claridge's, and it will be attended by the Queen. I would like you and your mother to pop in for a little while. I shall have someone furnish your mother with all the details.

I hope you enjoy your trip to Hamley's this year and to that end I enclose a cheque for £80.00, ten pounds for each year of your life. I hope we will be able to celebrate many more of our birthdays together.

Yours in gratitude,

Margaret

'Well, at least she didn't call herself *auntie.*'

'Hils, come on now, you got what you wanted, so you'll wear the dress tonight?'

Hils nodded and went back to playing with her new Power Ranger toys, violently hitting Billy, the Blue Ranger, with Kimberley, the Pink Ranger, while shouting insulting things to him. At least she wasn't swearing, thought Beth as she returned to the kitchen to refill her wine glass, glancing at the cooker to see the time; it wasn't even four o'clock yet. She needed to get Hils to practise her curtsey for the Queen and wondered what that was going to cost. She hoped Hils didn't need reminding to keep quiet about her visits to her dad. No amount of bribery could guarantee that, so from a young age she told her that if anyone found out she wouldn't see her dad ever again. Beth did consider that to be a strong possibility, so she had never told a soul. Hils loved her dad; it was a small price to pay, but sometimes she did feel like testing her mum's theory out. For someone of only eight years old she was extremely intelligent when judged against her peers; however, she lacked the basic social skills to interact with people her own age. Rarely was she invited to any birthday parties, and it didn't seem to bother her one bit.

Baroness Thatcher's party was a veritable "who's who" and Beth just about managed to contain herself when the organisers informed her of the details for the "meet and greet" with the Queen. Hils looked like butter wouldn't melt in her mouth; her long black hair was tied in a ribbon that matched her dress. It wasn't the dungarees she wanted to wear, but Hils desperately wanted a Nintendo Game Boy and they were over £70.00. She needed Margaret's cheque. The Queen couldn't have been more gracious, remembering who they were, though Beth realised she would've been forewarned. When Hils spoke, saying that she would tell her dad that she'd met her, the Queen responded politely, saying she spoke to her father in her prayers every night too. Before Hils could correct her, she had moved on to the next guest. Swerved that curveball, thought Beth.

The morning after the next full moon, Hils was indignant, proclaiming that her mother was a liar and that even telling the most important person in the world didn't stop her from vanishing.

Beth poured a drop of Bailey's into her morning coffee. 'That's because the Queen didn't believe you. I'm telling you that if someone were to investigate it seriously that it would be all over – they'd take you to some scientific lab, pull you to pieces and you'd never come home again.'

'Might be better than living here.'

*

'So, Sarge, how comes you're on patrol with me tonight? It's gone 2.30am already.'

'Standard for appraisal. How do you think it's been going?'

'Well, apart from Max being an absolute pedantic wanker, I'd say OK.'

'I didn't mean him, he's one of the good guys. Yes, he's fastidious because he wants to be good at his job. Isn't that what you want?'

Hils took a sip of her water. She knew she was good at her job and certainly didn't think she needed supervising by a boss who was the same age as her. It frustrated Hils that she wasn't able to get on the fast track as well, and that had nothing to do with her intellect, for which she knew she was in the top 1%. When querying her rejection, they'd stated that it was to do with her attitude. Hils had told the board that it was *their* attitude that stank, not hers, and threw her papers at them before walking out. Now, however, she had to play the game and get home by 3am.

'Sorry, Sarge, of course, it's just that I-I-I have some personal issues that I'm dealing with. In actual fact, I could do with clocking off early tonight, if that's OK with you.'

And there it was, just as Josh had thought. He needed to play his cards close to his chest. Make her think he was on board, then find some emergency of his own to stall her. He and Jess had had an inkling this would happen and had already thought up a couple of scenarios he could pitch if it came to that.

'Yes, sure, Hils, I'll see we can. Fancy a Maccy D? Not a lot happening at the moment.'

Josh pulled the patrol car into the twenty-four-hour McDonald's car park, went through the drive-in and then parked so they could eat their food. There was a couple of youngsters in a souped-up Honda Civic, parked on the far side of the car park, looking a little smoky in the interior.

'Have a word with those lads. I'll pop the bonnet – I need more water in the washers – and I'll be over in a mo if you need me. Don't be too long or your food will be cold.'

Hils looked at her watch – less than an hour till she needed to be home. It wasn't long before she'd dealt with the lads, deciding to send them off with a warning. It was only a bit of weed and after searching their car she couldn't find anything that would suggest more than personal use.

By the time she had come back Josh had loosened the battery terminal enough so that the vehicle wouldn't start. He prayed there wouldn't be an actual emergency call that would necessitate them attending. Settling back in the car, he began to eat his food. Jess wasn't a fan of fast food, so any opportunity he had, he took.

'Usual, Sarge, sent them off with a flea in their ear.'

'Great, eat yours, it'll be cold now. I'll get some fresh if you like, I could do with another coffee. I know about your dad, think everyone does, but I know nothing about your mum. What's she like?'

'What *was* she like? Died, a few years back, alcoholism. Funny story, she died the day Thatcher did! I can't get away from that woman. It never did me any favours. Think I resented her; after all, my dad would still be alive if it wasn't for the Iron Lady.'

'Sorry, I didn't know. I never knew my mum, was brought up by my sisters and my useless, bless him, dad.'

'Look, Sarge, all this "getting to know you" stuff is great, but I really do need to get home. My partner, Martin, well, he's unwell, he's unwell in the head,' she lied.

'Yeah, yeah, sure, another coffee and I'll be good to go.'

Hils looked at her watch – cutting it fine was an understatement. If Josh had another coffee, she could just get home on time. She was already surveying her surroundings looking for potential hiding places before realising all she needed to do was to get to the toilets in the restaurant. They'd have to open them for a serving police officer. Hopefully, she thought, it wouldn't be necessary.

Until it was.

By the time Josh finished his coffee and made a show of attempting to start the patrol car, she knew she had no choice.

'Sarge, I need the ladies' room – my stomach feels dodgy, so I may be a while! I'll have a look when I come back if you like. I'm pretty good with mechanical stuff.'

'Go ahead. I'll look, I used to fix up cars with my dad when I was young.'

Hils clicked her tongue. 'Never had that opportunity my first boyfriend was a petrol-head, but he was such a prick I never chose a guy like that again.' She laughed.

Josh made all the cursory pretence of looking for the problem. As soon as Hils was out of sight, he put the battery terminal back on and then followed her towards the toilets.

Looking at his watch, he saw it was 3.31am. Nine minutes, but he had to be in the loo when she appeared or it would be all for nothing. He thought it strange that she wouldn't care where she was when she disappeared, knowing how important it was for Jess to be laying in a bed, albeit any bed, but she always had to follow the same routine.

He decided to wait until 3.37am to go in so it didn't look suspicious to the night staff of McDonald's, engaging in conversation with a spotty youth whose name badge coincidently said "Josh" with four gold stars. It was a good talking point. The youthful Josh was telling him that his father had been a copper, but he didn't want to follow in his footsteps as he thought it had contributed to his parents' divorce. He'd studied psychology at university but felt that wasn't a path he wanted to follow either and was using this retail job while he decided what he wanted to do.

Adult Josh then made his excuses to go to the toilets. Whilst they were gender-separated, they sat in a little corridor so he wouldn't be seen entering the ladies. Three doors – he pushed the first two and they opened. The last one was locked so he climbed over the second one to open the third then stood just outside with the door open, waiting…

'And the magician's assistant reappears!' Josh laughed.

'WTF? Sarge, whatever you think you saw, you didn't. You're tired and imagining shit, and this isn't what it looks like.'

With that she lunged at him. Josh deftly took her arm before pinning her against the wall. 'Calm down, Hils. I'm not imagining anything. You don't know it, but you're a "16/87".'

'A fucking what? Loosen your grip, I'm not going to run or attack you.'

'That's not true now, is it, Hils? You and – I'm not sure how many others, but you were born on 16th October 1987 and at that moment your dad died too. Every full moon you get to visit him at 3.30am. I need to tell you that you're safe and so is your secret.'

'How'd you know that? Others? My mum always said I was the only one – it drove her to her death. Please, Sarge, Josh, I won't run, just please loosen your grip.'

Josh was so sure he couldn't trust her that he'd taken the precaution of locking them in, having procured the main door key from youthful Josh. He'd made up some convoluted story that he was concerned his colleague was taking drugs and he may have to detain her. He let her go and she darted for the door.

'Not going to run, Hils? Who do you think I am?'

Hils slid down the back of the door. For the first time in her life on Earth, she felt a sense of lightness about her body which she only ever felt when she was with her dad. Some big fat tears began to spring from her eyes. That was another emotion she wasn't used to. Normally it was she who made the boys cry, not the other way round.

'Oh God,' she sniffed, 'what do we do now? And what are you going to do with the intel?'

Josh pulled some toilet tissue from its container and walked over, putting a protective arm around her, dabbing away her tears. 'I'd like you to speak to my girlfriend, Jess. She is one of the "16/87s" too. She always thought she was the only one until we stumbled on the truth via my dead sister, Gail.'

'Freaky, totally freaky, but yeah, OK, I think I'd like that. Wow, it's a lot, it's really a lot to take on board.'

Josh took out his phone; he knew Jess would also be awake, so he hit her name on his phone. 'Hey, babe, Hils is with me, we're in Maccy D's toilets.'

'Very hygienic! All OK?'

'Yep, but I'd like to bring her home with me – there's a lot to talk about.'

'You're not on speaker, are you?'

'No.'

'Good, I thought you believed she was a total arse. I was just gonna leave her till last. Her cards don't look good.'

'I think they might be different if you did them again. We'll be a half hour, max, just need to pick her fella up on the way.'

'No worries.'

*

'I dunno about you, but I could do with a drink!'

'Sorry, Martin, this is an alcohol-free house. I'll make us all a cuppa, nice and sweet. That's better for trauma.'

Jess left Josh with the two visitors and went to the kitchen. When she considered that this was the beginning of the invitations, her heart lurched. Yes, it was what she wanted but now the process was actually happening she was terrified of the consequences. What if she was ruining the "space-time continuum" like her mum had always warned? She only had a month till her thirtieth birthday. If last night was the last time that she ever saw her dad she wished she would've known; she would've said goodbye. Her thoughts were disturbed by the kettle flicking off and she went about her task still feeling numb. Jess knew she had to alleviate any stress that Hils and

Martin were experiencing. For her, though, this was the second time that someone whom she didn't know had become privy to her secret. She expected to feel how she did when Josh had found out.

She didn't.

Josh had behaved in such an honourable way that she didn't doubt for one minute that he would keep her secret. Now, not only would two more people know, but as the net widened, every day was a potential threat. Who or what that threat was, Jess had no idea. What she did know was that if the authorities found out they could all end up as "lab-rats". It wasn't just herself she now had to consider, and yet it was her idea and she had to follow through with the consequences.

Or was it her idea? She genuinely couldn't remember.

TEN

HUNTER'S MOON

The familiar sound of the Ring doorbell rang out and Josh went to open the door to his friend Emilie. Jess was busying herself in the kitchen, feeling like she was starting to become some 1950's housewife. Recently she felt like she'd spent more time in the kitchen processing her thoughts than anywhere else in the house. Firstly, for Hils and Martin last month, and now Emilie. She'd tried to explain to Josh how she was feeling lately; it felt momentous and so exposing. He just kept telling her that it was what they were both supposed to do from the outset and now it was coming to fruition. Jess believed that while it was true, *he* wasn't the one experiencing the consequences, so how could he know how it was for her?

He couldn't.

Just before dawn, when Martin and Josh were snoring their heads off, Hils had confessed that she was too scared to ever have children in case they vanished too, and did Jess feel like that? She didn't, but only because she was looking for Mr Right first and had subconsciously decided that it wouldn't enter the equation until after that had happened. Now, standing in the kitchen, idly stirring the Bolognese, she thought about it. Josh seemed to be that "special one", but how and when she would know, she had no idea.

Emilie was absentmindedly shuffling Jess's Moonology cards, which had been on the coffee table, whilst making small talk with Josh.

'Fancy a reading, Emilie?' Jess laughed as she brought the hot pan with their supper into the dining end of their living room before placing it on the centre of the table.

'No, no, sorry, I didn't realise what I was doing. I don't like any occult stuff.'

'S'OK, I'm playing with you. Come on, let's eat.'

Emilie had grown fond of Josh, but this was the first time she was going to be in Jess's company for any length of time. She immediately felt comfortable in her presence though. Josh was right: she was trustworthy, kind and open. He'd invited her because he said Jess could help her with "something". What that something was, she had no idea. He had a get-out clause if her sister Adele wasn't a "16/87", but they thought that highly unlikely as he'd read the original case notes. Jess cut straight to the chase, though, seeing no reason to pussy-foot about.

'You know, Josh told me about your mum, but I know nothing about your dad – he couldn't foster you?'

Emilie was still chewing, which gave her a little time to

consider her answer to Jess's direct question. It didn't feel accusatory, but she never spoke about her dad. She vaguely remembered his face, but only because she'd had an old photo of him, which was long gone now. Jess and Josh had the confirmation they'd needed. Emilie's dad did indeed die the night Adele was born. He was on the Ugandan/Kenyan border of his home nation when the civil war began in Busia and was killed by an UPA insurgent.

When their guest excused herself to use the loo, Jess and Josh started hurriedly whispering to each other. They were deciding to reveal what they really thought had happened to baby Adele and how her mum, though heinous in her actions, went immediately to one hundred with the only explanation she could think of. Still engrossed in their discussion, they didn't hear Emilie return; she had been standing outside of the room listening.

'Do you want to tell me what's going on? I couldn't hear you properly, but it was quite obvious who it was about! Am I here under false pretences? Do I need to call a lawyer? Oh, yeah, I think I'll call myself—'

'Em, please, sit down, yes, we do have to talk, but it's all new to us and—'

'Oh God, you're not expecting to have a threesome, are you?' she interjected.

Fortunately, they all began to laugh, but it was Jess who called a halt to the proceedings. She was asking Emilie if she had seen her mum since her release from prison, and had she ever thought about what happened, but more importantly, did she have an explanation for her baby sister's disappearances?

'Enough with the questions. Think I do need a lawyer! Disappearances? What are you talking about? I've never said that.'

Jess didn't believe her; she may not have told them that part of the crime scene, but she knew she was right. Josh had said that her mother had made Emilie watch the carnage. He'd read the archived case notes which said that four-year-old Emilie told them her sister went away and when she came back her mum attacked her. The jury dismissed Emilie's account; they also decided that her mum was deranged and was experiencing hallucinations. They convicted her of murder due to diminished responsibility.

Emilie got up to leave with Jess begging her not to. She said she could prove that while her mum had behaved reprehensibly, her religious beliefs gave her the only logical explanation at the time. It certainly wasn't an excuse, but perhaps it was more understandable in the circumstances.

'I need a drink.'

'Please don't. I always want one too, but we need to face up to things – remember: "you and me, sobriety is free".'

Josh went over and gave Emilie a hug while Jess explained about the "16/87s". They both convinced her to stay over so they could prove it. Jess didn't particularly want to allow Emilie to see what would happen, but they couldn't think of another way to make her believe. They gave her some of Jess's nightwear and said they would wake her when it was time. From her experiences when she was young, Emilie was more street-wise than average. Sleep wasn't going to happen; she went into survival mode, like a cat with one eye open, ready to mount her flight-or-fight response. Running over everything in her mind, she didn't know what to believe. Josh had become her saviour; she often wished they were a couple, but she was always respectful of Jess. The pair seemed so genuine, and yet, it felt like a horror story she couldn't wait to escape. She decided to go along with the charade, but she wasn't going to sleep. Getting up, she wandered into the kitchen. There was no point in looking for alcohol so a glass of water would have to do.

'I can make you a cocoa if you like?'

Emilie jumped; she hadn't noticed that Jess was sitting at the breakfast bar.

'If I shared my mum's religious beliefs, I could assume you were the devil in a kind girl's body.'

'Emilie, I know this is incredulous, and I know what it has done to my mum. She's been in and out of mental institutions and I can't count the number of times she's tried to commit suicide. I'm tired, I'm so tired of it all. I want her pain to stop but I want her to live. Please just trust me.'

Emilie stared at Jess. She was wearing an old worn-out T-shirt: the lips of Mick Jagger were split and peeling off, the faded words "The Rolling Stones" barely visible. Jess's jet-black hair was piled on the top of her head in a messy bun. Her saucer-like eyes reminded Emilie of a painting that was on the wall in Auntie Adele's home. This looked as far removed from the devil as possible, but Emilie considered the possibility that if he did exist, he would be a master of disguise. Jess could see the fear in Emilie's eyes.

'Let's take our cocoa into my room – I have to lay on my bed. I'll only be gone ten minutes; Josh will be with you.'

'No funny business, mind,' joked Emilie.

The two young women smiled and Jess took her hand, prompting Emilie to roll her eyes in fake mockery of the potential ménage à trois. Within a couple of minutes of them all sitting on the bed, Jess had lit a candle and laid down with one hand on her heart, the other on her belly. She knew that Hils didn't care where she was when she *slipped*, but for Jess, she wasn't going to change her ritual.

She *slipped*.

Emilie looked at Josh with her mouth wide open, looking to say some words, but they failed her.

'It's OK, I've got used to it now. The first time I was drunk but soon sobered up!' With that he put a comforting arm around Emilie as she stuttered, 'H-h-how do you know it's not the devil?'

'Without a shadow of doubt, I know she's not. Jess *is* very special. She visits her dad, just as Adele did, and would've continued to.'

*

'Papa, I'm really struggling – there's a woman sitting with Josh who lost her sister and I have to prove I'm not the devil. I've met another one, Hils, who seems blasé about her *slips*. Why can't you tell me anything? Why do I have to be the "chosen one"?'

'Who said you were? It was just time, Jessie.'

'Time for what?'

'You'll see. I'm not being cagey, but this is how it needs to be. Tell your new friend that she was wearing a pink My Little Pony nightdress the last time she saw her sister alive.'

'If I'm not the "chosen one" – well then, who is?'

'Go now, tell her that everything will unfold exactly as it should.'

Jess closed her eyes and she was back on the bed; as soon as Emilie saw her, she leaped off and went for the door.

'Whoa, Em, it's OK, it's only Jess – hard to understand, but it's OK.'

'S-s-she has the mark of the devil... same as Adele.'

Jess then joined in the conversation; she knew better than to approach Emilie, but Josh did and held her, constantly reassuring her.

'Emilie, it's OK – the hair, that just proves Adele was also one of the "16/87s". It goes away after a couple of weeks, but I colour it. I'll do it now if you'd rather. Look, I have mascara here, couple of secs and it'll be gone.'

Jess wasn't used to seeing people in terror. In Josh's line of work, it was commonplace, and he seemed to know how to calm Emilie down. Sitting in front of the dressing table, she quickly set to work on her hair before turning back to Emilie. 'My papa says I must tell you that when you were with Adele that night, that awful night, you were wearing your My Little Pony nightdress – it was pink. He also said, "Everything is unfolding as it should." Does that make any sense?'

Emilie nodded, and as she did, she began nodding tears down her face. She turned to Josh and nuzzled into his jumper; he held her tighter. Jess walked over and hugged them both.

*

Jess scanned the cafeteria looking for Storm; she would be arriving soon. She'd started to notice what time Storm usually came in for lunch. She was a creature of habit, perhaps due to being in prison so long with a strict routine. Jess was idly flipping through the pages of a trashy magazine, not really taking much in. It was always the same – some Z-list celebrity breaking up with another Z-list celebrity, *again*. Some Z-list celebrity having piled on the weight was now slim and promoting the latest diet fad. Josh teased her for reading the "dross", as he called it, and for watching reality programmes like *Love Island*. Jess defended herself by saying that yes, it was her guilty pleasure, but she liked to unwind watching something that didn't need any brain power.

Storm was coming over now. Over the past week of observation, Jess had deliberately left as she arrived, exchanging pleasantries as they passed each other. She wasn't ready for the conversation.

Now, she had no choice.

Taking a deep breath and a sip of her latte, she indicated that Storm could sit with her. It had been less than a week since the last full moon and she was still dealing with the things her papa had said. Who was the chosen one? Maybe it was Storm.

'Hiya, how you doing? What did you do for your birthday?'

Storm's accent was very thick, and Jess had to really listen hard; she didn't think she'd ever met anyone from Scotland before. Crap, she thought, forgetting that she'd lied about her birthdate.

'Josh has blagged us some tickets to Lady Charlotte's gala – it's next Monday, so we'll celebrate then.'

'Och, that's my birthday. I'll be going nowhere fancy like that. The IT lads said they'd take me out for a drink. I still don't know many people down south.'

As she finished her sentence she ran her hand through her hair, dislodging a bit of the mascara covering her white streak.

Jess thought she would never make an elementary mistake like that. However, she realised it isn't unusual for women their age to start to go grey, so maybe that was the excuse Storm used. Jess had a few stray ones herself.

She was still pondering while Storm was laughing at the article that was open in the magazine. It seemed to her that the other "16/87s" so far were much more nonchalant than she. Three of them. Only a third was pedantic: Jess herself. She rummaged in her handbag for a packet of wet wipes before offering one to Storm to wipe the mascara from her hand. Rubbing it off, she began making a joke that she wasn't ready for the whole head dye yet when it was just a few grey hairs.

'So, didn't you at least go out for a drink?'

'We had one of Josh's friend's over for dinner. Sad story, her sister was murdered by her mum when she was a baby.'

'Oh, fuck! That's, that's heinous. I mean, I know you know what *I* did, but that was self-defence – whatever possesses someone to behave like that, I have no clue.'

'Do you believe that there could've been mitigating circumstances?'

'Absofuckinglutely not! A baby is defenceless.'

'Something terrified the woman.' As Jess said that she pulled another wet wipe out. With her left hand she took hold of Storm's.

'Do you trust me?'

'I don't trust no-one.'

Jess knew that may be the case, but she had to carry out what she'd set out to do. Taking a deep breath, she began to rub a little mascara off of her own hair, simultaneously speaking to Storm, not once losing eye contact.

'The baby disappeared, the mum was petrified and thought it was some voodoo at work. My birthday is 16th October – sorry, I lied, I didn't want to spook you before I was ready. My dad was killed by a telegraph pole that night – what about yours?'

Storm was used to fronting it out in prison. You had to; it was every woman for themselves. No real friends, as such, just people that would *do* for you as you would for them. Storm and her mum had spent their whole lives protecting the secret; now, in a puff of smoke, it was over.

Relief.

'Heroin overdose. Now what?'

'I wish I knew. Josh and I have been compelled to find the others – apparently we're called the "16/87s" on the other side and are like celebrities. We think we know of everyone now, but we've only met the sister of the murdered baby, one other and now you.'

Storm took hold of Jess's other hand. There was an instant connection between the two of them. She was normally always the driver of any conversations so that she could deflect and misdirect, if necessary, but she was lost for words.

'Don't you see? You were meant to be down south *and* in my workplace. Serendipity and all that. Once we've spoken to everyone, I want to get us all together. I'm sure that's what I'm supposed to do. Not just us but our families who know too. They've been through hell for nearly thirty years. Is your mum OK? Mine is currently back in a psych unit – it's second nature for me but still hurts. I guess I want to know how other mums have dealt with it.'

Storm's head was buzzing; she had so many questions to ask, but in that moment all she wanted was her mum. She was determined not to cry, not to show any weakness. 'My mum, well, she's made of Irn-Bru and haggis.' She laughed, hoping to lighten the moment. 'I genuinely don't know, but she did cope.'

'It's *a lot*, Storm, I know. It's ten months since I found out that I wasn't the only one. I'm here for you, I promise.'

'Look at the time – we'd better get back to work.'

'Only if you want to, we could bunk off for the afternoon.'

'Bunk off?'

'Yep, sneak out, like kids do at school.'

'Och, *dogging*.'

Jess started to laugh really hard and soon Storm was joining in. That wasn't Jess's understanding of that word, and after Emilie had joked about a ménage à trois, it felt like everything was rolling around to sex.

'Let's do it!'

*

Jess sat outside Miriam's house. She hated lying but she needed to find a way to talk to her. Josh didn't see the problem; he said she had no trouble initially lying to Storm, but that was only a date-of-birth lie. Pretending to be a friend of Miriam's deceased daughter, Joanna, seemed immense.

Even though the engine was turned off her hands were still gripping the steering wheel, as she steeled herself for Miriam's reaction. If she wasn't the "chosen one", why was it her responsibility to get all the "16/87s" and their relatives together? Her birthday was only a couple of days away now and they weren't even halfway through their list. Realistically, she knew the cold moon in December was the better choice for the gathering. Josh and Jess had decided to speak to both Charlotte and Daisy at the gala, but that still left Lexi, Jade, Kylie and, of course, Joanna's mum. 'Now or never,' she muttered under her breath.

Miriam held her so tightly. 'Anyone who was a friend of Joanna is a friend of mine.'

Jess felt the guilt piling on and she sat in an armchair, as directed by Miriam, before answering that she would love a cup of tea. She felt the time alone was both incredibly slow and yet super fast. Should she dive straight in? Make some small talk first? In any case she needn't have worried. Miriam was adept at small talk and proceeded to show Jess a photo album she'd made of Joanna's life.

'How did you say you knew Joanna?'

'I didn't. I just needed to speak to you – the month before Joanna died, I had this reoccurring dream—'

'So, who are you then? A psychic? Reporter? Police officer? I told them I wanted the case closed, I don't want to pursue the allegations she made, and I certainly won't talk to a charlatan or a reporter!' Miriam stood up. 'I think I want you to leave.'

'Please, just let me explain then I'll be out of your hair. Talking of hair, my white streak isn't visible at the moment.'

'Well, it wouldn't be, would it…' Miriam didn't finish her sentence. Unwittingly she'd let this Jess girl reel her in.

With more begging and cajoling Jess managed to get Miriam to listen to the story. Filling her in on the "16/87s", how she had been dreaming the same dreams as Joanna had talked about in her suicide note and that Jess's father's car was struck by a telegraph pole on the night of her birth.

Miriam was shaking her head. 'I didn't know what happened to Joanna's father until much later. How can you love and hate someone in equal measure?'

'Life is a strange one, that's for sure. I'm sorry I'm bringing all this up, but I *need* to, to, well, to complete this *mission*, whatever that is. As soon as I know more, I will be back in touch. I don't know what's going to happen, but I do know you need to be there. Can you do that? Please? Not just for me but for Joanna too.'

'OK, I'm not promising, but OK. How is your mum? And the other mums?'

'My mum has never been able to cope. I hope when I tell her it will somehow lift a weight off her shoulders, but I can't yet, she's not stable enough. I can't answer for the others – well, I know one of the mums is dead, but I've no idea about the others.'

'I just knew I shouldn't tell anyone. Joanna was never stable either, but…' Her voice trailed off as she recollected the day she went on holiday, when Joanna had taken her own life. Miriam had thought she was OK, thought she could leave her for a week and that she would be OK.

She wasn't OK.

*

'How do I look, Mo?'

'Gorgeous as always, the dress really suits you.'

'You can say *red* dress you know; my mum has always said the colours, and you don't look so bad yourself.'

Mo and Daisy laughed. He thought she judged him by his smell and touch, but Daisy's dad had shown her what he'd looked like when she first started dating him. She remembered joking with her dad that she had good taste.

'OK, Daiz, coming up shortly on your right is Lady Charlotte – she and her mum are greeting all the guests as they go in. I've just seen Lucy about five people ahead of us. It's like a spread out of *Hello* magazine in here. That girl Georgia Toffolo is in front of Lucy. There's a rumour she's going into the *Celebrity Jungle* series.'

'Who? Lucy?'

'No, *Toff.* Once we're in we'll find Lucy and say hi. I'll squeeze your hand when we're there. OK, so just for info, she has her hair piled high and has a tiara on, her dress is backless and, because you like to know, it's shocking pink. Behind her is a big sign about the fundraiser and it being her thirtieth birthday – I thought she'd done it for you! Though I don't know if hers is today. Her mum is in royal blue, very sleek and fitted. She looks like an older supermodel.'

Mo was always over and above considerate. Daisy felt it had nothing to do with her being blind; it was just the kind of guy he was.

'Good evening, so glad you could come.'

'I'm Daisy and this is my boyfriend Mo – Lucy Edwards extended her invitation to us.'

Daisy was saying all the right things, but her face looked troubled. Mo wasn't sure what was happening.

'Enjoy your evening, Daisy.' Then Lady Charlotte went to the next guests.

'What's up, Daiz? You look a bit disturbed.'

'Disturbed? How does one look disturbed?' She tried to laugh it off, but Mo was right, though she couldn't tell him why. She kind of expected her to smell of some really expensive perfume, like Creed for women, but Lady Charlotte actually smelt like her dad – weird.

'Let's get a drink, Mo, may as well enjoy the evening.' She smiled but inside she couldn't get rid of the thought: Mo was right, disturbed was exactly the adjective to describe how she was feeling right now.

'Jess, I think I've just seen Daisy going in, how do we look?'

'Like a dog's dinner! Nah, we look good, you in a tuxedo and me in this gorgeous emerald number. Wish I could've afforded to buy it rather than rent, but I'll probably never have an occasion to wear it again. Now, remember to sit on your hands when the auction starts – we don't want to do a Joey from *Friends* and end up with a yacht we can't afford!'

'You know I never really watched it, but yep, no worries, hands under bum! Here we go…'

'Are you nervous? I am.'

'Yep, just a bit, but we can do this. We'll find Daisy, I'll chat to the boyfriend, maybe I can separate them and leave you to it.'

'Thanks,' she said sarcastically. Jess really thought that he didn't have a clue how all this was affecting her. Thirty years on this Earth today, and in less than a year all manner of secrets were being revealed, taking the trajectory – well, this was the problem. She didn't know how it would change things.

There was a spare chair either side of Daisy and Mo, so Jess and Josh sat either side, boys to the left, girls to the right. Before they had a chance to introduce themselves, Daisy spoke. 'Oh, Lady Charlotte, have you finished greeting your guests?'

'No, sorry, I'm Jess and my boyfriend Josh is sitting the other side of your companion.'

'I'm Mo, and Daisy is beside you, Jess, nice to meet you both. Are you friends with her ladyship?'

'Ha, ha, no, Josh is best friends with Lady Charlotte's security officer, Jack. He blagged us an invite as it's my birthday today.'

Weirder by the minute, thought Daisy. This Jess also smelt like her dad, just as Charlotte did, and the birthday thing, she wasn't sure if it was coincidence. Besides which, this Jess might not be having her thirtieth; she couldn't see how young or old she looked.

'It's my birthday too, I'm thirty. What about you, Jess?'

Josh took that as his cue to whisk Mo away from the girls. He nodded his head towards Daisy, indicating to Jess that they should talk while he was gone.

'Yes, I'm thirty too. Take some deep breaths, Daisy, I promise you with all my heart that you have absolutely nothing to worry about.'

Daisy did as she was told and took stock. She always took her cues from the sound of someone's voice and Jess sounded trustworthy.

'Can I feel your face? It will help.'

Jess nodded before realising that she had to verbalise any answers. 'Yes, yes, of course.' With that she took Daisy's hand to place on her face. When she got to Jess's cheek she smiled, and Daisy knew she was genuine.

'OK, I assume you're going to tell me something that you think you know about me?'

'Not just you, Daisy, me too and Lady Charlotte, and there's more of us. Originally, I think there was ten of us, but two have died. Can I ask you why you thought I was Charlotte when I sat down?'

Daisy took her hand to Jess's face again to find her ear this time; cupping it, she whispered, 'You both smell like my dad.'

Jess, though shocked, began to explain about the "16/87s" and what she thought they all needed to do with the information. She asked Daisy if she would help engineer a meet-up with Charlotte and get her on her own.

'Does your boyfriend know?'

'Yes, and what about Mo?'

'No, my mum prefers it that way, but we want to marry, and I think it is about time. He's a good guy, he deserves to know.'

'My mum doesn't know that Josh knows. I'm preparing myself to tell her, but not yet. Gosh, that sounds like *Friends*, you know, the "she knows, he knows" one!'

'Love *Friends*, Mo's not a fan, though.'

'Neither is Josh, he never gets my references.'

'Every single thing in life can be related to a *Friends* episode.'

'*I know*,' replied Jess in the exaggerated way that the character Monica used to.

They were giggling when the boys returned with more champagne and an orange juice for Josh. This was his first proper test since quitting alcohol – so far so good, he thought. Jess squeezed Daisy's knee before saying that they were back.

'I know the smell of my own boyfriend.' She laughed. 'I'll see you in a bit, I need Mo to find Lucy for me.'

Jess and Josh waited for them to leave before she smiled at him.

'She's fab – reckon that was the easiest one so far. You know how she knew about me and Charlotte? We smell like her dad! Can you believe that?'

'Nothing surprises me anymore. So, I've just seen her ladyship out in the garden having a ciggie – grab Daisy, I'll go and have one near her.'

Jess knew he was right, but he seemed to be relishing in all these scenarios, with a feeling of amusement.

That wasn't how she felt.

She did as she was told, though…

'I've been expecting you two – sit down. Why don't you tell me what this is all about?'

Jess spoke first. 'Why were you expecting us?'

'Do you think I don't have all my guests checked out? It's par for the course, but I guess you wouldn't know that. You both have the same birthdate as me and both your dads have died. Anything else you want to share?'

Jess felt sick; she didn't know how Daisy felt, so she pinched her arm.

'Ouch! What are you doing, Jess? Or is it Charlotte? This isn't funny.'

'Me, sorry, why don't you tell her why you keep mixing us two up?'

'I don't think you can ask a blind girl those sorts of questions!'

'I can speak for myself, Charlotte. You both smell like my dad. I only found out tonight. You need to listen to what Jess has to say.'

Jess wished she had a pre-recorded speech as having to go through it all again seemed an ordeal; however, the audience was new and she had no idea how Charlotte would react. Jess finished by saying, 'Everything is unfolding as it should.'

'But we've never seen each other over *there*, Jess, how is that possible?'

'None of us know the ins and outs. We all have our own stories and that's all we know.'

'When I thought I was going to die I wanted to leave a memoir, confessing it all. It's such a monumental secret to carry.'

'I can see when I'm with my dad.'

Both the young women looked at each other before turning to Daisy.

'Wow! That's great, how does that feel?'

'Honestly, disappointing.'

Charlotte took hold of both Daisy and Jess's hands. 'We need to make a pact – how about "all for one and one for all", will that do?'

'How about "boyfriends come and go, but this is for life".'

'*Friends*, again, Jess?'

The girls laughed together.

Jess told Charlotte she would be in touch and gently guided Daisy back to Mo.

'Can we go home, Josh? I'm exhausted.'

'Don't you want to celebrate? It's all coming together. Chill out for a while, will you?'

'*No*, you can't drink, and I've got a shocking headache and I still don't know who the "chosen one" is.'

'*Chosen* what?'

'Never mind, Josh, let's just get home before I ruin this rented dress.'

'About that – I went back to the shop and bought it. You don't have to return it. Happy birthday, Jess.'

*

Penny pulled up the handbrake as she parked at her next patient's home. She glanced at the notes, being unfamiliar with this area. She was covering for one of the other community nurses and this was her last patient of the day.

> *Mick Monroe, DOB: 1/4/1957, aged sixty. Type 2 diabetes, uncontrolled, two gangrenous toes removed three weeks ago. Eyesight failing, neuropathy. Insulin doses increased as he won't regulate his food intake.*

His usual nurse had put a handwritten note at the end saying, '*Lazy – watch out, he's a bit handsy, wants everyone to look after him. Encourage him to do more for himself, express the importance of getting insulin doses correct and good luck with that!*'

Penny wanted to get home; it had been a long day and the last thing she needed was to attend to someone who she felt was costing the NHS unnecessary work. Her patience was wearing thin as she knocked on the door and waited and waited until, finally, she heard it being unlocked. Without looking up, she announced herself: 'I'm Nurse Penny, covering for Anita.'

'Penny, you say?'

Her heart felt as if it had stopped in that moment. His voice, there was something awfully familiar, and she was afraid to look up, knowing her worst fears could be true. Slowly she raised her head, hoping he wouldn't recognise her.

'No, no, it's Nurse Perry, like Katy Perry.'

'Who?'

'Perry, like Perry Como?'

He hadn't recognised her. Why would he? She was only nine years old when he'd last seen her, but he hadn't changed one iota.

She followed him into the sitting room, dazed but in full control of herself. This could be the opportunity she had waited for all her life.

'How are you feeling? Anita says you need help with your insulin.'

The room smelt of stale sweat and takeaway food. The empty cartons were strewn everywhere. Curtains were drawn and the carpet felt sticky under the thin soles of her shoes.

It was not her place to tidy up.

She was trying not to heave the contents of her stomach; her head wanted to spin but she was attempting to keep herself in check. To face your abductor twenty years later when said person had no clue who you were was an advantage. Penny just needed to pull herself together and put him out of her misery.

Literally.

'Anita says you need me to show you *again* how to administer your insulin. You need to count your carbs to determine how much bolus – fast-acting – you should take, and every evening take your basal – long-acting. It's important that you don't confuse them.'

As she said that she realised that there was never going to be another perfect opportunity like this. Mick Monroe didn't know it, but this was going to be his last day on Earth and Penny had no hesitations about her next course of action.

'I don't know if I can – can you do it for me?'

As Mick Monroe said this, he began to pull his trousers down; he wasn't wearing any underwear. 'I'm just finishing two lots of noodles. I prefer the injections in my leg. Can you do it?'

She duly administered the correct amount; now wasn't the time. She reminded him that he was supposed to inject fifteen minutes before eating, but that fell on deaf ears. When she'd finished Penny excused herself to wash her hands in the kitchen; she noticed the back-door key still in the door and now it was in her pocket.

Driving back in the middle of the night, she rehearsed what she was about to say and do. Not one part of her thought that she was wrong. The late afternoon that Mick Monroe had taken her from the streets back in 1997 happened to coincide with the full moon. Her friend couldn't remember anything other than that the van was white; she'd told the police that the driver had claimed to be a friend of Penny's parents.

Penny was glad this man wanted to take her home to surprise her parents. She wanted to get away from her new *friend*. She always preferred to play alone but her parents had suggested that Penny take the new neighbours' daughter, Bethany, to the park. She'd been fed up with her after about fifteen minutes.

Mick Monroe took her to the basement of his house. There was a mattress on the floor, a chair in the corner and a video camera set up to one side. He'd tied her tightly to the chair before pressing record for the first time. Mick Monroe returned in the early hours to begin all over again.

Penny disappeared in front of him.

When she came back, he was still there, but she was no longer tied to the chair and bolted for the unlocked door. The police found her wandering the streets. She never said a word.

She had a lot to say to him this time around.

Parking around the corner on the next street, she crept around to the side of this nondescript end of terrace house. Wearing surgical gloves, she quietly let herself in through the back door. Penny was going to go up the stairs, but she heard snoring coming from the living room. Mick Monroe was exactly where she'd left him earlier in the day. There were even more takeaway cartons scattered around; one of them was still on Mick Monroe's belly. As he breathed heavily the cardboard box raised, fell and wobbled, some of the noodles falling out each time. He wore no underwear, only his T-shirt which barely covered his enormous belly.

His insulin supplies were on the coffee table next to three empty two-litre bottles of full-sugar Coke. She dialled the fast-acting insulin pen to its maximum; Penny didn't want to take any chances and she injected all of it into his leg.

Then she woke him up.

He startled; the Chinese noodles fell on the floor along with its container.

She shoved the photo of her nine-year-old self in front of him before announcing her name. He instantly remembered Penny, for good reason.

'I was a *little girl* – you lied to me, you said you were friends with my parents. I got into your van. You kept me in your basement.'

'But you disappeared – you are a witch. You vanished in front of my eyes. I let you go.'

'*No! I ran!* And that makes it OK? Does it? You've ruined my life. They couldn't find you. I couldn't tell them where I'd been. I couldn't *speak*! Two years, I didn't utter a single word. You pressed the *mute button* on me.'

'I swear I never touched another girl after you – I destroyed all the tapes.'

Penny instantly recalled how she'd had the foresight to

rub some mud in her hair to disguise her white streak before anyone found her. She'd hoped that was enough.

She was nine.

Mick Monroe was beginning to slur his words now, but Penny wasn't going anywhere; she wanted to watch him till the end. She would've preferred to have stabbed him, shot him or at the very least beat the hell out of him, but she didn't want to be caught.

This solution was perfect.

Diligently she had replaced the insulin cartridge with a new one and primed a few units out of it to look as if he'd taken the correct amount. Stopping, she considered if the dose she'd given him was enough. She dialled up to the maximum again, just to be on the safe side, and jabbed it into his leg. When she primed another new one, she decided to swap the basal with the bolus, so it looked like he'd given himself the wrong one. The lids were colour-coded, so she swapped those too and put the empty cartridges in her pocket.

She had no qualms telling her dad later on the beach.

ELEVEN

BEAVER MOON

Jess was just about to go into the day room in the assisted living facility when she was stopped by a young man.

'Izzy has had a particularly bad night.'

'My mum's name is Isobel, and you are?' said Jess, glancing at his name tag. 'Billy.'

She could just see her mum through the porthole in the door, staring blankly into space and twiddling with her hair; every now and then she would yank some of it out.

'And that's why she looks like a zombie? I've told you all before not to over-medicate, but you don't listen.'

Jess had already decided she didn't like this Billy; he was new there and he gave off a bad aura – negative energy times ten, she thought.

'We had no choice; Isobel was very wild.'

An exasperated Jess made up her mind then that she would take her mum home and care for her, so long as Josh was OK with it. No, she decided, regardless of what Josh thought, this was what she *needed* to do.

'Mum, it's Jess, what's happening? You know you can tell me.'

'They're out to get me,' she slurred.

'Who is, Mum?'

'The moon people. That twat over there,' she said, pointing to Billy, 'didn't believe me, he was pushing me around…'

As Isobel tried to get her words out, they became lost and incoherent. Jess delved into her handbag and found a hairbrush and scrunchie. Moving out of her chair, she stood behind her mum, singing as she brushed her hair, looking to cover up the bald patch Isobel had created. With tears falling onto her mum's head, Jess was berating herself for allowing social services to convince her that the facility could help her recover rather than the sheltered housing she'd been in. Not that she spent much time in the flat; she was sectioned so often and taken into psychiatric hospitals that it was decided full-time care was needed. Jess's imagination was far bigger than any of the misdemeanours that were actually happening; nonetheless, it had crossed her mind to put some sort of spy camera in her room to discover the truth. After this morning's episode she realised that even doing that wouldn't appease her; she had to have her mum home.

'How about you tell Josh about the moon people? You like Josh, don't you?'

'*No*, we mustn't tell anyone. I was wrong, when I told Billy he wanted to kill me, we… we need… to keep… our…'

'*Our* what, Mum?'

'The… the pact.'

Jess put her arms around her mum and held her tightly. If Isobel felt like this, how could she tell her what they were up to? Isobel needed respite; Jess could ask for compassionate leave to look after her and hopefully get her well enough to come to the gathering of the "16/87s".

Maybe meeting other mums might be just what she needed.

*

'You're one missing, Jessie.'

'I thought you weren't supposed to tell me anything! What about this "everything will unfold exactly as it should" business, Papa?'

'Yes, yes, but you'll never pull this off by next month if you don't get a move on, Jessie.'

'Is that the only clue you're giving me? We've found ten – don't you think that's a nice round number?'

'Life doesn't work like that in round numbers. It is what it is.'

'Now you sound like someone from Love Island!'

They both laughed but Jess was wishing her memory was as good as Josh's. It must be someone who wasn't obvious from the spreadsheet.

'Take a trip to Wales.'

'Is that all I'm getting?'

'Checkmate.'

Jess smiled and then found herself back in bed with Josh.

'Wake up! Wake up, Josh!'

'Oh, come on, Jess.' As he glanced at his watch he could see it was 3.40am. 'I've got to go to work in… less than four hours.'

'Call in sick – get the spreadsheet out, we're missing someone. All I know is that the person is in Wales.'

'But that would make eleven, funny old number.'

'That's what I said.'

Josh rubbed his eyes and sat up. 'Don't need the spreadsheet. Penny Jones, Heather Evans and Melody Gethin – the only ones born in Wales, but Penny's dad is alive. Melody and Heather have "unknown" on their birth certificates where "father" should be.'

'Fancy a road trip?'

'Put the kettle on. I'll call work and we'll figure out the best route.'

'Well, we don't have to find Penny.'

'Sometimes people deliberately put the wrong father down, when they don't know or they do know but it's a secret. At this late stage I think anything is possible. Let's not discount anyone.'

By the time Jess had made their coffee Josh had chosen the route.

'First, Newport, then down to Barry Island.' He laughed. 'Maybe we'll see Gavin and Stacey! Then finally to Swansea. Bit of a trek but the traffic should be light as it's early and it's Sunday, and if we're lucky we might not have to do all three. Don't colour your hair, it's probably our only bargaining chip. Put your beanie hat on, and when we're ready take it off, I'll watch for recognition.'

Jess and Josh were packed within half an hour, ready for the first leg of their journey. With them stopping for petrol and snacks, he reckoned the first part would take just shy of four hours. Looking to entertain themselves, Josh asked if they should have a bet on which of the three it was.

'Well, we've got a 33.3333% or so chance of being right! I'm not a gambler but maybe at the services we should get a lottery ticket. We've never been away together before; this is our first couple holiday.'

Josh laughed. 'Think we can do better than that. Once all this is over, we should book something – where do you fancy?'

'Greece? Spain? I don't mind. Let's play a game – A for Ass.'

'B for Buffalo.'

Jess playfully punched his arm. 'No,' she laughed, 'B for Bum, C for Cock! Got it?'

'D for Dick.'

They continued with their game then Jess began pressing buttons on the radio as they'd lost the London stations. She stopped when she heard a Welsh voice talking about Barry Island.

'Nessa from Gavin and Stacey will be making a guest appearance this evening. Ruth Jones will be reprising her role as part of our fireworks display where she will be starting the party at around 7.30pm.'

Jess looked at Josh. 'Remember, no such thing as a coincidence – if I were a betting woman, I'd say our girl will be there. Which one is it?'

'Penny.'

'Yeah, but she's the one you would obviously discount.'

Josh parked up the car and turned to Jess. 'Ready? This is Heather's house. Got your story straight?'

Jess nodded; they'd gone over and debated their backstory for almost an hour of the journey. Her beanie hat was on, and they were out of the car and knocking on Heather's door.

'Heather Evans? Hi, we're Josh and Jess from the *London Local*. We're doing an article about the children born when the mines were being shut down and how that has affected your youth. Would you mind talking to us for a few minutes?'

'Bloody Thatcher – how'd you know my name?'

'Potluck. Our boss said we couldn't come unless we had some names. We randomly selected a few just to follow the lead. Did your dad work down the mines?'

Jess was amazed how easy Josh found it to sound convincing and that Heather was open to talking.

'Never met him when I was young, they weren't together, but see that pub down there? He's in there morning till night, him and his mates never got over them closing. I know who he is, but I wouldn't call him my dad.'

Josh touched his eyebrow. That was the signal Jess had been waiting for and she duly pulled her beanie hat off.

Nothing.

'OK, thanks for your time, you've been really helpful.'

As they walked towards the car, Josh turned off his camera.

'One down, two to go. I didn't realise you were videoing her.'

'I need to rewatch it – pretty sure there wasn't even a flicker of recognition, but I'll double-check before I delete it.'

The motorway was beginning to get busier; traffic was in full flow, but fortunately they only had about forty-five minutes to drive. Jess was particularly quiet on this leg of the journey. She'd started to wonder if the Welsh slipper was the "chosen one". It made sense to her as up until this point there had only been ten accounted for and eleven seemed a random number. They'd thought they'd finished searching for people, and now this. She dozed off with these thoughts running through her head. Jess was still feeling overwhelmed, not sure what to make of her predicament. Up until the start of the year, she'd known where she stood in life. Yes, her mum had always been a struggle to handle but Jess was able to live a relatively easy life. Now, she was managing Josh's sobriety and a host of other slippers who were looking to her for answers.

She had none.

'Wakey, wakey, sleepy head. Miss Penny Jones's home. Maybe she's related to Ruth.' He laughed. 'OK, so not every Jones is related but somewhere in history they probably are.'

Jess didn't really hear what he was saying. She took a facial wipe from her bag, pulling down the sun visor to look in the mirror before cleaning the smudged mascara from under her eyes. Popping her hat on her head, she said two words: 'I'm ready.'

Penny wasn't going to open the door; she was trying to get ready for work. She took a peek on the Ring camera in case it was the police. She could see a young casually dressed couple and doubted that they were. The police had been satisfied with her assessment of Mick Monroe in the last interview. Just a formality, they had said. Penny hoped that was over. She couldn't even be bothered to speak on the microphone.

'Let's sit back in the car. I'm sure I saw some movement, and if she were out, she would've spoken to us on the Ring. We're parked far enough away, and I'll keep watch in the rear-view mirror.'

'Not necessarily – I don't always.'

The pair started to bicker, both tired and irritated.

'Go, go, go!' Josh jumped out of the car.

'You're not at work, you arse! Got your battering ram too?' But she obliged all the same.

After Josh had said his rehearsed spiel, Penny surprised them by inviting them in.

'Look, I should be on my way to work by now, but I think I have been expecting you, though not as soon as this. Sit, sit, I just have to go to the laf.'

Jess and Josh looked at each other, raising their eyebrows in disbelief. Jess pulled off her hat; no point in carrying on with the façade. Jess's first instinct was that Penny was the "chosen one". She had said that she was expecting them – how else would she know?

They were sitting with their backs to the living-room door when Penny came in. 'Is this what you want to talk about? Yes, obviously, Jess, you too, eh?'

Penny had wiped the L'Oréal Root touch-up off of her hair, proudly showing the white streak.

'But you have a dad? Did we miss something? Did he die? Is this some sort of anomaly? Who do you visit?'

Jess's mouth had verbal diarrhoea. She'd begun to lose sight of the end goal and had become fixated on the fact that there was supposedly a "chosen one".

'Whoa! Slow down. The guy whose been married to my mum, Morag, for thirty-four years, isn't my dad. My mum had an affair and the guy died down the pit the night I was born.'

Penny went on to explain that her mum probably would've got away with it until she learnt to talk and would speak about her "real dad" whom she visited every month.

'Why were you expecting us?'

'Josh, I can't explain. Last night my dad said, "Everything will unfold exactly as it should," or something like that. I thought that was weird, but he wouldn't say any more. I thought you were the Jehovah's lot knocking,' she lied. '…and then I remembered what he said. I came out to see if you were still there and when you were I just knew. So, what happens now?'

*

Lexi was feeding baby Christopher but all she could think was how hungry she was herself. Belinda, her mum, was fussing around the house, tidying when she hadn't been asked to, and huffing and puffing her way around.

'I could've cooked us a nice lunch rather than that *junk* that Rachel will bring back. I hope you don't eat like that all the time, or you'll end up the same size as her!'

'*Mum!* That's cruel. Of course we don't, I just fancied a KFC today.'

Just then the doorbell rang.

'Can you get that? Rach probably forgot her keys, as usual.'

Belinda tutted then walked to answer it. Jess and Josh were at the door. They didn't know who she was.

'Hi,' began Jess, 'can we come in and speak to Lexi, please?'

'No strangers unless you have a warrant!'

Josh laughed. 'I am a copper, but not on official business.'

Just then Jess made her headscarf slip, accidently on purpose, and Belinda caught a glimpse of the tell-tale white streak.

'Oh, erm… I *guess* that would be OK. Come in, I'm Lexi's mum, Belinda.'

They introduced themselves and Belinda led them into the living room where Lexi was winding Christopher after his feed.

'Can I get you a cuppa? Lexi, these people want to speak to you, do you want to give me a hand first?'

With that Belinda tried to direct Lexi with her eye movements but she didn't pick up on the clue. She then moved to deliberately pick up Christopher so she could whisper to Lexi. 'Look at her hair, discreetly.'

Lexi couldn't do discreet if she tried and immediately was vocal. 'Do you see your dad too?'

'I do.'

'How did he die? They think mine was fighting back a mugger and he was fatally stabbed.'

Jess took her headscarf off; she was planning on a big reveal, but that wasn't necessary. 'A telegraph pole hit his car. There are more of us – we're called the "16/87s"—'

Rachel opened the door, her half-eaten bucket of chicken in one hand, keys in the other. 'Sorry, Lex, was a bit hungry on the… What the fu—'

'Rach! Don't swear in front of the baby. We've spoken about this – our swear box is so full that at this rate we'll get a holiday out of it.'

'He don't understand, but these fuckers do. *Get out!*' She threw the bucket directly at them. 'I remember you two, from the park. I was right, Lex; I knew they were up to no good.'

Rachel was going into full "Mama Bear" mode and wasn't listening to anyone.

Jess stood up to brush the chicken bits and pieces from her lap. 'Honestly, we're just bringing all of us together, nothing more.'

Belinda began to speak. 'Rachel, these people have been nothing but kind and it feels like a relief to share this secret.'

'*No!* Get out, now, before I throw the pair of you to the kerb!'

Rachel was getting desperate; she'd been thinking lately that Lexi was only with her because she knew the secret. They hadn't been getting on; she'd initially put it down to the lifestyle change of having a baby, but now she wasn't sure. If there were others, it might mean she would leave her.

Josh stood up too and went to leave, pulling out a card from his pocket. 'If you want to chat, Lexi, you can call us.'

As the pair were leaving, Jess looked back to see Rachel tearing the card up, muttering under her breath, 'Josh *Holmes*, that's a laugh, *Sherlock*. Pretending to be a copper!'

'Well, that went well,' said Jess sarcastically.

*

Emilie had long since forgiven her mum, not that the woman knew. She'd forgiven her mum for herself, not for her. It didn't change anything, it just enabled Emilie to heal a little, but the images of that night often interrupted her dreams. Now here she was standing outside of her mum's bedsit ready to talk to her for the first time in just over thirty years. Josh had managed to find out where she was living. Emilie didn't know if Hamisi would believe the story, but she felt she owed it to her to at least explain that it wasn't the devil at work. Knowing that Adele's death was needless seemed to hurt more; prior to that she could pretend that her mum was in some way correct in her thinking. Emilie was an atheist – there was no way she could believe in a god that was unjust or one that would forgive you for committing an atrocious crime. To Emilie there was no god or devil, but because it had been ingrained in her when she was small, remnants still existed; for instance when Jess had reappeared with the white streak in her hair. At that moment she'd reverted back to her four-year-old self, because at that age she'd believed everything her mum said without question.

Emilie knocked on the door, feeling her breath quicken. She almost turned on her heels and ran but then the door was opened.

'Hello, Hamisi, may I come in?'

Hamisi looked dishevelled and much older than her fifty-eight years. A dirty scarf was tied around her hair and her T-shirt was stained. Her feet were ashy, toenails too long and her swollen feet spilt out of the tattered sandals she wore that seemed at odds with this cold November day. The stench of marijuana hit Emilie as a breeze ran through the bedsit to the front door. She didn't know if it came from her mum's or another one of the rooms.

Hamisi stared at her intently, hardly believing her eyes. 'Emilie, is that really you?'

'Yes, it is me, Hamisi.'

'Why you no call me Maitũ?'

'You lost that right when you killed Adele.'

Hamisi invited Emilie into her room. It was a mess: Emilie had to move the duvet off of the sofa bed to sit down. There was one dining chair that you could just make out from all of the clothes that were hanging over it. Damp ran down the side of the wall nearest the kitchenette and the window was so dirty you could barely see out of it. Emilie had vague memories of the neat and tidy house they'd once lived in.

'Why do you live in a pigsty?'

'Why are you here?'

'You can't answer a question with a question, and I asked first.'

'Is that all you can say to your Maitũ?'

'You're doing it again! This was a mistake; I should never have come here.'

'So why did you?'

Emilie stood up; the woman before her was not the Maitũ that she spent the first four years with, the one who used to sing her traditional lullabies to send her to sleep but who also used to slap her bare bottom, hard, whenever she did anything wrong. Bringing herself back to her senses, she walked to the door to leave before turning around. 'Because I know why Adele kept disappearing. It wasn't the devil, but maybe you were for doing what you did. None of the other mums killed their disappearing babies. Goodbye, Hamisi.'

Emilie's mum followed her out of the door and watched her get in the car. Emilie drove away with her mum's yelling words in her ears: 'Others? What others? I didn't know! I didn't know, what was I supposed to think?'

Emilie found herself sitting outside of a pub. Life just seemed so difficult. She'd expected that the older she got the easier it would get.

It didn't.

She tried to take stock of everything that had happened lately, but nothing made sense. Even though she'd seen Jess disappear, and thirty years earlier when Adele had too, she was still looking for rational answers. Could Jess have spiked her cocoa? Emilie knew more than most that evidence had to be proved beyond all reasonable doubt. Had her eyes deceived her? She hit the phone button on her dashboard to call her sponsor, but then hit "end call" before pressing Josh's number. All she said when he answered was, 'I can't do this.'

*

Dear Journo,

Hi, it's me, Charlotte! It's been a while – OK, it's been a long while. I'm sorry, you must feel like a friend who was discarded to the side-lines because of a new boyfriend only for me to return when I've been dumped. I'm sorry.

Daddy says I should trust this Jess. I told him she said his favourite sentence and that was what convinced me. Whoops! Sorry, Journo, I haven't told you about that. I thought it was strange when I went through the gala guest list – well, not me personally, but it was brought to my attention that there were two others with the same birthday as me, and for the first time ever, and I guess it's because I've been confessing to you, I wondered… and I was right. Jess and Daisy are *just like me, and Jess says there are others. They want to have a meet-up next month.*

Mummy is really unsure; she worries it's a scam of some sort. I've told her she needs to come too so hopefully that will appease her.

Henry caused a fracas at the gala – well, he would, wouldn't he? It was quickly sorted. He thought one of the "plebs" (his words not mine) had taken his coke and wanted to know why I invited "them". The real problem is that his family is down on their luck, and he was bidding on the Hockney painting, just to keep face, and was scared shitless about the payment. Luckily, Spencer, one of Rupert's friends, stepped in – he says he'll sell it on and donate any extra money. Not to Henry! To the charity, obviously.

So, it appears that after thirty years I have discovered I'm not the only one who visits their dead father. Imagine if the press got hold of that – they'd probably say, 'Charlie takes the fizzy-lifting drink!' I could write the tabloid headlines myself! I asked Mummy why she hadn't sought to find out if I wasn't unique when I was younger. She said she was grieving and was too scared in case someone took me away from her too. It's only been recently that I've started to realise that she did love my daddy. LOL.

Anyhoo, I must get on and I'll end this by calling myself a "16/87" – which is apparently what we are called in the afterlife.

I'm glad I'm alive, Journo.

*

When Daisy told her mum what had happened at the gala she wasn't perturbed. Her problem was with Daisy's desire to tell Mo. Her mum thought that as there were others who had also kept the secret that they weren't a threat; however, she saw Mo differently. It didn't matter that Daisy explained that some of them were married with children or had partners that were privy to the information. The main question, which was probably one that had been asked hundreds of times, and not just by Daisy, was why the mums had decided to keep it a secret. She deduced that it was a decision made by fear and grief – that was the only logical explanation.

Daisy felt sorry that Jess's mum seemed to be the only one who couldn't cope. When Jess had told her about Emilie and Adele's mum, she'd been shocked to her core. Another one who couldn't handle it but who chose to deal with it in the most horrendous way.

She decided that she was an adult, and it didn't matter what her mum thought; this was her secret, not just her mum's. Daisy felt that as it was her who vanished that it should be her choice. Waiting until her mum had gone out with her friends, she had made Mo some dinner to sit and chat. She remembered when she first cooked for him; he was incredulously astonished. Having never dated a blind girl before, his assumption was that she would be incapable of doing such a task. Daisy had to explain the process of having most things labelled in Braille, a few handy utensils, but the most important thing was to be organised and tidy. Everything had to have a home and that it must also always be returned to where it lived. She'd joked that otherwise she would be pouring coffee over his dinner instead of gravy.

This was probably the first time Daisy wished she had sight – not permanently, but just for ten minutes, akin to when she saw her dad. She wanted to be able to see Mo's facial expressions, to be sure that not only was he OK with it but also that he wouldn't tell a soul.

Trust.

She would just have to trust him.

In the event, it was her that was shocked. Mo had said that he realised once a month she wouldn't let him stay over. He had produced a chart, mapping when she would and wouldn't let him stay. After a few months he'd noticed a pattern. Three times he'd watched her through her ground-floor bedroom window. The first time, he admitted, was because he thought she may have someone else over to stay, but when he saw her disappear and she didn't say anything he decided to double-check the following month. To be absolutely sure he did it one more time.

'And you never told me? Weren't you curious?'

'I guess so, but I love you so much, and if that was something you felt you needed to hide from me, well, I guessed you had your reasons…'

'And you never told a soul?'

'Nope.'

'I love you, Mohammed Abbasi.'

*

The old-fashioned bell chimed as Josh and Jess walked into Moonpie Bakery. There was a woman with her back to them cleaning the coffee machine. From somewhere in the back a voice with a northern accent called out, 'Dawnie, tell them we're closed. Let's get home and get the fire on.'

The woman who was being addressed turned towards them. 'You heard her.'

'My name is Josh Holmes…'

Jess nudged him and whispered that it was a bit formal, before speaking. 'Sorry about *Mr Holmes* there,' she said, chuckling. 'I'm Jess, nice to meet you, Dawnie?'

'It's Dawn,' she corrected Jess.

With that the lady from the back came out, turning sideways to get through the door due to her size.

'And?' she asked.

'Hang on a mo, Hels, just thinking… yes, are you Josh Holmes with two sisters, Anna and er, er, Gail? That's it, Gail.'

Jess could see the colour draining from Josh's face and squeezed his hand. She thought that maybe rather than finding out about Jade and Kylie it was their purpose today to find out about Josh's mum.

'My sister Gail passed away just before Christmas last year. How do you know us?'

'Excuse Dawn here, she has what's called a "photographic memory" – she absorbs everything she reads. Not so good with accounting, though, are you?'

'Helen! I'm still thinking. It'll come to me in a sec.'

The two women continued their conversation as if Josh and Jess weren't there. They were both standing looking intently at Dawn and Helen wondering what was coming next.

'Yes, yes, that's right, your mum went missing?' asked Dawn.

'Go on, tell us, Josh. I reckoned your dad did it – did he?'

'Shut it, Hels. I met your mum in the smoking room in the maternity hospital – she was a bit miserable, mind you, I had just dropped fag ash in her coffee cup!'

Josh tried to find the words he wanted, but his mind was racing. It wasn't his dad. The police investigation was so thorough that they even dug up their little garden – Anna had told him that when he was about eight or nine years old. It was eventually decided that she had just deserted the family. The police had said that it was often down to post-natal depression, and she may well come back. In later years, Anna had stated that their dad was never the same and she thought it contributed to his early onset dementia.

Josh finally answered, 'Is that all you know, Dawn?'

'Yep, when we took the bakery over there were piles of newspapers and I was looking at the 1987 ones and saw a photo of your mum on the front page. I guess my mind stored that story as I'd recognised her.'

'So, there's nothing else you can help me with?'

'No, sorry. More to the point, what was it you wanted? I can put the coffee machine back on – you look like you've seen a ghost.'

Just then the door chimed again as Jade and Kylie walked in giggling. They'd made up since the car-swerving incident and Kylie had conceded that with a bit of planning, Felix could move in with them. They'd been at the pub and had drunk far too much for the afternoon.

'Whoa! Kylie, that's the moon lady from the summer fete! I told you about her – she thought we were twins, how silly!'

Dawn and Helen were staring at each other; without saying anything they acknowledged that the "moon lady" was a strange name considering their circumstances. They'd spent the last thirty years keeping the secret. Every other time they'd had reasons to be suspicious they had been proved wrong, but this felt different.

Jess and Josh were still standing looking confused and not sure what their next move should be.

'Sit, sit, I'll make us all coffee. You two girls need to sober up too. Helen, got any of our famous parkin cake left?'

For a few minutes nobody said a word; it seemed like an eternity.

Then Jess spoke up. 'I do remember you from the village fete, I don't have a memory like Dawn and Josh, but *that* I do remember. The moon cards are supposed to be entertainment, but personally, I truly believe in them.'

Josh was being unusually quiet, but since he'd been the driving force behind Jess's meetings, she guessed she'd have to broach the subject.

'My birthdate is the same as yours, and your half-sister…?'

'Kylie,' replied Jade.

'And my dad died that night – a telegraph pole hit his car.'

'Ours died racing to the hospital.'

'Yeah, he was driving a stolen car.'

'Jade! Kylie! *Stop!* You don't know who these people are. Excuse them, Jess, they've had too much to drink.'

With that Helen got up and moved to lock the front door before continuing, 'And? Jess? What else do you want to say to trap my girls?'

'No entrapment, I promise.'

Jess went on to explain that she'd only found out at the beginning of the year that there were others and they called them the "16/87s". It was an overwhelming discovery, but she and Josh were determined to find them all. She was also able to ask Dawn if she knew anything else about Josh's mum as he was desperate to find out what the secret was.

'Well, it was probably one of his sisters who is his real mum.'

'Don't be daft, Helen, I met her, remember? She wouldn't have been there unless she was the one who gave birth! Sorry, Josh, I honestly know nothing else.'

'Woo hoo! We're in a special club, Kylie!'

'Jade, for God's sake, be quiet and drink that coffee! Helen and I have always had each other's support. How's your mum, Jess? Must've been hard.'

'It still is, to be honest. We have her staying with us at the moment. She's very fragile, always has been.'

Josh drained his cup before standing up. 'OK, think we'd better leave. We'll be in touch.'

Jess looked at him; she wasn't ready to go yet, but he seemed impatient. She did realise that he was still obsessed with finding out his family secret. Discovering all the "16/87s" had been relatively easier than they had thought.

Josh's mystery was harder.

She knew she had to do better for him.

Jess knew she had to speak to Anna.

*

Storm and Jess had formed an unlikely friendship considering they only had one thing in common. Jess was grateful, though; Josh hadn't been much fun since the bakery incident. She understood, but it didn't make it any easier. She'd been in touch with Anna, who'd informed her that her new boyfriend Romesh wanted to visit the UK for Christmas. She'd apologised for missing Josh's birthday and asked if they could stay with them. Jess had to say no because of her mum, so she ended up paying for a Premier Inn room as she felt bad. Isobel had been at their home for nearly a month. Jess had negotiated to work from home as much as she could whilst she took care of her mum. She'd met Storm for lunch to catch up. Jess was glad that Storm's mum was on board and was coming down for the meeting, which was due to take place, fortunately, on a Sunday.

The 3rd of December was the full moon, referred to as the "cold moon".

They'd all started a WhatsApp group and had decided to take the day off on the Monday, for those that were in work. Jess had asked Storm if her mum, Lizzie, would take Joanna's mum, Miriam, under her wing. From speaking to Storm, she knew that Lizzie's formal training enabled her to be very empathic. It was important to Jess that the families were all present. She would deal with her own mum herself. Josh and Jess had tried to tell her. Whilst her condition had improved immensely, she still had that level of disconnectedness and fear of the disruption of the "space-time continuum".

Charlotte and Daisy had also formed an unlikely friendship, though it did occur to Jess why she would consider all these new friendships unusual. People did seem to be paired off, though, in some sort of alliance. Jade and Kylie had already had that support since birth and both their mums did too. Her and Storm, Charlotte and Daisy, Hils… well, Emilie and Josh had welcomed her in, so they got the ménage à trois that Emilie had always joked about, though it didn't include Jess and wasn't of a sexual nature. Lexi and Rachel had each other too, but Rachel still hadn't come around to the idea yet. Lexi had telephoned Josh, telling him that Rachel felt threatened by the arrival of the "16/87s", but she was working on her.

Jess was telling Storm that she'd had a chat with Emilie the previous night about speaking to her mum again. She also confided to Storm that it was obvious that Emilie fancied Josh but hoped that they were both being respectful, and she had no reason to doubt that. From what Storm had learnt from her mum over the years it was quite common that those seeking to remain in sobriety picked someone in a similar situation so that they could keep each other on the straight and narrow, and that was what she relayed to Jess.

'I hope you're right.'

'So, is Emilie going to talk to *Hamisis*? Is that her name?'

'It's Hamisi, but I don't know if Emilie will really be comfortable having her in the room. I tried to tell her that when she's surrounded by the other mums, she may be able to make peace with herself if nothing else.'

'You're so generous, Jess, like, I don't know if I could be so forgiving. I can't forgive myself for what I did to Jason and his family. I apologise every night before I go to sleep, but it still feels raw.'

'Don't worry, Storm, everything will unfold exactly how it should.'

Storm began to laugh.

'What's so funny?'

'That's what my dad always says, Jess!'

'Mine too.'

TWELVE

COLD MOON

Lexi had put baby Christopher down for his afternoon nap when she heard a commotion coming from the garden shed. She knew Rachel was in there making the wooden train set she'd been painstakingly working on for a few months. Christopher had had a particular bad night previously and it was irritating her that Rachel was making a racket and she was going to give her a *piece of her mind.* When she opened the door and saw Rachel smashing her project up, she was about to shout at her. However, when Rachel saw her, she stopped and slumped over the workbench, sobbing. It was only the second time in Lexi's life that she'd seen tears fall from her wife's face.

Lexi didn't say a word, but Rachel did and started shouting, 'I know what's going on! I found it then I checked your phone!'

She picked up the hammer again and continued with her demolition of the train set.

'*Stop! Rachel*, I have no idea what you're talking about, and you'll wake Christopher, *please*, I'm tired, please stop.'

In between her sobs she continued, 'You got that Josh's card out of the bin, you texted him once and then you've been texting that Jess, because you feel *more comfortable* talking to her. *Of course you do…*'

'Stop it, Rach, it's not what you think.'

'And what do I think?'

'You tell me.'

'And then you said it would be easier if you were a single mum. I don't belong, I don't think I ever did, you only stay cos I know the secret and now you have the "16/87s" you don't need me.'

Rachel stopped talking and began sobbing again. Lexi's brow was furrowed as much as the Botox would allow, confusion written all over her face; it hadn't even entered her head that her wife might think she was "playing away". She'd only contacted Jess because she understood what her life had been like – a kindred spirit, that's all – but convincing Rachel would be difficult. She sat on the floor next to where Rachel was now sitting and put her arm around her.

Lexi was annoyed that Rachel had invaded her privacy by checking her phone, but she had to put that aside. She explained her side of the story and that she was sorry that Rachel had felt left out. Lexi reiterated that she was with her for life because of love, not fear, several times. She had to tell her, though, that this violent behaviour wasn't acceptable regardless of the truth. It wasn't something that she wanted Christopher to be a witness to, ever.

Whilst Rachel did begin to calm down, it wasn't over yet. She asked Lexi many questions in quick succession.

1. What did she see in her when she was just a "big lump of lard"?
2. Did she find Jess attractive?
3. Was she sure that she was with her for the right reasons?
4. Why didn't they have sex anymore?
5. Was she sure she didn't want a divorce?
6. Was she going to go to the "16/87" meeting with or without her?
7. What did her mum really think of her?
8. Why didn't they have sex anymore?
9. Why hadn't she paid the council tax this month?

Lexi began to laugh at the last question.

'Don't laugh at me, I'll wipe that smile off your face.'

'Whoa! Don't *ever* say that or I'll walk away now. I laughed about the *fucking* council tax!'

'Well, you know how to push my buttons and you owe the swear box some money now.' She laughed.

'*No*, Rach, not an excuse *ever*. So, it's OK for you to laugh, though? I find your "Mama Bear" routine hard at the best of times, but directed at me? I'll never, ever accept that.'

Lexi began to walk away, and Rachel began begging her to come back, profusely apologising and crying at the same time.

Lexi spun on her heels. 'I've always loved you because you are beautiful inside – I don't care how much you weigh. Jess is an attractive woman but not my type. I stay with you for love – as I said, love, not fear you'll reveal my secret. We don't have sex because I'm knackered looking after Christopher, just like any new mum. No, I don't want a divorce. Yes, I will go to the meeting either way, but I want you there. My mum has always loved you. I've already told you why we don't have sex. And I paid the council tax this morning!'

They both began laughing. Lexi wasn't happy with this conversation, but she understood why Rachel felt like she was being side-lined, which was the only reason she then gave her a big hug.

*

Hamisi was straightening her dress and her headscarf as she stood outside Emilie's front door. She was wearing her "Sunday best" church clothes. She had painstakingly hand-washed the orange and pink attire before borrowing an iron to press it to perfection. She had tried to clean her church shoes; they were a little scuffed, so she had filled in the marks with a black felt-tip pen. Under her arm was a scrapbook that she had lovingly filled over the years with the mementos that Auntie Adele used to send. There were copies of Emilie's high school certificates and photos, her graduation diploma, photos of graduation day, and even the odd newspaper clipping when she'd prosecuted some of the bigger cases.

Her hands were shaking as she rang the doorbell and she hoped Emilie wouldn't slam the door in her face.

Hamisi wouldn't blame her if she did.

She hadn't slept since Emilie's visit.

Over and over, she replayed the conversation they'd had. Who were these "other mothers" whose babies disappeared, and why didn't they think it was the devil's work? Her whole belief system had already been shaken after spending so much time in prison; she'd been released having no idea what theological truths she held. The only way she could justify her shocking actions was to believe that it was out of her hands. In those ten minutes before Adele had reappeared, she thought she would be liberating her from evil. Hamisi loved Adele as much as she loved Emilie, and in her mind, committing the crime was saving her.

Hamisi was brought out of her thoughts by Emilie answering the door.

'Yes?'

'Emilie, please can we talk?'

She directed Hamisi into the living room of her neatly kept flat before offering her a cup of tea. Emilie was pleased that she'd made the effort to look nice, but was she just a wolf in sheep's clothing? She wasn't sure but weirdly she knew that it was right to let her in. Hamisi put the scrapbook on the coffee table, and when Emilie returned with their drinks, she tapped it before explaining what it was.

'Adele has always sent me things and I wrote to you a lot; did you not receive them?'

Emilie had always burnt the letters Auntie Adele had sent on, never once opening them or wondering what they contained. Ignoring Hamisi's question, she responded, 'You mean Auntie Adele? The lady who was more of a mum to me than you ever were?'

Hamisi sunk into the sofa, wanting to make herself as small as possible; she knew she had no right to ask for forgiveness.

She had no intention of asking.

Once Emilie had explained, but not in detail, about life before Auntie Adele, she then clarified her position in relation to the "16/87s".

Emilie then took a final mouthful of her tea. 'You may not deserve to come to the meeting, but I think you should be there. You can't change the past, but perhaps meeting all the lovely mums who've kept this secret for thirty years may help you understand and… Well, I don't know, but maybe there will be some sort of revelation that you can seek to atone for?'

Hamisi took the details of the meeting and was almost genuflecting on her way out.

*

Penny went into the bathroom to retouch her white streak along with the greys that had started to pepper her curly, dark hair. Telephoning work, she pretended to be sick as she wanted to visit her parents and was soon in the car on her way for the hour's journey. Penny rehearsed what she was going to say over and over again, but when she knocked at their door, she completely forgot everything. She'd spent the rest of the journey looking back on her life. It was pretty unremarkable apart from the kidnapping and the "elephant in the room" of her evaporations every month. No-one had ever come close to finding out – well, except her abductor who had and now whose name she knew. Whether that was due diligence on the part of her parents or because she was a solitary person who didn't really have any friends, she didn't really know. Penny knew lots of people from work and the weekly quiz night she went to but regarded them as just acquaintances. People thought she was forthright and often quite brusque; she didn't care. In Penny's head, so long as she wasn't a timid mouse like her mum, Morag, she was doing OK. As for boyfriends or girlfriends, they'd never come into the equation. She hadn't told anyone, but she knew she had trauma-related genophobia.

Her dad only ever spoke Welsh; a proud and patriotic man, he always did what he felt was right, which didn't necessarily bring him happiness. When Penny was a teenager, she realised there was something amiss with her parents' relationship. There was a chink in the armour that had always been there, but when Penny was younger, she hadn't understood.

Until she did.

Her dad loved her mum, but he wasn't *in love* with her.

Penny thought her mum was lonely, that guilt made her stay as well as the love of their child, but that seemed to be her penance. Penny thought she would walk away in that situation, but how could she truly know? She didn't have any relationship experience; she read books, used Google and watched a lot of TV, which was where she'd gathered all her life information from. So many thoughts running through her head, but nothing made total sense.

Until it did.

'*Bore*, Penny.'

'*Bore, Tadgu.*'

Making small talk until her mum returned, Penny silently began to recite the Welsh alphabet in song. She realised the last time she had done that was when she was trapped in Mick Munroe's basement. She wanted them both to come to the meeting. She had never got close to her biological father, but her *Tadgu* was the real deal: the one who taught her to ride a bike, cleaned her grazed knees and cheered her on at sports day.

Penny coughed before she began to explain about the "16/87s". Her choosing to speak in Welsh gave her *Tadgu* cause for concern. He hadn't heard her speak it since she was a child, and then only up to the age of nine. When she finally began talking again at eleven years old it was always in English.

'*Sut ydych chi'n gwybod nad yw'n sgam?*'

'I don't know 100%, but I don't think it's a scam – what do you think, Mam?'

'I'll do whatever makes you happy.'

Penny knew her mum's stock answer; it was the same every time there was a decision to be made. The way she said it too, resigned to never having her own opinion, worn down by the weight of her guilt – definitely not a role model, thought Penny.

Her dad refused to come to the meeting. He expressed that whilst he loved his daughter dearly and had forgiven her mum, since he'd found out twenty-eight years ago about her mum's affair, it hadn't been easy. Going to the meeting was just a step too far but he thought her mam definitely should.

Morag never had a say in it.

She did as she was told.

*

Anna and Romesh had come back from dinner at Jess and Josh's and were getting ready for bed in their hotel room. Jess had warned her that her mum could be unpredictable, but Anna found her charming. Isobel indulged Anna's newly found hobby of chanting mantras and she fell asleep as she sang them to her.

'Do you think Josh and Jess were a bit cagey tonight, Rom?'

'How would I know?' He laughed. 'I've never met them before, and you were talking so much I hardly got a word in edgeways apart from moaning about the bloody cold weather!'

'It was your idea to come to the UK! I'm just thinking out loud here – I just felt an energy that seemed to be *off* and not in keeping with their physical actions.'

'You're reading too much into it. Ever since you did that "psychic energy course" you seem to think you're some kind of "all-seeing guru". You thought I was from India because we met there – you weren't psychic then!'

Romesh was being irritating, but it didn't stop Anna continuing the conversation until she realised he was snoring his head off. Going to the bathroom, she swore she could smell her sister's perfume. Gail had always loved the Daisy scent and was more liberal with it than necessary. After cleaning her teeth, the smell was still there when she climbed into bed. Anna began to doze off, but Romesh was keeping her awake. Every now and then, her body jolted. The third time it happened she saw Gail standing in front of her bed.

Anna rubbed her eyes, not sure if she was dreaming. Every time she'd imagined seeing a spirit, she expected them to be translucent. Gail's image was as formed as if she were still alive.

'Can I hug you?'

'No, sorry, sis. Look, I need you to tell Jess something, it's urgent, but I can't get through to her at the moment and I don't know why.'

'I was right! I told Rom there was something amiss, I'm really good at this psychic lark.'

'Anna, stop talking and *listen*.'

The younger sister did as she was told and was intently making sure she didn't miss a word that Gail said by repeating each sentence back to her.

Then she was gone.

Anna sat for a few minutes before looking at the clock – 2am. She looked at Romesh, whose snoring had subsided and who was now in a very deep sleep. Sliding out of the bed, she didn't even change her clothes. Anna grabbed her dressing gown from the chair and slipped her Ugg boots on before picking up her bag and the keys to the rental car.

She rang the bell several times but there was no answer. Rummaging in her handbag she found the key that Josh had given her to use when they were at work. As she opened the front door, she began calling out to them, to no avail. Upstairs their bed was empty and so was Isobel's.

'Come on, come on, think, where are they?' She was fully aware that she was speaking out loud, but it was in the hope that Gail may return and guide her. She sat in the kitchen racking her brains. The last time she'd been here, Anna had noticed there was a key on the dresser that was attached to an enormous key fob. It had said "cricket pavilion hall".

It wasn't there now.

'That's it! They must be there, thank you, Gail!'

She didn't even consider what time it was or why anyone would be using the place in the middle of the night. Anna immediately got out her phone to find out where the hall was and was quickly back in the car with the route map to guide her.

*

The hall was beginning to fill up; Jess and Josh couldn't believe that they were actually pulling this together, especially as they had no idea why. Storm arrived with her mum Lizzie, who'd come down from Scotland without Malcolm, who was still unaware. After the introductions Jess asked her to sit with Miriam. She then whispered in Storm's ear, 'I don't know why she's brought the cat in the basket – its name is Poppy, that's all I know.'

Storm smiled and directed her mum to the seats at the far end of the circle, joking to Jess that it looked like they were setting up a séance. Hils and Martin were still standing, speaking to Josh and Emilie, when Hamisi sheepishly popped her head around the door. Emilie had told Jess that she didn't think her mum would turn up, but there she was in her glorious technicolour church clothes again.

The next four to enter the hall were "the Moonpie Crew", as Josh called them. Dawn was rolling her eyes at Jess as once again the two younger women had been at the pub all night. They were giggling profusely, which seemed to be at odds with the sombre Miriam and her cat. Helen told the girls off, which made them snigger and make some barbed comment to each other.

Charlotte, Lilian, Daisy, Mo and a reluctant Josie were next to arrive, along with George. Despite her separating from him, Josie felt it was the right thing to do, especially as she was still upset with Daisy telling Mo and for insisting that he came too.

When Penny arrived, she announced herself and Morag to the group using their full names. Baby Christopher then began to cry loudly.

'The baby is not used to a Welsh accent?' enquired Penny.

Lexi whispered to Rachel that it was the loudness not the accent. They had been the first to arrive along with Lexi's mum, Belinda. Christopher had been peacefully sleeping in his stroller until then. The two wives had reached an impasse: Lexi was still exasperated with Rachel's reactions, not angry, just frustrated. Rachel, although remorseful, still felt uneasy about the meeting. It reminded her of the night she'd discovered that Lexi was a "disappearer". She wasn't supposed to be there, the pair of them weren't talking, but she'd wanted to be in the vicinity.

Just like now.

Penny was still making too much noise taking her seat and baby Christopher was still crying.

Dawn turned to her. 'Are you the Penny Jones who was abducted as a child?'

'*No*,' she lied.

'You and your memory, Dawn. There must be hundreds of people called Penny Jones. Though two out of three isn't bad.'

'Sorry, Hels, I just wondered. I'd say only one, as everyone knows Lady Charlotte, so Storm was the only one I remembered right.'

Then Jess clapped her hands. 'OK, I think we're all here now, so shall we sit?'

Jess then sat down herself in the hope that the stragglers would follow. She was sitting on her hands to calm her nerves. The shaking hands would be a dead giveaway. Jess thought it was expected of her to take control of the situation. She was so used to doing presentations at work that this event should've been easy.

It wasn't.

She'd put herself under too much pressure to get this right; however, there were no blueprints for what she was about to do. This would be the first time she would *slip* without being in a bed. She was wearing her dad's T-shirt with leggings rather than just her underwear and she had lit a candle. The majority of her own rules had been followed, but from speaking to some of the others they all seemed happy to be wherever they happened to be. Hils had told her lots of stories about the strange places she'd been in when she disappeared, but that still didn't appease Jess. It was especially discomforting when her mum was going on again about the "space-time continuum" being disrupted by the meeting. Jess told herself that her mum had no evidence for that and whilst she was improving, Isobel was still fragile. She looked at the time.

3.10am.

Twenty minutes to go.

She glanced at Josh, and he indicated that she should speak.

She took a few seconds to stand up, waiting for her breathing to normalise. Taking a sip of her drink, she began, 'I know you all have different names for what happens to us. I don't say disappear, vanish, evaporate or any other adjective; I am a *slipper* and I *slip* into another dimension. Almost a year ago I met Josh…'

Jess put her hand on his shoulder as she continued, 'It was that night that I discovered I wasn't the only one due to a bizarre set of circumstances to do with Josh's sister, Gail. We all have our own stories, of life, love, grief—'

Before she could finish her sentence, Josh pushed the chair away from himself and stood up as he saw the hall door open.

'I thought you locked it, Jess?'

'I thought you did!'

Anna was standing there in her pyjamas.

'WTF? You aren't invited! I don't want to speak to you now.'

'Wait, Josh, it's Jess I need to speak to, *now*, it's urgent.'

'Talk amongst yourself, gang, I'll take Anna in the kitchen. Josh, stay here.'

Whispers then began to chime around the hall, with everyone wondering who this woman in her nightclothes was who Josh and Jess seemed to know.

Jess surprised herself with her calmness. She had no idea what Anna would say next, but it felt OK. Yes, she thought, whatever it was, it was OK.

Anna began to explain that Gail had visited her and that her perfume preceded her. Jess knew she was telling the truth then. She said that Gail had told her to tell Jess about the day their mum disappeared.

And so began the story of how baby Josh was crying in their mum's room, which had woken Gail and Anna, who shared a room. They both went in and climbed into bed with their mum and Josh. Their dad was downstairs making up a bottle of milk. When he returned, he was laughing at the sight of them all lined up in bed. After giving the bottle to his wife, he picked up his camera and put a flash cube on top of it as it was still dark. As he took the photo of the happy family; the flash bulb went off at the same time that their mum disappeared, never to return. The police investigation was rigorous and damaged their dad's mental health. He was adamant that the girls should never, ever reveal what happened. They all stuck to their story that the mum had popped to the shops and never came back.

Anna said their dad always hoped she would return one day, but she never did.

Jess was left open-mouthed but now it all made sense. 'There must've been some sort of anomaly, Anna. I think Josh should've *slipped* but didn't and your dad survived. As he's the only boy, maybe he's the "chosen one"?'

'I don't think my brother is any kind of messiah!' She laughed. 'Gail said you were supposed to work it out yourselves, but she thinks you all got so caught up in the people-searching that it was there all the time, in plain sight, but you missed all the clues.'

'Grab a chair, Anna, and come and join the circle.'

Jess walked back into the hall and sat beside Josh on one side and indicating to Anna to put the chair the other side of him before instructing everyone to hold hands. Normally she would have one hand on her heart, the other over her belly. Instead, she crossed her arms holding Isobel and Josh's hands as if they were about to sing "Auld Lang Syne" before saying, 'OK, families, talk amongst yourself and we'll be back in ten minutes.'

She kissed Josh then quietly said in his ear, 'It's you, my darling. *You* are the twelfth *slipper*. We just didn't see it.'

Josh looked puzzled; he didn't *slip*, but... but... then it clicked. Detective Sergeant Joshua Holmes had his breakthrough just as the clock struck 3.30am.

*

Jess opened her eyes and saw her dad in front of her; he shouted, 'You did it, Jessie, you did it!'

Then she realised that he was holding hands with all the other dads. The beach was reminiscent of a line of people paper chains like she used to enjoy making when she was a child. It was only when Isobel let go of Jess's hand that it dawned on her that *everyone* had *slipped*. Isobel rushed over to her husband and enveloped him in a huge hug. Jess called out, 'Papa-Ji, this can't be happening – we can't touch, we've never been able to touch!'

Isobel wasn't letting go, so he released his arms to shrug his shoulders like the emoji with the upward-facing palms. He didn't know any more than she did. Jess felt glued to the spot; everyone had now broken free and collected themselves within their own families. She could hear a reverberation of apologies flying over her head. What struck her was that each of the conversations were being held simultaneously and yet Jess could hear each individual story.

Josh was cuddling Gail and meeting his mum for the first time in his life. Anna wouldn't let go of their mum. Jess could hear him asking Gail why she hadn't told him the truth when she was alive. She gave him many answers, but the one that stood out for Jess was just that they did what their dad told them to; he'd scared them so much, much like all the remaining mums had. Jess then caught his eye, and he blew her a kiss before his smile widened as much as his mouth would allow. Anna then asked why Gail couldn't cuddle her earlier in the evening. She replied by saying that whatever had just happened wasn't the way things normally worked.

Lexi was listening intently to her dad whilst Belinda was holding his hand. He was laughing as he explained that he saw baby Christopher before his wife did. Adult Chris reached out to Rachel, who was holding the baby, and embraced her. He could see she was feeling left out; he told her she was just as much part of the family as if she'd be born into it. Jess could see Rachel's face light up and she allowed a little tear to fall. She thought that was a huge breakthrough; Lexi had been telling Jess last week how much Rachel was struggling.

Jess also noticed that there weren't only dads in the "paper chain". There was a young man talking to Storm who she heard was Jason. She was expressing regret to him to such an extent that she almost fell over. What Jess overheard next shocked her. Jason said that he had intended to take his own life the night Storm had attacked him. He'd decided to have one more night of fun, telling Storm that if she hadn't killed him, he would've done it himself. Jess understood more than most that the façade everyone wore was mostly fake.

She overheard Storm's mum, Lizzie, say to Will, her dad, 'When I saw you last you said you were going to get us coffee – must be cold now – and you owe me a tenner!' They both laughed and hugged each other.

Miriam was handing Joanna the cat, which strangely had also *slipped.* She vaguely remembered Josh saying something about it being mentioned in the suicide note. Johan was making the loudest of apologies for his appalling behaviour as a young guy in the city, saying that he felt justice had been served to him when he died. He declared that it wasn't until Joanna arrived nine months ago that he realised how despicable he had been towards his daughter, and he had been trying to remedy it. Despite his horrendous previous conduct, Miriam inexplicably told him she still loved him. Joanna asked for forgiveness from her mother for taking her own life, whose only answer was that she wanted to remain with them both, that she had nothing to go back to.

Jess glanced back at her own dad, who was still cuddling her mum, deep in conversation. She decided to leave them be for a while as she continued to listen to all the verbal exchanges.

Daisy was able to look directly into Mo's eyes for the first time ever; she wasn't disappointed. Her dad, Tom, was thanking his brother George for looking after his wife and daughter but vehemently told him to let go now. Josie held Tom and said that she'd never stopped loving him. A tear began to fall down Jess's face as she saw Mo firstly ask Tom for his daughter's hand in marriage and then he got on one knee to formally ask Daisy.

Jess was becoming so overawed by all that she saw and heard, but like a voyeur she couldn't stop listening and looking. Just when she thought she couldn't be any more emotionally charged she heard the discussion between Lady Charlotte, her mum and dad. They were involved in what Albert called a "three-way-hug".

He stepped back just enough to gently lift Charlotte's chin; his eyes never left hers. 'You've been very brave, Charlotte, but you are going to have to be even braver soon, I'm so sorry.'

Charlotte buried her head in her dad's chest; she knew that the "cancer cloud" would be hanging over her head again with a "high chance of rain". Weirdly, Jess heard that thought process too. Charlotte also said she understood now that her parents loved each other deeply – she said it was obvious and she was sorry she ever doubted her mum.

Jess didn't expect to feel so attached to all these wonderful people, but she did.

The poignant words spreading around were lightened when she was listening to Hils and her family joking about Margaret Thatcher. Apparently once Hils reached voting age, Maggie had increased her cheques to one hundred pounds for each year of life on the condition that she voted Conservative. Hils told her dad she'd wasted all the money and never voted. Her father, Patrick, asked what she would've done with a three thousand-pound cheque for her thirtieth birthday if Maggie was still alive. Hils retorted that she would've gone to Hamley's and bought toys for under-privileged children, before bursting into laughter and saying she thought that Martin probably deserved a holiday after the way she'd been treating him. She also apologised to her mum for being such a bitch all her life and driving her mum to drink herself to death. Whilst Hils' mum accepted the confession, she did iterate that it was her alcoholism, not Hils, that caused her early death. Patrick told Hils in front of Martin that he had a feeling there would be a very special holiday soon, before winking at Martin.

'He's one of the good guys, Hils, don't let him slip through your hands.'

Hils nodded and kissed her dad's cheek before giving Martin a huge snog.

Hamisi was on her knees, kissing Adele's feet, begging her to understand why she did what she did, that she would forever be remorseful and would pay any penance due. Emilie had been standing on the side-lines observing everything, just as Jess was doing. She didn't remember her dad, and Adele was in an adult form she didn't recognise. She'd only seen her mum twice since she was four years old; everyone was a stranger to her.

Emilie took another step back.

She wanted to go home; she didn't feel that sense of belonging that seemed to be engulfing everyone else.

Jess not only noticed but felt Emilie's pain too. She made her fingers into the shape of a heart and directed it at Emilie. She didn't want to move yet; she hadn't spoken to her papa. Jess heard Jade and Kylie giggling and wrongly assumed they were still drunk. Terry, their father, was making his biggest contrition to Dawn for betraying her by impregnating Helen too, but the girls were laughing because, as they explained to Terry, they ended up with two mums who loved each other rather than a "deadbeat dad" with two "baby mammas". It crossed Jess's mind that a lot of people could benefit from the joie de vivre that Kylie and Jade seemed to permanently have. Jess realised it wasn't the alcohol but connection: they'd always had each other to share their secret life with. While Lexi and Rachel shared that bond, it wasn't the same because Rachel didn't *slip*.

Morag and Penny surprised Jess by their nonchalance. It was the first time Penny had seen her mum with her biological father, but there was no chemistry or love between them. Jess thought that maybe Morag had made the right decision thirty years ago but wished that she would forgive herself. It served no-one for her to be so downbeat. Penny was just glad Mick Monroe wasn't there.

Jess couldn't help but wonder who this "Mick Monroe" was that Penny had thought about.

The voices subsided and Jess took this as a sign that it was her time to speak to her papa. Isobel had let go of him, apart from holding his hand as if her life depended on it, which, in a way, Jess thought was true.

'Papa-Ji, so Josh was the "chosen one" after all?'

Jess's dad laughed. 'I never said there was a "chosen one", Jessie – they were your words, not mine. If I had to guess, though, I'd say it was Gail. She was the one who instigated all of this.'

'What if I don't see you next month? What if this is goodbye…?' Jess's voiced trailed off, her tone cracking under the weight of her potential future.

'Well then, Jessie, everything would've unfolded as it should've done in the beginning.'

The two of them hugged for the first time ever, neither wanting to let go.

With that he kissed her on the top of her head, and she was back in the hall with everybody else, except Miriam and the cat.

*

No-one was speaking; the families were all dumbstruck by the events that had just happened. The *slippers* themselves were used to being on the "other side" but had never seen their mums with their fathers before.

It seemed like an eternity of silence.

It was Penny who broke it with her sarcasm.

'Well. This. Has. Been. Just. Lovely.'

Kylie and Jade started to giggle again, mimicking Penny's accent.

'I'm leaving, we have a long drive back to Wales. I hope you all got what you were looking for.'

Jess felt that Penny was the only one whom she couldn't connect with and wished she could have spent more time with her. Also, she was still curious who this "Mick Monroe" was, whom Penny had thought about and was glad wasn't there. She wasn't going to give up on her, though.

'You're in the WhatsApp group, Penny, so please let us know when you get home. I don't know what we do next or if we do nothing, but thank you for coming down.'

With that, people started to disperse. As Lexi's family began to leave, Rachel gave Jess a hug and whispered in her ear, 'I'm sorry I ever doubted you.'

And then there were just Jess, Josh, Anna and Isobel left. They began tidying up, noting that the sun was now rising and the familiar sounds of the rush-hour traffic and numerous sirens filled the air.

'I wish it was as peaceful here as it is there, Josh. Are you OK?'

'It was *a lot*, but yeah, it all makes sense now.'

Jess moved towards the bin in the corner of the hall to dispense with the last of the rubbish from the gathering. Pressing the pedal to open it, she stood as if frozen in time, her arm raised ready to drop the empty packets in, but she stopped.

'Josh! Who dumped these surgical masks in here? And more to the point, why? I don't remember anyone with them, and none of them are doctors or nurses – well, apart from Penny. Strange, really strange.'

She shook her head as Josh joined her to peer into the bin.

'Maybe someone had a fancy-dress party the night before us, or a nail-bar convention – they wear masks in the salons. Who knows? Though everyone is supposed to take their rubbish with them. I think we need to get home and chill.'

Josh pulled out the black bag from the bin and tied it, carrying it to the front door, which was half open, before stopping in his tracks and turning to Jess. 'Listen! I can't hear anything.'

'What do you mean? You can hear me; we were just talking.'

'No, listen, where's the traffic? The police sirens? Nothing, WTF?'

Jess followed him as he went into the car park, walking to the far side before beckoning for Jess to continue in his direction.

'Turn around and look up.'

She did as she was told and immediately she could see the motorway flyover devoid of cars. Turning back to Josh, she began to whisper, 'OMG! Where are we?'

'I think it's more of a case of *when* are we? Why are you whispering?'

'I don't know, but look by that drain there – another one of those surgical masks, and over there by the kerb.'

Josh could also see a newspaper blowing around in the corner of the car park and ran over to it. 'Jess, what's the date?'

'Day after full moon, 4th December.'

'What year?'

'Don't be daft, 2017 – are you having a memory lapse?'

'No, it's a time-lapse of some weird sort – look at this.' Josh was pointing to the front of the newspaper he'd picked up. 'Read it!'

'17th April 2020.' As soon as she'd said it, she screwed up her face. 'And what's Boris been up to? He only left the mayoral office last year and now he's got a black mask on his face!'

Josh put his index finger to his lips to indicate that Jess should stop talking. He grabbed her hand and guided her back into the hall, before locking the door behind them. They both sat on the floor and spread the newspaper to get a better look.

'Prime Minister? Well, that's a joke. Coronavirus? Lockdown? Stay inside, protect the NHS? Essential workers only ones allowed out, hospital ICUs at breaking point, new Florence Nightingale hospital open in record time, UK death toll stands at 14,576 so far—'

'That's with only a four-week lockdown? If this is true, Josh, we need to warn someone.'

'They're never going to believe us – besides which, if we have just time-jumped over three years, how the hell do we know if we are going to get back?'

Isobel then began screaming hysterically; she had been listening from the kitchen. 'I told you! It's the "space-time continuum", we've ruined everything!'

Isobel began to hyperventilate, and Jess called out to Anna, 'Please sing to Mum – we need to figure this out and I can't think.'

Anna put her arms around Isobel and walked her gently into the cloakroom, singing to her as if she was a baby, stroking her head and telling her everything was going to be all right. Anna had no idea if that was true; she was petrified herself.

Both Jess and Josh's phones then started frantically beeping. It was the WhatsApp group:

Daisy:	*What's going on? I was listening to the news on the radio and WHERE ARE WE? Mo's changed the stations but they're all saying the same…*
Storm:	*Don't you mean WHEN are we??*
Lexi:	*Rach popped to the shops and was shouted at*

	for not wearing a face mask. She ran back, she thinks it's a zombie apocalypse.
Hils:	*Just turned the TV on. What do we do???*
Josh:	*STAY WHERE YOU ARE. I need to think.*

'OK, let's look at the evidence and figure out what we do next.'

Josh then separated the newspaper, roughly half each, and passed Jess her part. 'Let's read everything, every single word, and take photos, grab your phone – we need as much evidence as we can. I'll go outside and take a photo of the flyover.'

'No, don't leave me, Josh, I'm scared. Of all of the things that have happened since we met until now, life made sense. Weird sense, but it still made sense to me. I grew up visiting my dead dad every month, and that still made sense, but this? You thought last night was *a lot*, but this? Hold me, Josh.'

The two of them held each other for what seemed to be the longest time before agreeing not to go outside. Anna had made them a cup of tea each and they settled down to read the newspaper. The WhatsApp group was still alight, constantly beeping.

'Turn it on silent, just while we think.'

'No, Josh, I'll give it to Anna to read them – it might be important or valid.'

'OK, let me memorise the lottery numbers first!'

'*Josh!* Quickly then.'

'16, 28, 32, 37, 45, bonus balls 1 and 11.'

'So, we know that there's some contagion coming, but if it's already killed that many, who knows how many more it will, and more to the point, *how* can we do anything?'

Isobel started sobbing from the kitchen: it wasn't fair to leave Anna to deal with her mum, so Jess went to take over. As she did, she heard Josh open the door and call out, 'Traffic is back!'

The WhatsApp messages immediately began coming through in a flurry again, all confirming that normality had been restored.

'Mum, it's OK, we're back. It'll be OK, I promise,' Jess lied; she had no idea if that was true.

'Jess, did you take the newspaper with you?'

'No, you had it.'

'It's gone, and... yep, and the masks in the car park too. Ten minutes.'

'Ten minutes what?'

'We were in 2020 for ten minutes, just like when you *slip*.'

'Let's go home.'

The journey back to their house took place in total silence. Anna was trying to take in the weirdest night of her life since she was ten years old. Thirty years of not having a mum and there she'd been in front of her; she wished she could get her dad to understand. Even if he did, he'd soon forget. Maybe having dementia was easier than this, she thought. She also wanted to ask why all the thirty-year-old women now had white streaks in their hair. No-one had said a word about that.

Isobel was rocking in her seat, chanting to herself the mantra Anna had been using earlier. She couldn't decide if it was better or worse that she'd been able to hug her husband. She wanted to get better, she really did, but everything always seemed so crushingly difficult. The new therapist Jess had organised was lovely, but Isobel couldn't tell her the truth, so how could she help?

Isobel had never told the truth to any of the therapists over the last thirty years.

She couldn't.

The silence was disturbed by Josh as he pulled up outside of their house: 'What's your Romesh doing sitting on our front wall? He looks bloody freezing.'

'Probably looking for me! It's not like I left him a note – I'm still in my PJs, for God's sake!'

Romesh was hugging himself, drawing his newly bought winter coat tightly to his body. His legs dangling off the wall, his woollen bobble hat pulled down past his ears, and he was rubbing his gloved hands together to try to generate some heat.

'Cold enough for you, Rom?' joked Josh. 'How long you been there?'

'Only ten minutes.'

Romesh didn't even ask where they'd been or why Anna was still in her nightclothes. She had warned him when they flew back from India that he needed to prepare for the cold, but he'd never actually experienced it before and didn't imagine it would be like this. Anna didn't miss the UK winters and was looking forward to going back to the place she now called home.

As soon as they were inside, Jess took her mum up to bed; she'd had enough excitement for one day. Jess considered, yet again, that their roles had always been reversed, more so the older she got. However, without her Auntie Viv she probably wouldn't be as well-adjusted as she was. Auntie Viv was her rock; she had wanted to tell her the truth so many times but always stopped short because of her mum's "space-time continuum" theory.

Maybe Isobel was right.

After the monumental experiences this evening, she couldn't be sure. Nothing seemed to have changed in this world, but she knew it was going to.

The biggest question in her head was *why*? For what purpose was the meeting? Did they somehow need to "save the world"? Or maybe it was as simple as to say goodbye to their fathers and the time slip was just an anomaly?

She kissed her mum. "We're going to be OK, Mum, goodnight.'

She had no idea if they were going to be OK or not.

Jess came down to find the three of them around the table drinking tea. It still concerned her that Romesh didn't seem to be inquisitive about their unknown adventure. She hoped that if Anna did tell him the truth that she would do it without mentioning her. That was Jess's prerogative, not Anna's.

Jess wanted to lighten the conversation after the unbelievable night they'd had.

There would be time for Jess and Josh to debrief later.

'So, Romesh, we don't know much about you, apart from how much Anna is *always* going on about how wonderful you are.'

'Have you got ten minutes?' He laughed.

'Don't you want to take off your hat and coat? Didn't your mum ever say that you won't feel the benefit when you go out?'

'In Sri Lanka? Not something we had to worry about!'

They were all laughing now, and Jess thought that was the respite they'd needed.

'OK, I was born on 23rd November 1978.'

Nothing, not a flicker of historical memory from the British threesome.

'We lived in Batticaloa, nicknamed Batti.'

Josh sniggered as Romesh continued, 'You don't know your history, do you? That was the day the cyclone hit. They only had *ten minutes'* notice; more than seven hundred people died when the cyclone hit land.'

Still nothing.

He desperately needed to give them some information, but they had to understand first.

'My dad died in the cyclone as I was born.'

Josh was furrowing his brow as if you could see the cogs turning in his brain. They all *slipped* for ten minutes. They were in 2020 for ten minutes. Ten minutes Romesh said he'd been waiting outside. Ten minutes to tell his story. Ten minutes' notice the Sri Lankans had been given… the realisation dawned on him. Romesh stood up and took his bobble hat off, revealing his white streak of hair. He held out his hand to shake Josh's before saying, 'There's twelve of us too. We're the "23/78s".'

Jess then stood up before Romesh continued, 'Welcome to the Chronos Club.'

ACKNOWLEDGEMENTS

It takes an army to support an author and I'm grateful for everyone in my battalion!

It goes without saying that my daughter Antonia and my husband Steve are the generals to my field marshal.

Coming up the rear are my publishers, my family, and friends, without whose support none of this would be possible.

Felix, as promised, I used your name. It's in Chapter Six. Love you and your sister Beatrice more than you will ever know.

I also want to thank everyone who bought my debut novel, *The Gift of Time*. Having that be so well received made me believe in myself to write another.

Follow me on Facebook and Instagram: @juliewalkerauthor

Twitter: _julie_walker_

WATCH OUT FOR THE SEQUEL TO *SLIPPED*...

Every day, I'm grateful to be alive.
Live presently, be brave.

Had I the heavens' embroidered cloths,
Enwrought with golden and silver light,
The blue and the dim and the dark cloths
Of night and light and the half-light,
I would spread the cloths under your feet:
But I, being poor, have only my dreams;
I have spread my dreams under your feet;
Tread softly because you tread on my dreams.
W.B. Yeats (1865–1939)